Curling her shaking fingers around the whitewashed banister of her mother's front porch, Emma sucked in the humid August air and studied the chipped red nail polish on her left hand. She didn't remember when she'd last painted them, so the fact some color lingered made the wheels in her mind spin like the teacups at an amusement park. Had she painted her daughter Sophie's nails lately in an attempt to cheer her up, and then half-heartedly done her own? Had her sister done them before the funeral?

No, the color would have faded by now. She slid her gaze to the gold wedding band she still wore. Six months passed since Luke died, and nothing faded from her mind or her heart. The only thing that dimmed was her damn nail polish.

She tightened her grip and the pale, thin skin around her hand choked her knuckles like the emotions threatening to close off her windpipe. Coming home was the last thing she'd ever expected. For over a decade, her life existed on the other side of the state. The flat farmland of northwest Ohio was a place for family visits and long-ago memories—not the place she planned to raise her children.

Until Luke died.

I0526236

Praise for Danielle M. Haas

In COMING HOME, Danielle Haas spins a heart-warming romance filled with tenderness, loss, and how love and grit can pull you through anything. A truly touching and unforgettable read.

~Samantha Wilde, author

~*~

COMING HOME, the third book in Danielle Haas' Sheffield family saga, is full of all the warm and fuzzy feelings we all need, especially right now. It's full of loyal family members, delightful children, a heartbroken woman trying to move ahead after unspeakable tragedy, horses, and a hot Greek god of a hero. Kudos to Danielle for imagining this story.

~Becky Lower, author of *Sweet Caroline*

~*~

From devastating heartbreak to true love, and all the ups and downs between. The rollercoaster ride for Emma and Antonio keeps a reader on the edge of their seat. Will they ever find happiness together?

~ Celeste Cook

~*~

A heartbreakingly sweet story of love and resilience that won't let you stop reading until the last Sheffield's story is told.

~ Brenda Hill

Coming Home

by

Danielle M Haas

The Sheffields, Book 3

This is a work of fiction. Names, characters, places, and incidents are either the product of the author's imagination or are used fictitiously, and any resemblance to actual persons living or dead, business establishments, events, or locales, is entirely coincidental.

Coming Home

COPYRIGHT © 2021 by Danielle M Haas

All rights reserved. No part of this book may be used or reproduced in any manner whatsoever without written permission of the author or The Wild Rose Press, Inc. except in the case of brief quotations embodied in critical articles or reviews.
Contact Information: info@thewildrosepress.com

Cover Art by *Tina Lynn Stout*

The Wild Rose Press, Inc.
PO Box 708
Adams Basin, NY 14410-0708
Visit us at www.thewildrosepress.com

Publishing History
First Edition, 2021
Trade Paperback ISBN 978-1-5092-3807-1
Digital ISBN 978-1-5092-3808-8

Published in the United States of America

Dedication

To my family. My parents, Mike and Brenda, and my siblings, Josh and Caitlin. Thank you for giving me a home of love and laughter. The Sheffields came to life because of you.

To my in-laws, John and Twila, thank you for always welcoming me to your family with open arms. I'm proud to call myself a Haas and call you my second set of parents.

To Rusty and Megan. Your love story will live on forever.

Other Titles by this author

A Place in This World
Second Time Around

Chapter One

The old porch step squeaked under Emma's weight. How had she ended up back in Smithview, Ohio, after all these years? She glanced at the swing hanging from rusted chains at the end of the porch and the wicker chairs huddled around the small glass table. Everything appeared exactly the same, but everything in her life had flipped upside down. Her throat tightened, and she fought to keep her tears at bay.

Curling her shaking fingers around the whitewashed banister of her mother's front porch, Emma sucked in the humid August air and studied the chipped red nail polish on her left hand. She didn't remember when she'd last painted them, so the fact some color lingered made the wheels in her mind spin like the teacups at an amusement park. Had she painted her daughter Sophie's nails lately in an attempt to cheer her up, and then half-heartedly done her own? Had her sister done them before the funeral?

No, the color would have faded by now. She slid her gaze to the gold wedding band she still wore. Six months passed since Luke died, and nothing faded from her mind or her heart. The only thing that dimmed was her damn nail polish.

She tightened her grip and the pale, thin skin around her hand choked her knuckles like the emotions threatening to close off her windpipe. Coming home was the last thing she'd ever expected. For over a decade, her life existed on the other side of the state. The flat farmland of northwest Ohio was a place for family visits and long-ago memories—not the place she planned to raise her children.

Until Luke died.

Now she needed to come home to her family and rebuild her shattered life. A barking dog and squeals of delighted laughter turned her away from the house she'd grown up in.

Sophie, her three-year-old daughter, ran circles around her sister's Australian Shepherd.

Anderson, her son, toddled around before falling on his bottom. He brought his chubby hands together, clapping and giggling at his sister.

At the sound of her children's laughter, she smiled, her heart lifting higher than the white clouds that dotted the clear, blue sky. Laughter wasn't a part of her life lately. Nothing but pain, sorrow, and a life she couldn't maintain on her own defined her days. But life was about to change—again. She needed to be strong for her children and give them a childhood filled with love and laughter and family. Even if their family would never be the same.

"They're happy to be here." Annie stepped out of the house and locked her gaze on the kids.

Her mother's voice was heavy with happiness. Too heavy, as if she were trying too hard to make everything seem right.

A gentle hand squeezed the tension from Emma's stiff shoulder. The long drive zapped her energy, even as the hours in the vehicle made her children bouncing bundles of vibrating limbs. Sophie's long, blonde hair streaked across the yard, and Anderson's arms circled the air like the industrial windmills that now littered the surrounding farmland.

Emma released her death-grip on the wooden railing and placed a hand on top of her mom's. Years of working in the garden had toughened them to leather. "They're happy to be out of the car. We all are."

"Have they eaten lunch?"

"Besides the cookies and chips I used to bribe them to be good on the way here?" Emma turned and found herself staring into sapphire blue eyes so much like her own. But unlike the bloodshot eyes and dark circles she'd carried around for months, her mom's were bright and filled with compassion. Her mom's wide mouth tipped up at the corners, and she brushed a piece of ash blonde hair from her forehead. Annie Sheffield was not a vain woman, but she'd keep her hair color until her dying day.

"Do you want me to make them something while you get some rest?"

Emma shook her head, and loose curls whipped into her face, sticking to the beads of sweat dotting her hairline. "You don't have to. How about I make lunch while you keep an eye on them?"

"Call if you need help." Annie rushed down the stairs toward the children. "Did you hear that, my little darlings? Grandma has to keep an eye on you. I don't have on my glasses, so you better stay close."

"Grandma!" Sophie hurled herself into Annie's open arms.

Annie squeezed her tight, and then scooped Anderson close. All three collapsed onto the ground and broke into a fit of giggles.

Nora barked and covered them with slobbery affection.

A rush of happiness flooded Emma. Smithview might be the last place she imagined she'd end up, but she had no doubt it was exactly where she needed to be. She savored one more second of her happy children and then stepped into the house. A black shoe mat sat beside the oak door, and Emma slipped her flip-flops from her feet and set them neatly on the fleur-de-lis print. After her mom transformed their home into an inn when Emma was a kid, cleanliness and organization were always a top priority. Those priorities stuck with her, even if they hadn't with her brother and sister.

She slapped her bare feet against hard wood, and the sound echoed off the high ceiling. Thank God for air conditioning. The frigid air blasting through the old farmhouse caused goose pimples to erupt on her arms. The sweat on her brow evaporated. Memories overwhelmed her like a flashflood breaking over the edge of a riverbank—fast, furious, and with no way to stop them. She avoided the familiar rooms she'd spent countless hours in with Luke and made a beeline for the kitchen. Instead, she focused on the smooth wood grains in the hardwood floors.

Granite countertops gleamed against the distressed white cabinets she helped her mom pick out a few years ago. Burlap-covered wire baskets filled with freshly baked bread and cookies sat on the large island in the center of the room. Emma inhaled, filling her lungs with the familiar scents of her mother's kitchen. If Annie wasn't in her garden, she was baking, and the walls oozed the smells of every delicious morsel she'd baked over the years.

Emma ran a hand over the smooth surface of the island and inched her fingers toward the breadbasket. The warmth of the bread caressed her palm, and the pit of her stomach let out a groan of desire. She grabbed the plastic handle of the knife in the wooden block by the sink, and the empty coffee pot caught her attention. The craving in her stomach morphed into a growl of desperation.

The sandwiches could wait. The kids probably weren't even hungry and would whine if they had to cut playtime short. She could make a pot of coffee to go with lunch and maybe slip in a little quiet time with a quick cup before calling everyone inside. Tossing the bread and knife onto the counter, she filled the machine with water and added coffee grains to the pot before sitting on the high-backed stool at the island.

The *plip-plip-plop* of coffee dripping into the pot stole her focus. Blessed numbness calmed her frazzled mind. She was so damn tired. Exhaustion weighed her down until her eyelids collapsed and her head bobbed forward. Her chin collided against her chest, and she jerked up her head. She fluttered her eyelids like the wings of a hummingbird to keep them open. All she needed was a quick jolt of caffeine to drag her through the afternoon. She'd just nestle her head in the crook of her arm and relax for a quick second until the coffee was done. Just one…quick…second.

A baby's cry pierced through her blank mind, and she jerked her head off the not-so-soft pillow of her elbow. The muscles in her neck screamed in protest, and she kneaded at the pain with her hand. She glanced around to get her bearings. "Is Anderson awake?"

"Sounds like it, but I'm sure Meg's got him. She's

watching him and Sophie in the living room. You know how those kids are with your sister. They don't want anything to do with me when she's around." Annie clucked her tongue and wiped off the counter with a dishrag. "Can I get you anything for lunch? We finished a little bit ago. I can warm up something."

"When did Meg get here?" Emma sat straight and arched her back to stretch her muscles. "How long did I sleep?"

"Meg got here a little over an hour ago. We ate outside so we wouldn't wake you." Annie pressed together her lips—eyes crinkled down at the corner. "I thought about getting you to your room, but I figured you wouldn't get back to sleep."

"You're probably right." Emma rubbed at the knots in her neck and winced. "I wish you would have tried, though. My neck will be a wreck for days."

Annie let out a small laugh. "Sorry. Did you want some food?"

She shook her head. "I'm not hungry."

Annie nodded. "Meg hoped to take the kids to the fair later. Would that be okay?"

Her heart swelled. Meg always had her children's needs in mind, which is one of the reasons she made the difficult decision to move home. "Of course. I bet Anderson will get a kick out of it this year."

"Do you want to come with us?"

Emma hesitated, and a knot formed in her stomach. Since Luke's death, she hadn't seen a lot of her old friends and neighbors. She wasn't ready to deal with the pity in their eyes and their heartfelt condolences. They'd mean well, but she'd relocated to Smithview to start fresh. She didn't need their sad faces to remind her of everything she'd lost.

Frowning, Annie fisted her hands on her hips. "You mean to tell me you're considering not getting homemade ice cream? You crave it all year."

"I forgot about the ice cream." Emma groaned. "I guess I can go for a little bit. Seeing Sophie have fun would be nice. Getting her to smile since…" Tears filled her eyes, and grief ebbed through her. She closed her eyes, warding off the pain. Once the initial wave passed, she opened her eyes and wiped away her tears.

"Once some time passes, she'll be back to her rambunctious self." Annie paused and threw her dishrag over her shoulder. "You kids bounced back after your dad died. I know our situation was different, you were older than Sophie, but it all boils down to the same thing. You both lost your daddies long before you should have."

Emma stiffened, a stab of longing filled her heart. Her dad missed so much of her life. Her children would always have the same pain, and that she could do nothing to ease their broken hearts killed her.

Annie crossed the distance between them and rested a hand on Emma's arm. "You'll help her through this, Em. And the rest of us are here, too. Now, we have a few hours before we leave. The kids are in good hands. Take a little time for yourself while you can."

Sliding off the stool, she padded outside to grab some of her luggage then hauled it down the small hallway. She entered her old room and lost herself in the mundane tasks of hanging up clothes and putting away toiletries. The simple chores kept her hands busy and her mind distracted until everything was put away.

"Are you ready to go?" Meg leaned against the

doorframe and glanced around. Her long, blonde hair hung in a braid over her shoulder, and she crossed one tennis shoe over the other.

Emma didn't have to see her hands folded across her chest and tucked under her arms to know dirt would be caked under her nails.

Meg darted her gaze around the room. "Nothing's changed much in here, has it?"

"Not a bit." Emma chuckled. She ran a finger over the stickers she'd placed on the closet door as a child. "Mom kept everything exactly the same. I hope I can talk her into getting rid of these twin beds and buying a bigger one. Sophie climbs into bed with me at night. A small bed won't be comfortable."

"I'm sure Mom won't mind. Do you want to push them together for now? I can help."

"You don't have to." She smoothed an imaginary wrinkle from the baby pink comforter. "Maybe she'll stay in her room tonight since Anderson will be in there with her."

"Sounds like wishful thinking."

Emma gave a small shrug. "Maybe, but I don't really mind having her with me at night. The nights get pretty lonely."

Meg crossed the room and rested a hand on Emma's shoulder.

Emma glanced down and smiled at Meg's dirty nailbeds.

"Do you want me to crawl in there with you and snuggle like we used to when we were little? I always loved cuddling up to my big sister." Meg widened her eyes.

"I hated that!" Emma laughed and brushed Meg's

hand from her shoulder. A bit of tension uncoiled from her neck. Meg could always lighten her mood. "You always stole my blankets."

"Sophie doesn't do the same thing?" Meg's eyebrows rose together, and she puckered her lips.

"Oh, she's way worse than you ever were." She swiped a towel from the bed and threw it at Meg. "Are Sophie and Anderson ready?"

"Yep. I even got the diaper bag all set. We need to hurry if we want to make it before the parade starts."

Emma took a deep breath before she followed her sister out the door. She could stand tall and face the town she loved before hightailing it back home. Seeing Sophie happy, even if just for the evening, would make all the awkward attention worthwhile.

****

Circus music blasted over speakers set up in the courthouse lawn on the town square. Food trucks and carnival games littered the roads and sidewalks. The smell of fried sugar sweetened the air. What had to be the entire population of Smithview milled about, clogging the walkways. Emma tightened her grip on the handles of Anderson's stroller. Anxiety pitched back and forth in her stomach like the giant ride rocketing into the air in front of her. She hated crowds. "Sophie, don't let go of Meg's hand."

"Can Meg-Meg take me to play games? I want a unicorn." Sophie jumped up and down.

Excitement coated Sophie's sweet voice, and Emma melted into a puddle of goo. "What about the parade, honey?"

"We've got a little time." Meg put a hand on Sophie's head, halting her frantic movements. "I'll take her to play while you find a spot to watch it."

"Oh, and I see some of my friends. Let me take Anderson so I can show him off." Annie grabbed the stroller and took off in the opposite direction from Meg.

So much for safety in numbers.

Keeping her head down and her gaze trained on her black flip-flops, she made her way to where the parade would pass. The skin on her neck tingled from the stares she attracted with every step. Her shoulders tensed and heart pounded. The parade needed to start so everyone could stop staring.

"Emma!"

She braced herself for the assault of sympathy and turned toward the voice. Her brother's new stepson ran toward her. His dark hair curled around his ears and bounced around like the floppy ears of an overgrown puppy. The contagious smile lighting his face lifted the corners of her mouth.

"Hi, Sam, how are you?" Sam's mother, Jillian, married her brother, Jonah, in March, and she hadn't seen him since the wedding.

He wrapped his arms around her waist and squeezed. "I'm sorry about Luke. He was a real nice guy."

Emma leaned down and hugged him close. His words stabbed her chest. "Thank you, honey. He really liked you and wanted to get to know you better." She straightened and came face to face with Antonio, Sam's dad. He had the same dark hair as his son, only his curls were a little tamer on the nape of his neck. His velvety brown eyes met hers, and dimples appeared in the shallows of his cheeks when he smiled. "Hello, Antonio. Nice to see you again."

She had met him before, but only spoken with him briefly. His involvement last fall in her brother being set up for arson still left a bad taste in her mouth, and she'd kept her distance whenever he was around. Even if he hadn't played as big of a part in the mess as originally believed.

Antonio nodded. "Hi."

"Where's Sophie? Will she watch the parade or ride any rides?" Sam glanced around.

"She's by the games with Meg." Emma leaned over and pointed. "She's coaxing Meg into winning her a pink unicorn."

"I'm really good at the games, aren't I, Dad? Can I go over there and win it?" Sam bounced up and down on his toes.

"Do you have any money?" The corner of Antonio's mouth hitched up, and his dimples deepened.

"That's what you're here for." Sam grinned and held out his hand.

Antonio placed some bills in his palm, and then ruffled his dark hair. "You're not getting any more cash for the rest of the night. Spend it wisely."

"Okay, okay. Will you stay here with Emma until I get back? Then I can watch the parade with Sophie."

Antonio glanced at Emma with arched brows.

She offered him a weak smile. She didn't want company, but at least he wouldn't pry. He'd hardly said two words whenever their paths crossed.

Antonio shrugged. "All right, but don't be too long. The parade will start soon."

Without another word, Sam sped off in Sophie's direction.

A moment of awkward silence passed. She had no

idea what to say to this man. Emma darted around her gaze before resting it on her feet. She shifted them back and forth, and then glanced at Antonio. "Sam's really good with Sophie. Having him around will be nice."

"Who would think an almost ten-year-old boy would be so enchanted with a three-year-old girl?" He chuckled and rubbed the back of his neck.

Emma lifted her gaze to sky. The white clouds of earlier were now a muted orange with the fading light. "She has that effect on a lot of people." Another moment of silence passed.

"I'm sorry about your husband. Being alone really sucks."

She inhaled in a sharp breath and jerked her gaze to his face. His words slapped like a splash of cold water. They were brutal, honest, and refreshing as hell.

Chapter Two

Heat crept up Antonio's neck and settled in his cheeks. He bit into his lip. *Oh, man*. His statement was insensitive. Dread filled his gut. After the nightmare last year when he'd tried to win back his ex-wife, only to accidently have a hand in helping a guy with an axe to grind burn down a barn and frame Jonah Sheffield, being around any of Jonah's family made him uneasy.

Hell, his involvement with Jonah's mishap made it difficult to be around most people in Smithview. The year before, he'd moved back to town in hopes of reuniting his family—a family he'd always longed for. Instead, he'd alienated almost everyone in town and spent most of his time either alone or with Sam. His relationship with Sam was better than ever, but he needed more. He just wasn't sure how to get it.

He glanced through the corner of his eye. Emma's lips curved up at the corners, and his dread melted away. Waiting for her response, he tilted his head and wrinkled his nose.

"You're right. Being alone does suck." She drew in a shaky breath.

"I'm sorry. I shouldn't have been so callous." The words trickled from his mouth.

She shook her head, and hair fell in her eyes. Hooking the strands behind her ears, she kept her gaze fixed on the road. "Everyone's tripping over themselves to tell me we'll get through this tragedy. But not one person has said how much being alone sucks."

He fidgeted with some loose change in the pocket of his jeans and peered down the road, waiting for the parade to start. The smell of fried food wafted up his nose. His mind was blank. He met her husband once or twice, and Luke seemed like a nice guy. But his instant attraction to Emma's petite frame and the sexy waves that bounced in her shoulder-length hair the first time he met her led him to avoid both her and her husband anytime they were around. His attraction still burned warm, causing guilt to gnaw at his conscience.

Sam ran over and stood between them. "I won Sophie the unicorn. She's so excited." Redness stained his normally olive cheeks, and small beads of sweat clung to his forehead.

Emma glanced around. "Where is she? The parade's about to start."

"Meg wanted to grab a drink first. We ran into Annie, too, and she said she would be over in a second with Anderson." Sam swiveled his head from side to side.

A groan rumbled deep in Antonio's throat, and he swallowed hard. Watching a parade with all of the Sheffields wasn't how he wanted to fill his evening. When he moved to Smithview almost a year ago, he intended to spend more time with his son and win back his ex-wife. But Jillian's love for Jonah was something he'd always battled.

When Jonah returned home from Iraq, he convinced Jillian into giving him a second chance which left Antonio pining for the family he'd always wanted. His jealousy led him to some stupid decisions not many in town were quick to forget. Jillian and Jonah were now happily married, and he was stuck in a small town with no friends and very little social life. "Do you want to watch the whole parade?" He couldn't stop how his tone dipped low with annoyance.

Sam nodded. "Definitely. All the good candy comes at the end. Doesn't it, Emma?"

Emma wrinkled her nose. "It sure does. Last year was the first time Sophie enjoyed the parade, and she insisted we stayed until the end. Unfortunately, that meant sticking around to watch every emergency vehicle in the tri-county area drive by at two miles per hour. I swear we were here for two hours."

He dropped his jaw. "You've got to be kidding me." He'd never survive being surrounded by Jonah's family for that long. They were always nice, but he could never relax with them all around.

"Not kidding." Sam grinned. "But if you don't want to stay and watch the whole thing, I can watch the parade with Mom and Jonah. I go back to Mom's house in the morning anyway." He shrugged. "I could go home with them tonight instead."

"How do you even know they're here?" Tension wound around his neck.

"Because they're right behind you with Annie and Anderson." Sam leaned to the side, bending at the waist, and waved.

Every muscle in his body stiffened. Turning, he faced Jonah's tight jaw and rigid stance.

Jonah's arm wrapped around Jillian's waist.

A silent agreement to remain civil was established, but their relationship would never go beyond niceties. Jonah made Jillian happy, and he was good to Sam.

Antonio didn't need to know anything else.

"Hey, everyone." Annie moved the stroller back and forth while she talked. "Did you two run into each other?"

Antonio glanced at Emma and waited for her answer.

"Sam caught sight of me a little earlier and wanted to know where Sophie was." She dipped her chin in his direction. "Antonio was kind enough to stand with me and help keep our spot while Sam played games with Meg and Sophie."

At that moment, Meg and Sophie stepped up beside Annie. A giant pink unicorn dragged along the ground beside Sophie.

"Look, Mom, Sam won the unicorn." Sophie broke free and ran to Emma. She wrapped herself around Emma's legs.

Words spilled out of Sophie's mouth faster than he could understand. She spoke with elaborate hand motions, and her high, squeaky voice rambled on. He watched her excitement, and his tension slipped away. He shifted his gaze, and his heart skipped a beat. Emma smiled sweetly as she listened to Sophie, but something in her eyes made him want to take her in his arms. A glassiness turned her sapphire eyes vulnerable and sad.

She secured Sophie in her arms. Moisture pooled at the corners of her eyes, and the illusion of happiness unraveled. He glanced away before he did something stupid, and he landed his gaze on Jillian.

Jillian narrowed her gaze and thinned her lips before she curved them up. "Has Sam been good?"

"He was a little impatient to get here, but he's been great. He mentioned something about staying with you so he could watch the whole parade. Would him going home with you be okay?" With his hands still in his pockets, he rubbed a coin between his thumb and forefinger.

A hard glint sparked in Jillian's green eyes, and she tilted her head. An uneasiness hummed through him. She knew him too damn well. He needed to stay away from Emma, or Jillian would see his attraction as clearly as the pink unicorn now lying at Sophie's feet.

"You don't want to watch the parade?" She hooked up an eyebrow.

He cleared his nervousness from his throat. "I wouldn't mind watching a little bit, but maybe not the whole thing. I have an early flight in the morning and don't want to get home late. If Sam spending the night with you is a problem, I can take Sam home." He shifted his weight to his left foot and the toe of his right foot pointed toward home, as if his subconscious told him to get out of here. He needed to get away from Emma and her sad eyes and forget the nagging feeling to comfort this woman he hardly knew.

"Jonah and I will be here anyway. Sam can stay with us." Jillian glanced down the street. "Do you plan to come to Sam's birthday party at the inn next weekend?"

"I wouldn't miss it." Seeing more of Sam was the reason he moved back. He missed too many birthday parties throughout Sam's life. How uncomfortable he might be once he got there didn't matter. He owed it to Sam to be present in his life.

Jillian squeezed his arm. "Good. Make sure and say bye before you leave."

Antonio returned his focus to the street. Decorative

floats and a gaggle of tiny cheerleaders marched past. Thank God. Making small talk with Jillian and her new family was awkward as hell. He was an outsider. He stood quietly and prayed the loud blasts from the sirens didn't add to the headache already building in the center of his forehead.

Twenty minutes later, he'd had enough. "Sam." He leaned down and tapped Sam on the shoulder, making sure not to disturb Sophie who sat beside him on the curb.

"Yeah, Dad?" Sam's gaze never wavered from the parade.

"I'm taking off. Your mom said you could watch the rest of the parade and go to her place tonight. I'll see you later this week, okay?"

"Okay, see ya."

"Wow, what a heartfelt goodbye." Antonio laughed and rubbed the top of Sam's head.

"Stop." Sam swatted away his dad's hand and laughed. "Sorry. I'll see you later." He stood, gave Antonio a hug, and returned to his seat.

A light touch brushed against his arm, and goose bumps broke out where the sensation lingered. He faced Emma. She was so close he inhaled the citrusy scent of her shampoo, and his stomach muscles clenched. He stepped back.

"Are you heading home now?" She widened her eyes and crossed her arms over her chest.

He ran a hand through his hair and scratched the top of his head. "I've had my limit of small-town excitement for the night."

"Did you drive here?"

"Sam and I walked. I only live a couple of blocks

away." He cocked his head to the side. "Why?"

Emma scrunched her nose then dropped her gaze. "I hoped to get a ride home."

"Oh." A rush of adrenaline shot through him, causing the word to come out too loud. "Getting you home isn't a big deal, but we need to walk to my place first. My house is probably closer than wherever you parked your car."

Emma gave a snort of laughter. "You're probably right. Are you sure you don't mind? The kids want to stay, and I can leave my car with my mom if you drive me."

"Not at all." He answered quickly—too quickly. He shouldn't spend more time than was necessary with her, but what harm was there in a short drive home?

"Great." Emma exhaled a long breath. "Let me say goodbye and let Sophie know I'm leaving. She won't even notice I'm gone. I don't exist anyway whenever Meg's around."

He waited a few feet away while she spoke with her family.

Annie grabbed her hand, and Meg nodded as Emma spoke.

Jonah's shoulders tightened, and his gaze found Antonio's. He gave one shake of his head and worked his jaw.

Antonio forced a tight smile and gave Jonah a little wave before he sought Emma.

She gave each of her children a kiss before making her way to his side. "Ready?"

Nodding, he put his hand back in his pocket and turned toward his house. He weaved between crowds of people who huddled together talking and children running in all directions. The smell of corndogs and fried cheese on a stick practically clogged his arteries.

Emma kept her head down, never pausing to talk to the people who stared.

Pivoting, he blocked her from the gawkers. Small towns had their charm, but the disregard for others' privacy wasn't something the citizens of Smithview cared about. He made it past the crowds and to the neighborhood sidewalk. The music faded in the background. "Did the fair excitement wear you out?"

Emma shrugged. "Today's been long, and I'm not in the mood to be around a bunch of people. I'll deal with everyone and their pity at some point, but I don't have the energy tonight."

"I understand. Letting the kids experience the fair for a while was nice." He kicked a rock off the path.

"Seeing Sophie having fun was enjoyable. She's been so sad and distant since Luke died. I hope being here will help. We need to heal and move forward, even if both seem impossible."

She shivered despite the heat of the August air. Antonio was silent for a minute and continued to walk beside her. The stillness of the warm summer night surrounded him, even as the sounds of laughter trailed behind him.

From the corner of his eye, he stole a glance and studied her profile with the soft glow of the lamp light that shone down. Damn, she was beautiful. "I've never experienced the death of a loved one, but I have dealt with loss before." Pressure squeezed his heart. Losing Jillian was like losing a limb. The pain of their divorce lingered, even if she'd moved on, and he knew they weren't meant to be. "When you're ready, you'll heal.

All of you. No right or wrong way exists. No timeline dictates these things. You were happy once. You'll be happy again."

Emma stopped and tilted her head. "You've said exactly what I needed to hear twice tonight. Thank you."

His chest tightened, and he gave his shoulders a small shrug. "I just say what I think. I'm surprised no one else hasn't said the same thing."

"Everyone is so worried about saying the wrong thing to the poor widow that all they say is the same reassuring nonsense over and over again. Don't get me wrong, my family is amazing. They want to help. What they don't understand is nothing they do will help." She wiped a tear at the corner of her eye. "I'm tired of explaining how I feel or what I think. The kids and I need to find our new normal. I can't do that when everyone acts like I'm a fragile piece of glass about to break. Trust me, I already shattered into a million pieces the day Luke died. Now, I have to figure out how to put back together the pieces."

Antonio took off toward his house again. His divorce left him broken, but he'd picked up the pieces and moved on. Emma would do the same. "I don't know much about you, Emma, but I know you're not fragile. And your daughter is an awful lot like her mother. She'll bounce back. I have a feeling Sam has made Sophie's happiness his new mission. He adores that little girl."

"The feeling's mutual. He's wonderful with her. If putting a smile on Sophie's face is his new mission, I sure hope he succeeds soon."

Silence wove through the air, but this time he

didn't search for the right words. He didn't need to. He continued until he reached the driveway and opened the passenger side of his sports car. Once they were both secured with seatbelts, he drove toward the inn.

Emma ran her fingers along the black interior that lined the door.

He tightened his hands on the soft leather of the steering wheel. Her long, slender fingers caressed the material. His pulse beat in his throat. The movement was so casual, yet so damn sexy, he forced his gaze to focus on the road.

"Luke loved his sports car. His big dream was to own one. He said all he ever wanted was a beautiful wife, loving children, and a nice car. He bragged about being lucky enough to get all three." Her voice caught, and she let out a shaky breath. "I guess his luck ran out."

"Sounds like he had more luck in his short time here than most men have in an entire lifetime." Sadness pinched his chest. Luke had everything Antonio fought so hard to get back—something he'd foolishly let slip away. He'd do anything to belong to the type of family Emma and her husband created and cherished.

She placed her hands in her lap. "Are you uncomfortable when I talk about Luke?"

He cast her a quick glance before returning his attention to the road. "No, why should it?"

"I don't know. Most people act uncomfortable when I talk about little things he liked or funny things he used to say."

The red eyes of a deer glowed by the side of the road, and he decreased the speed of the car. "To be honest, I didn't really know him. Hell, I don't really know you. Think of me as a clean slate. Whenever we run into each other, feel free to say whatever you want. No judgment or making me uncomfortable—just an innocent bystander who's willing to listen to whatever you need to get off your chest."

Emma chuckled. "An innocent bystander, huh? Don't most people call that a friend?"

Antonio grinned. He didn't have many friends these days. "I guess they do, but don't you already have enough of those around here?"

Emma cleared her throat. "I have a lot of family, I have some life-long friends, but I don't have anyone who I don't have to worry about how my feelings affect them. Having someone I can vent to would be nice."

Surrounding herself with family and loved ones she couldn't let her guard down with wasn't fair. But she wouldn't want his pity. "Emma, I can be whatever you want me to be."

Emma laughed so hard she swatted his arm and then wrapped her arms around her stomach. "Your statement sounded pretty darn intimate from a man who doesn't even know me." Her words came out between gasps for breath.

He groaned. He should say things in his head before speaking. A chuckle broke through his throat. Her laugh was infectious. "I've said something stupid in front of you twice tonight."

Emma waved away his words and then wiped the tears from her eyes. "Don't worry. Laughing felt good. Thank you for sounding like an idiot."

Antonio drove down the long, tree-lined driveway toward the inn. His heart sank. He didn't want to leave her. Most of his free time was spent with a soon-to-be nine-year-old boy. A long time passed since he'd been in the company of a smart, attractive woman. He banished those thoughts from his mind. She needed a friend right now. She didn't need the ex-husband of her brother's new wife to add any more complications to her already messy life.

"Thanks for the ride."

Her gratitude cut into his thoughts. "Not a problem. I hope you get some rest."

"Yeah, me, too." She sighed. "I'm glad we ran into each to each other. I'll see you next week for Sam's birthday party."

Antonio's heart gave a little pitter-patter at the thought of seeing her again so soon. "I'll be there."

Emma smiled. "Good. Have a nice night."

He sat in his car and waited for her to unlock the front door and let herself inside. Once she disappeared, he put the car in Reverse and made his way back to his big, empty house. Nothing waited there but loneliness. But tonight, with his mind centered on the one woman he had no business thinking about, loneliness echoed through his body in a way it hadn't in years.

Chapter Three

Sunlight streamed through the window, and the heat of the morning rays slid over Emma's face. Fatigue made her eyelids heavy, but a sharp kick against her side snapped them open. She'd spent four nights at her mom's house, and Sophie ended up in her tiny, twin bed every single night. She should take Meg's suggestion and push together the two beds.

Stretching her arms high above her head, Emma loosened her tight muscles and muffled a yawn. To relish the soft tug of sleep leaving her body, she closed her eyes, and an image of the man she'd dreamed about flashed in her mind. The man didn't have kind green eyes and a lopsided grin but eyes the color of melted chocolate and dimples that deepened at the smallest quirk of his lips.

Nasty tentacles of guilt wrapped around her and threatened to swallow her whole. She grabbed the framed picture of Luke from her nightstand. His black-framed glasses stared, and she ran a finger down the smooth glass. If only touching him again was so easy—or to see him again. A lump lodged in her throat, but she couldn't tear away her gaze from the man she'd loved for so many years. She needed his face to be the one in her mind when she drifted off to sleep and the first one she imagined when she woke in the morning. Anyone else just wasn't right.

"Mommy, is it morning?"

Sophie's usually high voice was deep with sleep. "It sure is, honey pie." Emma let her gaze linger for a beat on the picture of Luke from their last vacation before she set down the photo then stared into the wide, blue eyes of her daughter. If she wanted to see Luke's face, it definitely wasn't in Sophie's smooth, pale skin and bow-shaped mouth that were identical to Meg. No, Luke's features were more visible in his son.

Sophie popped a thumb in her mouth and wrapped her fingers around the frayed edges of her pillowcase. "Is Anderson up?"

Emma tossed off the comforter and slipped into her robe. The soft cotton covered her shorts and tank top, and she slid on a pair of slippers. "Let's find out." She opened wide her arms for Sophie to jump into.

With Sophie, her pillow, and her blanket nestled against her hip, Emma stepped into Anderson's room.

"Mama, Mama, Mama," he murmured over and over.

"Soph, can I put you down?" She smoothed away a piece of hair from Sophie's soft cheek and placed a kiss on her nose.

Sophie scrambled to her feet.

Anderson lifted his arms.

"Good morning, little man." She picked him up and nuzzled him close then changed his diaper. The baby shampoo she'd used the night before lingered in his hair, and her ovaries squeezed at the familiar scent. A tug on her robe shifted her attention back to Sophie.

"I'm hungry, Mommy."

"Well, then, let's get some breakfast. I hear Grandma in the kitchen already. I bet she's making something yummy." She squished together her face with enthusiasm. Excitement lit Sophie's eyes.

Sophie ran out of Anderson's room.

Emma followed, making sure not to step on the blanket trailing behind Sophie. She rounded the corner into the kitchen, and saliva filled her mouth. The scents of cinnamon and sugar mixed together and wafted in the air. Coffee was her usual breakfast of choice, but not when her mom's homemade cinnamon buns sat cooling on the stove.

"I'm surprised you three took this long to find your way to the kitchen. I've been baking for hours." Annie wiped her hands on her apron.

"Do you ever sleep?" Emma placed Anderson in his highchair, and then helped Sophie climb into a chair at the large farm table that dominated one side of the kitchen.

Annie cut a cinnamon bun in half and placed the pieces on plastic plates. "Not when I have guests who want breakfast."

"Thanks." She grabbed the plates, placed them in front of her drooling children, and then grabbed their sippy cups from the refrigerator.

"The coffee's fresh." Annie rummaged in the bottom cabinet. She stood and placed a silver mixing bowl on the island.

"One of the perks of moving in with you." Emma kissed her mother's cheek and then grabbed a mug from the cabinet above the coffee pot. "I have a question."

"Sure, what's on your mind?"

"Do you know where I can get a job?" She sat on a stool at the large island, turning on the seat so she could keep one eye on the kids. She pinched off a piece of her cinnamon bun and popped it in her mouth. The warm, gooey icing tasted like heaven.

Annie knit together her brows and mixed the dry ingredients for another batch of rolls. "Why do you want a job? I thought your finances were taken care of."

"Luke made sure money wouldn't be an issue in case something happened. The sale of the house helped, too, but I still need to contribute." She licked her lips, cleaning off every last morsel of pastry.

Annie waved a hand through the air. "Don't be ridiculous. This old house was paid off years ago, and I make more than enough money to get by."

"What about when Meg takes her horses to Dylan's farm? Once they open Gilbert Farms this fall, she won't have a reason to do lessons here." Meg and her boyfriend were busting their butts to create a travel destination for fun for all ages at his family's farm. They hoped to have it ready in a month, and then her mom would lose the income Meg earned with her horses when the guests at the inn couldn't take spontaneous riding lessons.

"If you ask me, she should take those darn things to Dylan's now. She's there all the time anyway. Coming back and forth is a waste of her time. We both know she'd rather be in the brand-new barn Dylan built." Annie stopped mixing and placed her hands on her hips. "Maybe I should discuss moving the horses. I would hate if she delayed because she thinks the move would upset me."

"I'm sure she'd appreciate you discussing it." Emma swooped Anderson's sippy cup from the seat of the highchair and placed it back on his tray. "But can we get back to my issue? I need a job."

Annie furrowed her brow. "Why do you need a job? You stayed home and took care of your kids before. Why does your employment have to change?"

Emma sighed and pushed away her empty plate. "Things are different. Yes, the kids keep me busy, but I don't have a house to maintain now. I also want to make sure I'm in a position to take care of things financially before I buy a home."

"You already plan to move? You just got here." Annie plunged her hands back into the bowl and dropped her gaze.

Emma cringed, guilt squeezing her chest at hurting her mom. "I don't plan on moving anytime soon. We need time to adjust to our new life as three, and being here is best. But we can't live in your house forever, and I want to be prepared for whatever the future holds. I need to make sure I can provide for my family." She hesitated for a beat. She once had big dreams of designing homes and building a business. Finally putting her interior design degree to use would be nice. "I need something a little more fun to focus on."

"And a job will give you fun?" Annie chuckled.

"Would you stop grilling me and just offer some suggestions?" Praying for patience, she sucked in a deep breath and wiped crumbs from the countertop. She wasn't used to explaining herself. Heck, her mom hadn't asked this many questions when she was a teenager.

Annie sighed and leaned forward on the island. Small clumps of dough dripped from her hands. "What about interior design? You loved decorating when you graduated college—before you had Sophie."

"I did love my job." Emma twisted her lips. "But

one of the reasons we moved was because Cleveland offered more opportunity for our skills. Do you really think I could make a living as a designer here?"

Annie shrugged. "You never know until you try. You might pick up a job here and there while staying home with the kids most of the time."

Mulling over her mom's suggestion, Emma was silent for minute. She did love letting her creativity flow in a new space. She missed playing a part in helping people fall in love with their homes. "What if I need more than a side job every now and then?" She glanced over her shoulder to make sure the kids hadn't smeared icing on the walls.

"What if you don't?" Annie returned her focus on her baked goods. "Why don't you give it some thought? You don't want to rush into anything. For now, you can help Jillian and me with Sam's party this weekend."

She raised her brows. "You mean you don't already have his party all planned and put together?" Her mom loved to put on a party and often went overboard.

"I've taken a backseat on this one, and not jumping in with both feet is killing me." Annie released a groan. "I don't want to scare off Jillian by being the overbearing mother-in-law. She mentioned a pirate theme, and I haven't heard anything else. You and Jillian are good friends." She glanced up and wiped her chin on her shoulder. "I'm sure she'd be happy if you helped."

"Sounds like fun. But do you want to keep me busy this week or use me to get Jillian in gear?" Emma picked up her coffee and took a long sip. While she studied her mom, she kept her hands wrapped around the mug and suspended in the air.

Annie lifted her chin and pursed her lips. "I have no idea what you're talking about."

Smiling, she sipped her coffee and let the caffeine rush into her bloodstream. "Well, thanks for the suggestion. Since the party is this weekend, I should talk to Jillian as soon as possible. Do you mind if I run to Jillian's bookstore?"

"No problem. I won't get a new guest until this evening. I'll finish here soon, and then I can enjoy my grandbabies for a little bit."

Emma jumped from the island and reached for another cinnamon bun.

Annie smacked her hand.

Laughing, she yanked back her hand. "Thanks, Mom. I'll be back soon." She leaned forward and kissed Annie's cheek, hugged her children, and then darted from the kitchen. Anxiety dipped in her stomach. As much as she wanted to find something to fill her time, this was one more step toward a new life—a life without her beloved husband.

****

A few days later, Emma drew in a deep breath, and the humid August air stuck to her lungs like the hair glued to the back of her neck. The party hadn't even started, and she was already exhausted. She'd spent the rest of the week planning the pirate-themed party for Sam, right down to the water-filled balloons for the boys to use as cannon balls and throw off the side of the deck. The wide-eyed smile on Sam's face when he'd arrived earlier made every detail she'd toiled over worth the energy.

But now kids were arriving, and a few more snacks

needed to be carried out from the kitchen. She hurried inside through the French doors off the deck and wished she could take a minute to enjoy the cool breeze blowing through the overhead vents. Pushing back her desire to soak in the frigid air, she grabbed the last bowl of chips on the counter, spun on her heel, and slammed a shoulder into a hard chest. She tightened her grip on the bowl, and chips sloshed over the side and onto the floor. She shot up her gaze and dark, hooded eyes stared. Her breath caught.

Antonio.

He steadied the bowl, and his fingers brushed over hers.

An involuntary shiver ran down her spine, and she jerked away the bowl. "Oh, hello. I didn't see you arrive." Her voice came out at the same octave as a teenage boy before puberty hit.

He rubbed a hand over his jaw and then let his arm fall to his side. "A sign said to come in."

"I'm glad you can read." To hide her shaky breath, she forced a short laugh. She hadn't expected to find him in the kitchen, and his closeness set her nerves on edge. Especially when images of her stupid dreams invaded her brain, reminding her of how much he'd been on her mind since he'd given her a ride home. "Do you want to come out back? I think everyone's here. Sam said he wanted to do the scavenger hunt first, so we'll probably start soon."

Antonio's eyebrows arched high. "Scavenger hunt?"

Emma grinned. "Didn't Sam tell you this was a pirate birthday party?"

"He must have forgotten." Antonio fished out a

chip from the bowl still held between their bodies.

Enjoying the easy banter, she grinned. "Don't worry. Eye patches and black hats are available outside."

Antonio cringed and roamed a hand over his hair.

Emma dropped her gaze to the floor. His dark good looks were dangerous enough. He'd be downright lethal if he donned a pirate getup.

"I'm down for a hat, but I might have to pass on the eye patch."

Emma cleared her throat and then hurried to open the backdoor. She waved an arm through the open door but kept her gaze on the potato chips. "Right this way."

Antonio strolled outside.

Emma followed, placed the bowl on the table with the rest of the food, and scanned the crowd in the backyard.

"Do you know any of these people?" Antonio leaned close.

"Some are familiar." Emma glanced toward the giant oak tree in the back yard. Meg spun Sophie in a wide circle, while Dylan held Anderson. Of course, Sophie would be with Meg.

"None of them look familiar. Maybe some of the kids, but not the parents." Antonio rubbed the back of his neck.

"I need to talk to Meg." She took a step and then stopped. She'd been the odd man out in a new place more times than she could count. The feeling wasn't fun. "Do you want to come?"

Nodding, he fell into step.

His hand brushed against hers. Butterflies danced in her stomach. She should pull away her hand but couldn't. The soft, warm skin on hers caused a tingling sensation to shoot up and down her arm. Her lips tugged up, and she did a mental eye roll.

Meg narrowed her gaze and tilted her head to the side.

Emma gave a slight shake of her head. She made sure Meg was fine watching the kids and then cleared her throat. "Hello, everyone." She shouted over the screaming boys crowded on the deck. "I'm so glad you came to Sam's party to help celebrate his ninth birthday. Our first activity is a scavenger hunt. We have treasure maps for everyone." She pointed toward the table holding the maps. "The first team to collect all of the treasure wins. Everyone pair up, and good luck!"

Boys ran around searching for a partner and then grabbed their maps as fast as they could.

Sam rushed over with his friend, Tom. "Will you play, Dad? Mom and Jonah are playing. They're on a team. You should play, too."

Antonio winced. "I would, but I don't have anyone to be on my team. I'll watch."

Sam waved a hand in Emma's direction. "Emma can be on your team. She knows where everything is, but she won't cheat. She can hold the map while you hunt for the treasure."

"I wouldn't be a very good partner." Emma laughed and ignored the excitement in her stomach over spending time with Antonio.

"It's fine." Sam scrunched up his face. "He's a grown-up, so he doesn't need as much help."

"His logic is hard to argue with." Antonio shrugged.

Heat crept up her neck. Thank God the weather

was so warm. No one would guess Antonio's simple gaze caused the warmth spreading through her.

He rocked back on his heels. "What do you say? Will you be my map carrier?"

"I guess. I wouldn't want you to treasure hunt by yourself." Emma heaved a heavy sigh and shrugged but couldn't keep the smile from her voice.

"See, I knew Emma would do it." Sam nodded then ran off with his friends.

"All right, partner, go get that map." She watched Antonio make his way across the lawn and up the stairs. His long legs strode across the yard, and his demeanor screamed confidence. An internal battle warred. He laughed at something her mom said, and the sound caused goose bumps to ripple up her arms. Her reaction was crazy. Antonio was only her friend.

Heck, he was barely even an acquaintance. He was a nice guy and Sam's dad. She definitely shouldn't be taking note of him—especially with his history with Jonah. Not to mention she was a widow, not a young girl who got caught up in senseless fantasies with handsome men. Even if his dark looks and straight-to-the-point personality were sexy.

Antonio hurried back and grinned, waving the map in the air.

Her knees swayed. Lord help her.

"What will it take for you to tell me where everything's hidden?" He wiggled his eyebrows.

"Trust me." She smirked. The easy banter lifted her heart. "You couldn't handle my rate."

He grinned. "I have no doubt." He glanced at the map before placing it in her outstretched hand. "We're getting a later start than everyone else, so we should work backward."

Emma grabbed the map and twisted it in her hands. "Good plan. We should head behind the horse barn." Without another word, she took off in the direction of the barn. The inn was located on a large piece of property, with the barn on the south end of the property. She held her breath, waiting for his hand to brush hers again. Another feel of his warm skin didn't happen, and disappointment filled her.

The farther away she ventured from the house, the quieter it became. Emma handed him the crumbled paper. "I'll sit here and see how long you take to figure out the map." She strolled to the split-rail fence that corralled the horses and stepped on top of the handle of a rake lying on the ground. She shot out her arms to steady herself.

Antonio reached for her.

She hit his cheek before he could duck. She whipped around her other arm to grab him, throwing them both even more off balance. "Oh, no!"

Antonio wrapped an arm around her waist.

The impact of her body sent them both flying to the grass. She erupted into laughter and rolled to a stop beside the open barn door. Gazing into his brown eyes, she sucked in a breath. She ached to release the smile, but her muscles refused to cooperate. She dropped her gaze to his lips, and her mouth went dry. What would kissing those full, sensual lips feel like? The familiar pangs of guilt echoed through her, but she didn't want to leave the warmth of his embrace.

She shifted her gaze back to his. The brown of his eyes melted, and she searched for the strength to either pull away or dive in.

Lowering his head, Antonio gently placed his lips on hers.

She closed her eyes, and heat melted her core. The echoes of guilt shouted to stop, but she quieted them for another day when she didn't have to choose between loneliness or grief. Both were her constant companions, and for one minute, she just wanted to be held by a pair of strong arms.

He broke away.

Her heart lodged in her throat. She opened her eyes, and the longing in his gaze scolded her. Whether it was right or not, she wanted him. Fear spiked in her gut, and she swallowed hard.

He wrapped his arms around the small of her back.

A soft sigh escaped her mouth, and she laid her head on his rapidly beating heart. The scent of sandalwood and citrus tickled her nostrils.

Oh boy, she was in big trouble.

Chapter Four

Antonio danced his fingers along Emma's spine and willed his thundering pulse to slow. Her breath seeped through the fabric of his T-shirt—its heat scorching his skin. Her head lay nestled on his chest, and he moved his fingers so he wouldn't bury them in her hair and devour her. Desire pulsed through him, but he kept himself in check. He shouldn't have kissed her in the first place, but he couldn't resist. Even if she still grieved for her husband.

Emma lifted her head and rested her chin on his sternum. "Well, that was unexpected."

Her lips curved into the sexiest damn smile he'd ever seen. He huffed out a laugh. "I'm sorry."

"Please, don't apologize." She smoothed her hands over the front of his shirt and followed the motion of her fingers with her gaze. "The kiss was nice."

He arched an eyebrow. "Nice?" Crimson stained her sun-kissed cheeks.

She buried her head in his neck. "I don't know what to say."

"You don't have to say anything." He flattened a palm on her back and rubbed circles over her shirt. The fabric bunched beneath his hand. "This shouldn't have happened."

"Do you really think kissing me was a mistake?"

Her voice muffled against his chest. Of course he

didn't. She was everything he ever wanted in a woman. The need to roll her over and touch every inch of her body rumbled through him.

Her head snapped up, and her eyes widened. "Did you hear that?"

He lifted his head and strained his ears. Laughter echoed through the barn and drifted out the back door. The hairs on the back of his neck stood up. "Jillian."

Emma scrambled to her feet.

He jumped up behind her and brushed off dirt from the back of his pants.

The laughter morphed into squeals of protest. Jillian and Jonah wandered through the barn door. Jillian slapped Jonah's hand off her hip.

He growled and pulled her into his arms.

Jillian's arms snaked around Jonah's neck, and she lifted her gaze, and her eyes widened. She stepped away from Jonah and cleared her throat.

"What's wrong?" Jonah ran a palm over her arm.

Jillian lifted a finger and pointed behind him.

Jonah glanced over his shoulder and scowled before turning to face them. "What are you two doing back here?"

Antonio grabbed his treasure map from his pocket and held it in the air. "We're on a treasure hunt. I assume that's what you two are doing here as well."

Color flooded Jillian's face, and she dropped her gaze to the ground.

No way they planned to find a couple gold coins.

"What we're doing is none of your business." Jonah took a step toward them.

A baseball hat sat low on his head, but it couldn't hide his hardened expression or the anger in his voice.

"Well, I could say the same thing to you." Antonio's voice was tight, and he ground his teeth together.

Jonah's gaze sought Emma's. "Why do I keep finding you with this guy?"

Emma held up a palm and then planted her hands on her hips. "I don't really care who you find me with. What's with the attitude?"

Jonah took another step forward.

Jillian placed a hand on his arm and gave a small shake of her head. Her long, honey colored hair fanned around her shoulders at the motion.

Antonio tightened his grip around the map so he wouldn't slap the stupid expression off Jonah's face. He couldn't stand Jonah's holier than thou attitude.

Blowing out a long breath from his nose, Jonah hung his head. "Sorry. I didn't expect to see anyone back here, and seeing you all chummy with Antonio threw me for a loop. You know what he did."

Blood pulsed in his ears. Jonah had some nerve. The guy didn't even know him. "What do you mean? I'm not allowed to be friends with Emma?" The lines of Jillian's face were smooth and calm, but the slight twitch of the muscles above her eye sold her out. She was irritated. Whether at him or Jonah, he wasn't sure.

Jillian stepped between him and Jonah. "No one is saying you and Emma can't be friends. That's ridiculous."

Jonah snorted.

Jillian swiveled to face him.

The back of her head didn't reveal a lot, but Jonah's face contorted into a mixture of annoyance and resignation. Antonio coughed to stifle a laugh.

Jillian whipped back around.

Lightning bolts flashed in her green eyes. He swallowed hard.

"What's ridiculous is this entire conversation." Emma stared down Jonah until he lowered his gaze and concentrated on his shuffling feet.

Pride swelled in Antonio's chest. Emma was a petite little thing, but she had spunk.

"I'm a grown woman, and I can spend time with whoever I want. Now, I suggest you get the stick out of your butt and find Sam. This is his day, and there's no reason all of you should be back behind the barn." Pressing her lips together, she raised her brow.

His lip twitched, and he fought a grin from taking over his mouth.

Jonah stormed out of the barn. Dust lifted into the air behind him, catching the rays of sun shining through the open door.

The side of Jillian's lip hitched into a half-smile before she followed.

Antonio glanced at Emma, and a bark of laughter took over. "You can be pretty scary."

She faced him, hands still resting on her hips, and rolled her eyes. "So I've been told." She lifted a hand and pointed a finger at his chest. "You need to be nicer to Jonah."

He lifted his hands in the air. "Are you kidding? I'm sorry, but your brother's a jerk. I didn't do anything."

Emma lowered her chin and pressed her lips into a firm line. "Really? You didn't egg him on? I know all about your history with him and Jillian. I also know you didn't tell Blake to set Dylan's barn on fire, so trying you for another man's crimes is pointless. Unless you're still harboring feelings for Jillian, you both need to grow up and get over it. The rest of us have."

"I'm not harboring feelings for Jillian, but why should I be any different around Jonah?" He scowled and kicked the dirt like a child. "We'll never be friends. We have to tolerate each other for Sam's sake and nothing more."

"But you are friends with me, which means you'll be around him even more. Unless you want more uncomfortable encounters, you two better figure out how to be more civil."

His heart lurched. She still considered him a friend, even after they kissed. He mentally shook his head. He shouldn't have expected anything else. She was honest about where she stood. Hell, her husband had only been gone a few months. Emma and he shared one simple, little kiss. Just because it had shaken his senses and left him breathless didn't mean it'd had the same effect on her. Obviously, it didn't.

"Jonah and I could get along a little better. I'll try harder." Like hell he would, but Emma didn't need to know he didn't plan to be nice. Jonah would always be the guy who ruined his marriage, even if he was over his ex-wife.

"Good." She bit her bottom lip and glanced toward the door. She dropped her hands to her sides and fidgeted with the front of her shirt.

"Are we okay? I overstepped, and I'm sorry if I made you uncomfortable." He buried his hands in the pockets of his jeans to keep from touching her. Unshed tears hovered over her lashes. Guilt sliced through his gut.

She sniffed back her tears. "We're good. Just forget about it." Her voice trembled, and her hands shook as she wiped her eyes.

Unable to resist, he grabbed her shoulders and secured her close to his chest. He wrapped one arm around the small of her back and the other brushed her light brown hair off her face. "Don't cry, Emma."

"This is stupid. I have no reason to be upset." She folded her arms over her chest. "I mean, I didn't do anything wrong. But I can't stop this crushing sense of betrayal in the pit of my stomach."

"You're right. You didn't do anything wrong. But you weren't ready for something to happen. We've talked about this and already decided we both need a friend. Nothing more. I got caught up in the moment, and things progressed too far."

She inhaled a shuddering breath, leaving his shirt damp. She pulled away, and the tears had dried in her bloodshot eyes. "Let's get back to the party. The boys should be here any minute, and I need to check on the kids."

Even though his insides rattled, he forced a smile. "Sounds good." He led her to the front of the barn.

A swarm of boys ran toward them. Sam stopped and threw his arms around Emma's waist. "This is awesome. Best birthday ever!"

Emma squeezed him tight, and laughter bubbled out. "I'm glad you like it, buddy. Now go get some more coins."

Antonio watched Sam run after his friends and disappear behind the barn. His heart hammered against his ribs, and uneasiness took hold of his stomach. As much as he wanted to be friends with Emma, he needed

---

to keep his distance. She was too tempting, and he couldn't resist her forever. He'd proven that by kissing her in the barn. Sometimes he was such an idiot.

When the boys were out of sight, he and Emma walked back toward the house. His uneasiness grew, causing an upset stomach. He passed on the food and only stayed until Sam opened his presents and everyone sang happy birthday.

Now was a good time to slip out. He said goodbye to Sam and weaved around the side of the house toward his car. He dug his hands in his pockets and kept his gaze on his feet. The feel of Emma's lips on his was branded in his mind.

His chest tightened as he climbed into his car and drove out of the driveway. Living in a place where no one missed you wasn't fun. He didn't regret his decision to move back to Smithview. He wouldn't trade the relationship he'd rebuilt over this last year with Sam for anything. But being alone still sucked.

The closer he got to home, the tighter his chest became. He couldn't go back to his big, empty house. Not tonight. He drove past his street and headed into town. The only time he ever visited uptown was with Sam. Smithview was a close-knit community, and gazes always followed him everywhere. He was an outsider who came to town and tried to ruin the relationship between two of the town's beloved people. No one would ever see beyond his mistakes, no matter how much time passed.

But he couldn't leave. Not when his son was here. He had to find a way to fit in and become a part of the community. Maybe doing that would push away his constant loneliness.

He parked his car and slid into the hot, muggy air. Sweat pooled at the back of his neck, and he wiped it away. He stepped onto the sidewalk and rushed toward the bar. He'd never been inside The Village Idiot, but it was the only bar in town, and he needed a drink. He grabbed the metal handle, and it scorched his hand. Throwing open the door, he hurried inside. The cold air from the air conditioner slapped him in the face, and his body shivered.

The crowd inside was thin. Soft music played from a jukebox. A couple tables in the back were taken by families eating dinner, and one man sat at the bar. A tall, dark-haired beauty tended bar, and her breasts all but poured out of the deep v of her shirt whenever she leaned over the bar. Red lipstick accented the heavy pout of her lips, and her deep, husky laugh should have warmed his blood. But it didn't. Her over-the-top sexuality stood in stark contrast to Emma's understated beauty, and right now, his body hummed for Emma. Hesitation left him standing by the door.

The bartender lifted her heavily shadowed eyes. A wide smile split her face. "Have a seat. We won't bite."

He chuckled and rubbed the rough whiskers on his face, taking a seat at the closet bar stool.

The bartender sauntered over and put her hands on the bar, angling forward. She arched her brows. "Can I get you something to drink?"

"I'll take a whiskey on the rocks."

She smirked and nodded. "Well, all right then. Most guys around here stick to beer. I like a man who can handle his liquor." Her hips swayed from side to side as she grabbed a glass at the far side of the bar and filled it. She fixed her gaze on him.

He squirmed in his seat. One sparkling eyelid winked shut, and she placed the cold glass in his hand. Her fingers brushed up against his, lingering a few seconds too long. He cleared his throat, slid away his hand, and lifted the glass to his lips. He wanted no part of whatever she offered. "Thanks."

A soft chuckle sounded from the man down the bar. The brown-haired guy scanned him with cool blue eyes, and then fixed a wide grin on his face. "Hey, buddy. Long time no see."

Antonio tightened his grip on his glass and bit back a groan. He hadn't seen or heard from Blake in months, and he didn't want to deal with him now. He tipped his head in a silent greeting and gulped down the rest of his drink. The whiskey burned his esophagus, and he winced. He placed the glass back on the bar and batted it back and forth between his hands. "Can I get my check?"

"Leaving so soon?" The bartender frowned.

Heat crept up the back of his neck. Damn, she made him uncomfortable.

The chuckle returned, and Blake slid over to the empty stool at his side. "No hello for an old friend?"

Antonio ran his tongue over the top of his teeth. This guy caused nothing but trouble a few months before, but people weren't exactly lining up to get to know him. Taking a deep breath, he decided to test the waters and see what Blake had on his mind. "Haven't seen you around. Last I heard, you skipped town."

Blake widened his eyes and frowned. "Taking off was a mistake. I screwed up big time, but now I'm here to make things right. I served some time and have a ton of community service to take care of. I'm sorry I dragged you into my mess, man. I really am."

Antonio stared into his empty glass. He wasn't sure if he should trust Blake, but he didn't have many other options for friends right now. Besides, he made some stupid choices, as well. Blake seemed remorseful for his actions, had paid for his crimes, and maybe deserved another chance. "You put me in a hell of a bind, but I played my part. I'm not blameless in the whole mess."

"Do you still want your check?" Sally arched her brows.

He sighed and lifted his glass. "I'll take another."

"That a boy. I hate drinking by myself." Blake grinned and slapped him on the back.

Sally grabbed his glass and brought him a full one.

Blake lifted his beer bottle and clinked it with Antonio's glass. Amber liquid spilled over the top and sloshed on the bar. "Here's to a fun night spent with friends."

Antonio forced a tight smile before taking a sip. Blake wasn't the friend he wanted to spend his Saturday night with, but his company was better than nothing. Antonio had lived here for close to a year, and it was about time he got out of his house. Blake might have burned him once, but everyone deserved a second chance. Sitting at home alone night after night was depressing. Maybe having drinks at the local bar on a Saturday night was a turning point, and he'd finally become part of this small-knit community.

He kept his glass held high in the air, and his smile widened. "To friends."

Chapter Five

A week had passed since Sam's party, and not a day went by without Emma's thoughts wandering toward Antonio. Humid heat beat down from the blue sky, the perfect backdrop to the red barn and grain silo at Meg and Dylan's farm. Emma tightened her fingers around Sophie's little hand.

A stone caught on the toe of Sophie's pink, knee-high cowgirl boot and skittered across the smooth pavement.

Sophie lifted her gaze long enough to watch it fly off the edge of the sidewalk then hung her head once more.

A vise squeezed Emma's heart. "Aren't you excited to ride Meg-Meg's horse today, honey?" Forced cheerfulness made her voice an octave higher than usual.

Sophie's shoulders hunched upward, and then dropped again.

Emma's heart split in two. "Your new boots are fabulous. You're the cutest little cowgirl I've ever seen." She swung their hands back and forth, but Sophie's palm lay limply in her grip. Biting back a sigh, she opened the door to the viewing room inside the barn.

Jillian sat on a worn armchair in the corner with her feet propped up on an old coffee table—her attention fixed on the book in her hands. She peeked over the top of the leather-bound pages, held up a finger, and fixed her gaze back on her book. "Okay, I needed to finish the page." She threw the book on the table and smiled. "Hi, Sophie, how's my favorite niece?"

Sophie curved up her lips in a half-hearted smile, and she greeted Jillian with a wave.

"What are you doing here?" Emma scooped up Sophie and set her on a stool that faced a large picture window looking into the arena.

"Sam's taking lessons." Jillian nodded toward the window.

Emma turned her head in the direction Jillian indicated.

Sam bounced along on Meg's white mare, Snowball.

Emma took a seat on the faded sofa beside Jillian. Flowers etched over every inch of the fabric. She ran her fingers across the lumpy cushion and laughed. "Where in the world did Meg and Dylan find this ugly thing?"

"The couch was in the house Jonah rented before we got married. Meg and Dylan bought some of Mrs. Price's old furniture after Jonah moved in with me. He hated the couch and cringes every time he sees it." Jillian grinned.

"I would have loved to see him lounging around on this thing." Emma nodded toward the window. "When did Sam start taking lessons?"

Jillian ran a hand through her hair, pushing the strands from her forehead. "At the beginning of the summer. He needed something to do once school was out. He loves it so far, and Dylan has him doing chores around the farm in exchange for the lessons. Working for his lessons is a good learning experience."

"Dylan getting some extra help will be nice. They're opening soon. I hope they'll put me to use to get everything ready for the fall." Emma leaned against the lumpy sofa and crossed her legs.

Jillian raised her brows. "Meg will love to boss you around for a little while."

"Yeah, she never has a problem telling me what to do." Emma raised her gaze to the wood beams lining the ceiling.

The door from the arena burst open. Sam ran in, a trail of dust coating the floor with every step.

Sophie jumped off her stool and flung her arms around him. "Hi, Sam. You did real good on Snowball."

Sam squeezed Sophie. "Thanks." He crouched to eye-level with Sophie. "Meg says you'll ride her next. Are you excited?"

A huge grin took up Sophie's face, and she nodded, her exaggerated movements causing her ponytail to sway back and forth.

The smell of dirt and hay trailed into the room. Emma's heart melted like butter.

"Will you watch me?" Sophie clutched his hand.

Sam glanced at Jillian. "Can we stay, Mom?"

Jillian scrunched her nose. "I'm sorry, buddy, but we can't. I have to get back to the store, and I told your dad I'd drop you off when you were done. You're staying with him tonight, remember?"

"Oh yeah. I'm sorry, Sophie. Maybe next time." Sam frowned.

Sophie's face fell, and she kicked at the floor, a smudge of dirt marring her pink boot. "Okay."

Emma glanced at Jillian. "What if I took Sam to his dad's when Sophie's done with her lesson? He can sit with me, and I can drop him off on my way home." Her pulse picked up. She hadn't seen Antonio since Sam's birthday party. She'd picked up her phone to call him a hundred times but didn't know what to say. Taking Sam to his house would give her a perfect excuse to see him.

Something strange flickered in Jillian's eyes. Emma tensed, as if clenching her muscles would keep Jillian from sensing her excitement.

Jillian furrowed her brow. "Are you sure you don't mind?"

"Not at all. Sophie will be so happy if Sam's here watching her." She pasted on an easy smile and held her breath. Jillian couldn't know how much she wanted to see Antonio. She didn't want to explain her feelings.

"I don't see why not, then. I'll text Antonio and let him know you'll drop off Sam in a little bit." Jillian gathered in Sam for a big hug and then kissed the top of his head. "Be good for your dad tonight. I'll call you later."

Sophie ran over and wrapped her arms around Jillian's legs. "Thanks, Jilly."

Emma snorted out a soft laugh. Her daughter picked up on everybody's nickname.

"You're very welcome, little lady. I'll see you soon, okay?" Jillian kissed Sophie's forehead then waved goodbye on her way out the door.

Meg popped her head through the open doorway attached to the arena. "Where's my munchkin?"

"I'm right here, Meg-Meg." Sophie waved an arm

in the air. "And guess what? Sam's staying to watch me ride."

Meg beamed. "Fantastic. Do you think Sam would want to stand in the arena with me during your lesson?"

"Really? I can be your helper, Meg." Sam bounced on his toes.

"You sure can. Now both of you rug rats get in here." Meg waved her arm then held open the door. "We'll be done in thirty minutes."

Emma walked to the window and leaned a hip against a stool, crossing her arms in front of her chest.

Meg buckled a helmet under Sophie's chin and then lifted her onto the saddle.

Sam stood in front of the window, turning to stick his tongue out at Emma, and then focused all his attention on Meg and Sophie.

Laughing, Emma perched on the stool to watch the lesson. Sophie's smile grew each time she made a lap. Thirty minutes flew by.

Sophie and Sam ran back into the viewing area, while Meg led the horse out of the arena and toward her stall.

Emma stretched her legs in front of her and then stood. "How'd you like it?"

Sophie grabbed her hand and jumped up and down. "I had so much fun. Did you see me? I rode all by myself, and I even steered the horse. Meg-Meg said I'm a natural."

Warmth spread to her toes. Moving back home was the right decision. Sophie showed more excitement in the last couple of weeks than she had in the previous few months. She squeezed Sophie's hand. "I did see you. You were amazing."

Sophie beamed. "Thanks, Mommy."

"Are you two ready to head out? I'm sure your dad's anxious to see you, Sam." She smiled at Sam.

"Yep, but can we say bye to Meg first?" Sam asked.

"Good idea." Emma led them through the door and over to the wide aisle where Meg housed her horses.

Meg secured Snowball in the middle of the aisle and hoisted off the large saddle. She set it on a nearby sawhorse then faced them with hands on hips. "Do you guys want to help me brush her?"

"Maybe next time." Emma ignored Sam's and Sophie's groans. "I have to take Sam to Antonio's and then get back to the house. Mom has some things to do in town, and I need to take charge of Anderson."

"Okay, on your next lesson you rug rats can groom before and after your lessons. And if you're really lucky, I'll let you muck out her stall." Meg winked.

Sam giggled.

Sophie scrunched her nose.

"Great, now I won't get her back here." Emma clapped her hands together. "Okay, say goodbye, and then climb into the car please. We have things to do."

Meg snuggled Sophie in a bear hug and whispered something in her ear.

Sophie covered her mouth and giggled.

"I'll see you soon, Sam." Meg ruffled his hair, then picked up her currycomb to brush Snowball.

"Thanks, Meg. We'll see you later. Love you." Emma waved goodbye and followed the kids out of the barn.

The bright glare of the sun blinded her. She squinted her eyes until the shadow of the car cast over her. She opened the back door, buckled in the kids, and slid into the driver seat. Katy Perry sang from the radio on their way to town. Sophie's squeaky voice joined in on the chorus, and a smile touched Emma's lips. A small bit of pressure released in her chest. Everything would be okay.

Antonio's dark eyes and dimpled grin flashed in her mind, and butterflies swarmed in her stomach. He'd left Sam's party before she said goodbye, and it dinged her pride a little he hadn't sought her out. They survived the awkwardness of their kiss, and she was eager to prove she could set aside feelings and build their friendship. Once the air was cleared for good and they moved forward, he wouldn't be invading her thoughts anymore.

She drove onto Antonio's driveway, and her palms grew damp around the steering wheel. She put the car in Park, stepped out of the driver's side door, and then wrangled the kids from their seats.

Sam ran up the sidewalk and bounced up the two steps to the wide porch. He pounded twice on the brick-red door before opening it wide and running inside.

Emma stood rooted to the spot with her arms resting on Sophie's shoulders.

Sophie peered upward. "Are we going inside, Mommy?"

With Sam inside, she didn't really need to go to the door. Maybe Antonio would think she was intrusive stopping by without an invitation. She was only supposed to drop off Sam and head straight home. Unsure of what to do, she bit her lower lip. She clasped her fingers around her keys and locked her arms around Sophie. "Let's just head home."

The screen door creaked, and Antonio stepped onto the porch.

Emma lifted her gaze. Her feet transformed to lead, and she swallowed hard as lust swam in her veins. His wavy, dark hair was slicked back, and he rubbed a towel across the back of his neck. Gym shorts hung low on his hips, and his chiseled abs glistened in the sunlight. Her mouth went dry. His bronze skin beckoned for her to touch him, and she tightened her hold on Sophie.

"Ouch. Your keys hurt me, Mommy." Sophie squirmed and lifted Emma's arms from around her neck.

"Sorry, honey." She kept her gaze glued to Antonio.

He lifted a water bottle to his lips and strolled toward them. A trickle of water slid down his neck.

Good God. She ran a hand through her tangled hair and tucked it behind an ear. Why hadn't she done something with herself today? He was the walking embodiment of a Greek God, and she was happy she remembered to brush her teeth before she left earlier.

A smile settled on his face, and he dropped his arms to his sides. "Hi there. Sam said you guys were coming in. He wanted to show Sophie his room."

The swarm of butterflies from earlier dive-bombed her stomach lining.

"I want to see Sam's room. Please." Sophie pouted her lips.

"Sure, but we can stay only a minute. I need to get back to help Grandma." She glanced at Antonio. "We don't mean to intrude."

He waved away her words, and his towel flapped

in the air. "Nonsense. I appreciate you bringing Sam home. Come on inside."

She followed Antonio up the steps and into the house. She focused all her attention on the back of Sophie's head so her gaze wouldn't wander to inspect the way his shorts clung to his backside or to the muscles of his broad back. Of all the days to show up, why did it happen when he was half-naked? God must be punishing her or tempting her beyond reason.

Sam stood on the first step of the staircase in his bare feet. "Come on, Sophie."

Sophie kicked off her boots and ran upstairs behind him without a word.

"Would you like something to drink?" Antonio turned down the hall. "I need to refill my water bottle."

"Water would be great." She darted her gaze into the darkened rooms on either side of the hallway as she followed him into the kitchen and dropped her jaw. Wood floors gleamed beneath her feet, and high vaulted ceilings rose above her. "Your house is amazing."

"Thanks, I like it. Do you want a tour?"

"I'd love to see the house." She leaned against the marble countertop on the center kitchen island. Coldness seeped into her fingers as she grazed the top. "This is beautiful. Did you pick it out?"

Antonio laughed. "I haven't picked out anything in this house. The place was renovated right before I bought it. I wanted something already furnished so I didn't have to deal with buying furniture, but no furnished homes were available when I moved here. I fell in love with this house and had to have it. The rest will come together eventually."

"You haven't furnished the house at all. Are you

crazy?" She gaped, unable to imagine not throwing herself into the details that made a house a home.

Antonio set a glass of water in front of her and placed his water bottle on the counter. He shrugged. "Decorating is too much of a hassle. I have what I need."

Emma entered the family room located off the kitchen and gasped. "All you have in here is a couch, a chair, and a television. The furniture doesn't even match."

He stepped beside her.

A shiver ripped through her. The heat from his body rubbed against her, even though his skin didn't. The musty scent of sweat tickled her nostrils.

"They're comfortable. Why do I need them to match?" He shrugged.

She dipped her chin low and wrinkled her nose. "I'm afraid to see the rest of the house."

A deep chuckle purred from his throat. "Seriously?"

Facing him, she placed her hands on her hips. "Did you know I use to be an interior designer?"

"No kidding?"

"I stopped working after I had Sophie." She tapped a toe on the wooden planks, the sound echoing across the room. "I've wanted to get back into it. Maybe I could help you."

Antonio shifted his weight and pivoted to face her. "You want to decorate my house?"

A rush of adrenaline shot through her, and her pulse picked up. She bounced up and down on her toes. "I want to help you decorate your house. I'd never do anything you didn't like. You'd have the final say on everything. We could do something really amazing."

"Sounds like a lot of work." He twisted his lips.

"But finding all the right pieces will be so much fun. We can go shopping to get an idea of what you like. Decorating won't seem like work at all."

Rubbing his jaw, he scowled. "Shopping does not sound like fun."

She slapped his arm and laughed. A jolt of electricity scorched her hand, and she yanked it back. Maybe spending more time with Antonio wasn't a good idea. The thought of decorating his house brought an excitement she hadn't known for a long time. But she wasn't sure if part of her excitement was because she'd be spending more time with him.

Smiling, his damn dimples deepened again.

He flicked his gaze to her hand, and then back. "All right, Emma. You're hired."

Chapter Six

Antonio glanced up and down the wide aisle in the home goods store. Normally, an afternoon spent shopping for decorations would be very low on his list, but he'd enjoyed his time with Emma more than he should. He'd agreed to let her help decorate the house two days before, and already he'd spent hours with Emma, poring over details he'd never considered before—details that would have bored him to death had he been with anyone else.

"What do you think about this knick-knack?" Emma held up a giant animal skull.

"It's a dead animal." He wrinkled his nose and kept his voice flat.

Emma held the skull in front of her face and hoisted it up and down as if it were talking. "I promise I won't bite if you bring me to your house."

A deep belly laugh boomed from his mouth. "Put down that thing. It's creepy."

Emma set the skull back on the shelf and grinned. "I didn't think you'd scare so easily."

"Hey now. I don't know many people who wouldn't be a little freaked out by whatever that thing was." He moved alongside her as she continued scanning the shelves. She'd dragged him to several stores to get a better understanding of his style. As if he had any. He could care less what his house looked like.

He just wanted to spend more time with her.

She smirked. "The skull's not real. The decoration is perfectly harmless and screams masculinity."

He dipped his brows together. "No, it screams, why is my head in his living room?"

Emma giggled and crouched to inspect some candles on the bottom shelf. She glanced over her shoulder. "Do you like candles?"

He shrugged. The only reason to have candles was to seduce a woman, which wouldn't happen any time soon. An image of Emma lying in his bed while candles burned low, casting shadows over her body, flashed in his mind. Heat spread through his body, and he cleared his throat. "Yeah, I like candles."

She stood with a candle in each hand. "What about these? They smell nice, and the colors are rich. They'll go well in the family room."

The scent of pine needles and eucalyptus wafted up his nose. "Sure. Let's get them." He glanced around, avoiding eye contact as he battled to beat back the lust still lingering in his gut. "Do you want me to grab a shopping cart?"

"No. We weren't supposed to get anything today." She hoisted the olive-green candles in the air. "But the candles are too good of a deal not to pick up. Did you want more than two?"

"Two's good. Are we done?" Shopping wasn't his favorite pastime, especially with no intention of purchasing anything. Décor and More was the third store they'd been to, and boredom set in an hour ago. He buried his hands in the pockets of his khaki shorts and rocked back on his heels. "Are you hungry?"

"Starving. Do you want to grab some lunch?"

Emma carried the candles toward the front of the store.

He followed. "How about purchasing some sandwiches and eating outside? A park has to be close. Do you know of a place?"

Emma tilted her chin and wrinkled her brow.

He grinned. She was so damn cute. He scrunched his hands into fists in his pockets so he wouldn't skim her button nose with his index finger. A flash of light sparked in her eyes.

"I do know of a place. I haven't been there in years, but we can check it out."

"Great. Let's hurry up, buy these, and get out of here."

Emma handed the saleswoman the candles.

Antonio grabbed his wallet from his back pocket. He took the bag and carried his purchases to the parking lot. Stopping on the sidewalk, he pulled his sunglasses from his back pocket and settled them on the bridge of his nose. "A sub shop is a couple doors down. Do you want to grab something from there?"

Emma nodded and headed for the sub shop.

He opened the door and glanced down to watch the way her skirt inched up as she stepped over the threshold and into the shop. Smooth, creamy skin came into view, and he suppressed a groan. He had to stop fantasizing about Emma. She was a friend and nothing more. Imagining her in his bed and staring at her rear were not the ways to treat a friend.

A fresh tray of buns came out of the oven, and the scent of warm wheat bread filled the small space. Saliva filled his mouth. His stomach growled. "Sorry, I haven't eaten all day. Do you know what you want?"

"I think so." She stepped up to the counter. "I'll

take a turkey sub with lettuce, cucumbers, and mayonnaise." She rummaged in her purse.

He placed a hand on her arm and shook his head. "I got this. You were nice enough to accompany me while shopping and spending my money." He shot her a wink before placing his own order.

Once they were inside with their seat belts hooked, he placed his hands on the wheel. "Where to now?"

She pointed out his window. "Take a left. A park should be a couple miles up on the right-hand side. Last time I was there was in high school, but there used to be a nice lake with a path. If I'm not mistaken, a few benches sat along the path."

"Sounds perfect." He drove past four stoplights, craning his neck to see what lie hidden on the side of the road.

"Right here." Emma extended her hand and gestured.

He pressed down his foot on the brakes a little too hard and lurched forward as he swung the car to the right. He instinctively shot out an arm to brace her, and the curve of her breasts brushed against his arm. Goose bumps erupted on his skin, and the desire that settled in his bones physically pained him. He gritted his teeth and jerked his arm away. Heat scorched his skin. He glanced at Emma out of the corner of his eye, and a deep blush settled on her cheeks.

She clicked her tongue. "Well, that's the most action I've gotten in a while. You just got to first base."

He whipped around his head, and his jaw fell open.

She sat ramrod straight and smoothed down the front of her cream-colored skirt. She glanced up through heavy lashes.

His heart raced in his chest.

Emma burst into laughter. "Get your gaze back on the road, or you'll cause an accident."

He tightened his grip on the wheel and swallowed hard. "Sorry."

"I'm teasing. It was an accident. Now turn into this parking lot, and we can find a bench to sit and eat."

He exhaled a long breath and parked in the nearest empty spot. His pulse pounded like a drum inside his ears, and he stepped out of the car. The sun shined down on his face, and he closed his eyes and lifted it toward the warmth. His even breaths calmed his racing heart and steadied his nerves.

When he opened his eyes, he was captivated by Emma's coy smile. He arched one brow. "What?"

"Nothing." She shook her head. "Just wondering what you're thinking about. You had the weirdest mixture of serenity and pain on your face."

"I was thinking about you." He slid his lips to the side. Amusement deepened Emma's grin. He grabbed the bag from her hand and walked toward an empty bench in front of the lake.

Carrying their drinks, Emma followed then set them at his feet before sitting beside him. She held out a hand.

He placed her sandwich in her palm.

She set her sandwich on her lap. "You know, you're refreshingly honest."

He snorted and unwrapped his sandwich. "Why?"

"Most people would have made up something, but not you. You don't even hesitate to admit you're thinking about me."

He shrugged. "What's the point of lying?"

Emma took a bite of her sub, and then set it on a napkin on her lap. "Was your brutal honesty ever a problem with Jillian?"

Sweat pooled at the back of his neck. Talking about his past relationship with Jillian was never easy, but discussing it with her new sister-in-law caused his blood pressure to spike. He rubbed his neck, and then wiped the moisture on his thigh. "No, her lack of honesty caused an issue."

"She lied?" Emma's voice pitched high.

He sighed. He didn't want to get into the dynamics of his relationship with his ex-wife. "Jillian lied to herself for a long time. Hell, I lied to myself, too. We both knew she didn't love me the way she loved Jonah. She was my best friend, and I loved her with everything I had. I fooled myself into thinking she felt the same way about me."

"Did you know about Jonah from the beginning?" She took a sip of her soda.

"Jillian confided in me about her entire past when we were just friends. We ended up sleeping together, she got pregnant, so we decided to marry. I was ecstatic, and I hoped she'd learn to love me the same way she did him. I mean, hell, I was the father of her child. But it never happened." His heart ached at the memory of the short marriage and the mistakes they both made.

"Why did you think her feelings would be different when you came back to town?"

"You really know how to cut to the chase, don't you?" He rubbed a hand over the scruff on his chin and stared into the clear, blue water. A tiny ripple surfed from the middle of the lake up to the shore. "So much time had passed, and my feelings for her were still so strong. I wanted my family together again, and I hoped she'd put her past with Jonah behind her. I never would have guessed he'd return to his hometown with the same intentions. Her picking him hurt, but just like before, I never stood a chance."

"I'm sorry."

He stared and tucked in the corners of his mouth. "You're sorry I didn't end up with Jillian? I'm sure your brother would love to hear you say so."

She smiled. "Jonah and Jillian were meant to be together. I'm sorry you got caught in their path."

"Well, if I hadn't gotten caught in their path, Sam wouldn't be here, so no regrets on my part." He put the last bite of his sub into his mouth, and then wadded the wrapper in his hands. "I'm glad she's happy now. Being in such a small town and not knowing many people is tough. Between the time I spend at work and the time I spend with Sam, I don't socialize much." Not that anyone wanted to spend time with him anyway. His expectation of moving to a small town and reuniting his family, growing old with close friends and community connections, was quickly replaced by a lonely reality with no end in sight. A depressing thought he tried not to dwell on.

"Even if you had time, Smithview doesn't offer much socializing." She leaned forward and grabbed her drink.

He landed his gaze on the straw as she placed her lips around it and took a sip. Every muscle in his body constricted.

She sighed. "I know how being new to town feels, though. Not having close friends can be very lonely."

He cleared his throat and forced his attention back on the lake. "Everyone loving Jonah and Jillian and looking at me as the bad guy doesn't help. A lot of people aren't in line to strike up a friendship."

Emma placed her drink back on the ground and smiled. "I'm here."

Warmth spread down to his toes. "You are, and your friendship means a lot. Especially since you're Jonah's sister."

"Trust me, Jonah doesn't have much influence over the choices I make. Definitely not about who I choose to be friends with." She cocked her head to the side. "Is it weird I'm Jonah's sister?"

He shook his head. "Not really. Your sister and mom are friendly, so I never expected anything different from you. I'm still not comfortable being around your family, Jonah in particular, but my feelings are on me. I need to get past them. With you as my interior designer, I have no choice but to put up with a Sheffield."

She chuckled and clasped her hands on her lap. "Well, I'm a Harris so you don't have to worry about spending time with a Sheffield." Her voice caught, and she dropped her gaze.

The muscles in his stomach clenched. He hadn't meant to make her uncomfortable. Silence fell while Emma finished eating. He grabbed her empty wrapper and threw away the trash. He returned to the bench and stood in front of her.

Blinking back tears, she glanced up.

Tears glimmered in her eyes like the ripples that glimmered in the water. "Are you okay?"

She drew in a deep breath through her nose. "Every

once in a while, I say something or a memory surfaces, and reality hits me. I'm a widow, and I'll never again see my husband." She wiped her eyes with the backs of her hands. "I don't mean to be a downer."

"Trust me, Emma, you're never a downer." He ached to take her in his arms and comfort her, but touching her was too risky. Instead, he clasped his hands behind his back. "Are you ready to head home?"

Emma glanced at her watch and laughed. "Oh wow. We just finished lunch, and it's close to dinner time. I guess we should get going…"

He waited for her to finish. Was she dreading ending their day together as much as he was? "We could walk around the lake first. Maybe if we work off the subs, we'll be hungry for dinner when we get home."

"I doubt I'll eat anything more today, but the exercise is worth a try." She rubbed a hand over her stomach. "I'm sure my mom will make an elaborate meal tonight and will fret like crazy if I don't eat. She's driving me nuts. Every night she makes enough food for ten people, and then she's all over me if I don't eat much. She's trying to fatten me up."

He laughed. She was so tiny. No amount of food would put extra meat on her bones. "Then we better start walking." He held out his hand to help her stand. Her fingers clasped onto his, and a spark of fire burned his skin and traveled up his arm.

She gasped, and her gaze met his.

He sucked in a breath, and he tightened fingers around hers. A fist squeezed his heart. He should drop her hand and walk away. He should forget this stupid idea of hiring her to decorate his house. Instead, he helped her to her feet, and her body brushed against his. He smiled. "Let's go." A tremble raced down his spine. Spending more time with Emma might not be wise, but he couldn't walk away—his heart wouldn't let him.

Chapter Seven

The sun hung above the horizon and settled behind a small gathering of clouds. Golden rays beamed down on either side of the full, white clouds. The once-blue sky turned magical as deep pink and orange swirls danced overhead. As she strolled along the dirt path around the lake, Emma couldn't tear away her gaze. Dust kicked up from her feet and settled in her lungs. Coughing, she covered her mouth with her hand as the heavy dust tickled her nose.

Easing her grip from his, she was oddly aware of her hands swinging back and forth by her sides. Her hands weren't often free of Sophie and Anderson. Should she put them in her pockets? Or just keep them dangling? The heat of Antonio's hand beside hers had her yearning to slide her fingers between his. Her skin still throbbed from his earlier touch. The electricity that shot through her almost changed her mind about their walk.

She dropped her gaze from the sky and tilted her chin to glance at him from the corner of her eye. The muted light caused his naturally bronzed skin to appear darker than usual. His hooded eyes and tightly pressed lips made him look like he belonged on the wall with the Night's Watch, not enjoying an early evening stroll. "You're very serious right now."

He glanced at her and then returned his focus ahead

of him. "Sorry. I was thinking about what you said earlier about your husband. Is remembering him always painful?"

A smile touched her lips. "I think about him all the time, and the memories usually make me happy instead of sad. We had a good marriage and a lot of great times together. I would be devastated if thinking about him always made me sad."

"You're lucky you guys were so happy. Having those memories to look back and share with the kids must be nice."

Smiling, she shrugged and made the turn around the bend on the path. "The memories are nice. My heart breaks that the memories are all they'll have of their dad, especially Anderson, but I can't dwell on what he'll miss." Her gut twisted.

"Was moving back here hard after being gone for so long?"

A familiar longing for the home she shared with Luke seized her heart, and she took a deep, shaky breath. "Yes and no. We had such a happy home, and it was beautiful. Luke worked behind a desk, but he was good with his hands. As soon as we could afford it, we bought an old house and transformed it into exactly what we wanted." Unshed tears burned her eyes, and she blinked them away. "I wanted to keep the kids there and raise them in the house their daddy built, but being there was too hard."

"Because of the constant reminders of him?"

A soft chuckle tickled her throat. "I don't need to be in our old house to have constant reminders of Luke. Those are everywhere, even here." She halted and nodded toward the lake at their side. "He loved the water. It didn't matter what plans we had, if an excuse came up to be on the water, he took it. Boating, fishing, or swimming…he didn't care." Antonio's gaze burned the side of her face as she stared at the lake. Sharing so much with him about her life with Luke felt so natural—so easy. Having someone to listen lifted the heavy burden from her shoulders.

"Sounds like we would have gotten along. I love the water, too."

She smiled, imagining splashing in the lake with Antonio. Clearing her throat, she forced the image from her mind. "Luke got along with everyone. He always thought you seemed like a good guy, the few times you met."

His brows snapped together. "Really? Well, the feeling was mutual."

She started walking again.

Antonio fell into step beside her.

"I moved back home because being in the house alone was too hard." She kicked a pebble from the path. "Maintaining the property and two children all on my own was exhausting. Not to mention figuring out our finances and dealing with Luke's death. We stayed a little over six months, and I fell apart one day. Then I realized I didn't have anyone around to pick me up anymore."

"You didn't have any friends or family in the area? What about his family?"

His loud voice carried over the lapping waves. "I had some good friends, but they had their own lives to deal with. Luke's parents lived thirty minutes away, and they were lost in their own grief. His brother lived nearby, but we've never been close. Moving in with my mom and starting our life over in Smithview seemed like the best answer." A heaviness settled over her. She was convinced she made the right decision, but the constant barrage of emotions wasn't any easier to deal with.

"I bet your family is happy to have you home, even if the reason why sucks." He bent down and picked up a large, smooth stone. He turned it over in his hand and made the last turn on the path.

"They are, and having so much help with the kids is nice. I'm a little at loose ends, though, figuring out what to do with my time." As she spoke, she watched a flock of birds soar overhead.

"Is that why you want to decorate my house?" He stepped off the path toward the water.

His lips curved up at the corners, and sexiness oozed from his pores. She followed and stopped when she arrived at the shore.

He tossed the rock in the water, and it skipped across the surface three times before plunging out of sight.

A wide grin split his face, and those darn dimples peeked through. She cleared her throat and concentrated on their conversation. "I've toyed with the idea of starting my own business. I figured your house would be a start. Plus, your house is way too gorgeous to sit empty." A tight smile took over his mouth, and a flash of pain melted his chocolate eyes. His dimples disappeared, and a stab of disappointment pierced her gut.

"Having the house finished will be nice," he said. "I never intended to be the one to decorate it. I'm glad I have you to help."

"Oh, I didn't think about your plans when you'd bought the house." He'd planned on living there with Jillian and Sam. No wonder he hadn't done much with it. God, she was an idiot. She forced a bright smile and looped an arm through his. Little bursts of excitement erupted, but she ignored them and walked back to his car. "The house will look great when we're done. I promise. Now let's head home."

He stopped beside his car and opened the passenger door.

She climbed in and settled into the seat. A wave of sadness hit her, but she couldn't tell if it was from talking about Luke or because her day with Antonio was over. Either way, she was already too comfortable with a man who wasn't her husband. She'd continue the job Antonio paid her for, but she needed to keep her distance whenever possible. She couldn't cross a line that would destroy her—a line that meant betraying the memory of Luke.

****

"Mommy, you're home!" Sophie ran and threw herself in Emma's arms. Sophie's wide eyes stared. "You were gone so long."

Holding back a chuckle, she kissed the top of Sophie's head and inhaled the baby shampoo that lingered in her hair. She'd only been gone for a few hours. "Didn't you have a good time with Grandma?" She cast her mom a questioning glance, but Annie didn't notice from her spot at the kitchen stove.

"Yeah, but I missed you."

Guilt ate away at her conscience. She'd enjoyed her time with Antonio, and missing her children hadn't even entered her mind. Being away from them for a day and enjoying the company of a nice, attractive man had been nice. The guilt grew. She was a horrible person. She squeezed Sophie tighter, and then set her on her feet. "Where's Anderson?"

Annie turned from the stove with a whisk in her hand. "Meg took him outside. They're sitting on the deck. Did you have a nice time?"

Warmth heated her cheeks, and she sat at the table. "We had fun. We shopped at a few stores then grabbed some sandwiches."

"That's nice, dear." Annie grinned at Sophie. "Would you like to take a couple of cookies out to Meg?"

Sophie's gaze darted to Emma, and then back to her grandma. "Before dinner?"

"I don't see why not. You've been such a good girl today." Annie glanced at Emma. "Is Sophie having a cookie okay with you?"

Sophie clasped her hands under her chin and bounced on her toes.

Emma laughed. "Sure, honey." Uneasiness formed a lead ball in the pit of her stomach. The only reason her mom would give Sophie cookies was to get rid of her for a few minutes. The only reason to get rid of her was to talk about something she shouldn't hear.

Annie filled a bowl with some cookies, handed the bowl to Sophie, and then scooted her out the back door. After she closed the door, she took a seat at the table across from Emma. "You and Antonio are spending a lot of time together since you've been home."

Annoyance flared in her chest. She crossed her arms in front of her and narrowed her gaze. "I've run into him a few times, and now I'm working for him.

What's your point?"

"You have no reason to be defensive. I'm merely making an observation." Annie lowered Emma's hand to the table. She linked their fingers and squeezed. "Making a new friend is a good thing. You need friends."

"I'm sorry. I guess our relationship is a sensitive issue."

"Why?" Anni drew together her eyebrows. "Is your brother giving you a hard time? We all know Antonio's not to blame for what Blake did."

Emma pulled away her hand and waved it in the air. "I can handle Jonah. I guess I feel guilty I've enjoyed spending time with Antonio."

Annie furrowed her brow. "You haven't done anything to feel guilty about. You're spending time with a friend who happens to be a man."

She dropped her gaze to the table, and the heat in her cheeks grew to a small fire. She hadn't done anything, but her thoughts were more complicated. Moisture gathered in the corner of her eyes. "If Luke were here none of these problems would be happening."

"Honey, if Luke were here, he'd want you to be happy. Of course, everything would be so much easier because you'd still be in Cleveland with him, and life would be perfect. But he's not here, and you and I both know he wouldn't want you to feel guilty about spending time with Antonio." Annie lifted Emma's chin so they were eye to eye. "Even if that means you aren't spending time with just a friend."

Emma dashed away her tears with trembling fingers and stood. She paced across the worn wooden floor. "Having these feelings for anyone is too early."

Shifting her legs to sit sidewise, she held her stare. "Having another man stir feelings within you isn't a bad thing. You had a very happy marriage, and wanting to find another good relationship again is only natural."

She stopped pacing and waved a hand toward her mom. "You never remarried. Dad's been gone for so long, and I've never once seen you with another man."

"I had three little mouths to feed and no way to make a living—with no one to help me. Finding my footing took years." She lifted her shoulders. "By then, I'd found my happiness. But you, you have so many years ahead. If you're lucky enough to find someone to make you happy in a time of darkness, don't be afraid to hold on."

She squeezed shut her eyes and held on to the back of the kitchen chair for support. Guilt and confusion collided in her mind, and a dull ache pulsed behind her eye. She sighed and opened her eyes. "Antonio's my friend and nothing more." She rubbed her eyes as the pain grew. "Do you mind if I step in the shower for a minute before dinner?"

"Not at all. Meg can watch the kids while I finish cooking." Annie stood and pulled her into a hug.

Emma nestled her face against her mom's neck. "Thanks for everything, Mom. I love you."

"I love you, too. Now go wash off that stink."

Locking herself in the bathroom, she sniffed back the tears clogging her throat. The conversation with her mom zapped her energy, and she leaned against the door after she closed it. She took a few deep breaths, slowing her heart rate. Pushing herself off the door, she peeled off her clothes and turned on the shower. Steam filled the room, and she stepped into the scalding water. The water rolled over her, and she winced, and then relaxed her muscles as her skin absorbed the heat.

The pressure of the water beat down, and she sank to her knees. The tears trapped in her throat spilled out and mingled with the droplets of water that cascaded down her body. For once, she let herself go. She cried for the loss of her husband, she cried for Sophie and all the joy robbed from her life, and she cried for the innocence ripped away from Anderson. He didn't understand the magnitude of the loss he'd been handed, but one day he would.

As she unleashed all the grief she'd bottled deep inside, she cradled her stomach to soothe her aching soul. She lay down in the bathtub and let the water wash over her after all her tears were shed. She closed her eyes, and an image of Luke appeared. He waved, wearing a huge smile. His hair was cut short, and a soft breeze pressed his white linen shirt to his strong, lean body. He lifted his hand, blew her a kiss, and then turned and walked away.

Squeezing her eyelids harder, she strained to refocus a picture of a memory she didn't know she had. A sense of peace washed over her. Mom was right. Luke would want her to be happy. She opened her eyes and stood to turn off the shower. She stepped out and dabbed a soft, cotton towel against her warm, wet skin. She had a life to get back to, and she needed to live it to its fullest.

Whether or not her life included Antonio as more than a friend, she wasn't ready to discover. For now, she had her family waiting, and for the first time in a long time, she was finally excited to start living again.

No matter what anyone thought of how she chose to move on.

Chapter Eight

Antonio sat at the bar in The Village Idiot. He brought up his bank account on his phone and winced. A couple of weeks passed since he'd hired Emma to decorate his house, and the expenses added up. Anxiety threatened to seize him. He'd put off placing his personal stamp on his house for long enough. He just hoped he wouldn't be broke by the time he was done. He might have given Emma a budget, but he hadn't been prepared for watching the money fly out of his bank account.

He brushed a strand of hair from his eyes, and Sally's shapely form skimmed along the bar to where he sat.

"What'll it be tonight? Whiskey on the rocks?" Grinning, she shot him a wink.

He met her sultry gaze and lifted the corner of his mouth. "Is it sad you have my order memorized?" He'd started making appearances at the bar in hopes of mingling with more of the locals. So far, only Blake and Sally noticed his presence.

Pulling a glass from under the bar, she laughed. "Not at all, darling. I'm good at my job. Besides, I'm glad you're finally coming around." She leaned a hip against the counter and slid his glass forward. "Are you meeting anyone?"

He took a sip, and the whiskey burned his throat.

He placed his drink back on the bar. "Yeah, Blake."

"Him I see all the time." She leaned forward. "I'm more interested in getting to know you."

Sally used her biceps to shove her cleavage together. He swallowed hard and stared into his drink. Sweat dampened his palms, and he cradled his glass. The coolness seeped into his skin. He squirmed in his seat and cut his gaze to the door. Where was Blake? He didn't want to be alone with her. The door remained closed, so he glanced at Sally and pressed his lips together. "Making new friends is always nice."

She grazed a fingertip up and down his forearm. "I don't need any more friends."

Disgust rippled over his skin. He kept the muscles in his face loose so she couldn't see how much she rattled him. "A friend is all I need right now."

"Maybe for now." She tossed her hair over her shoulder and sauntered away. Her hips swayed and heels clicked as she made her way to the other end of the bar.

A hand slapped him on the back.

Blake sat. "Hey, man, how's it going?"

Relief seeped through him. Blake was better at dealing with Sally's advances. Hopefully Antonio wouldn't have to deal with her for the rest of the night. "Things are good. How 'bout with you?"

Blake signaled for Sally. "I'm good. Glad you texted. I had nothing going on tonight."

Sally brought over Blake's beer.

Antonio picked up his drink. Sipping his whiskey, he tried to forget about Emma. She'd pulled back after they'd spent the day together. He'd hoped discussing such personal issues would bring them closer together, but the opposite happened. He hadn't seen her since. Instead, she sent texts with pictures and made purchases online. His chest ached. Damn, he missed her.

Blake grabbed his wallet from his back pocket and handed a credit card to Sally. "Keep my tab open." He focused on Antonio again and took a pull from his bottle. "Do you have to work tomorrow?"

The question snapped him back to the present. "No. I have a weird schedule."

"Must be nice not to work on a Thursday." Blake lifted his bottle and stopped it halfway to his mouth. He lifted his chin. "Dude, I don't even know what you do."

Antonio chuckled. "Not many people around here do. I'm an airline pilot."

"Seriously?" Blake's eyebrows rose to his hairline. "That's so cool. Do you fly all over the world?"

"I used to, but not so much anymore. I switched to mostly domestic flights." He missed those long flights, but the change was worth it. Since he'd moved back, he'd spent more time with Sam than he had in the past five years combined.

"Sounds a lot more exciting than selling cars. I'm forced to paste a phony smile on my face all day and kiss up to everyone who comes in." His clean-shaven face contorted into a snarl. "I hate it."

"Why do it then?"

Blake shrugged. "After the trouble I got in, I'm lucky to have a job at all."

"True." He swirled his glass, and the ice cubes clinked together.

The front door creaked open, and familiar laughter spilled in from outside. His heart hammered against his rib cage. Emma stepped into the bar with Meg and

Jonah. She threw back her head and laughed a deep, full laugh. He followed her with his gaze.

She stopped laughing.

His pulse quickened. He raised a hand and waved. She set her mouth in a hard line, narrowed her eyes, and stalked toward the back of the bar. Meg cast a hardened glance his way, and Jonah shot daggers his direction before following her to a table.

Blake snorted. "The Sheffields are so dramatic."

Sally sneered at Blake. "Your ex just walked in. Will you say hello?"

Blake picked up his bottle and drained it. He slammed the tinted brown glass on the counter and wiped the beer dripping from his chin with the back of his hand. "Shut up, Sally."

Blake's tone dropped an octave, and his voice was as hard as rocks. Antonio's senses tingled, and his muscles clenched. Menace mixed with Blake's words, and he experienced a glimpse into the side of Blake he wanted to stay away from.

Sally laughed and blinked her lashes. "Don't be mean, Blake."

A throat cleared loudly at the other end of the bar.

Sally groaned.

Emma stood rigid with her arms across her chest and lips pursed.

Annoyance radiated from her, even from a distance. He waited until Sally was done taking her order and pushed up from his seat.

"Where you going, man?" Blake asked.

"I'll be right back." His palms grew damp as he moved toward Emma, and he wiped them on the front of his jeans. Her sleeveless shirt showed off her toned arms, and her muscles stiffened as he stopped beside her. "Hey."

"Hey." She stared straight ahead.

Anxiety prickled the back of his neck. He racked his brain for what he'd done to make her mad but came up empty. "I haven't seen you in a while. How've you been?"

"I just texted you yesterday." Her gaze flickered to his. "I didn't know you were still friends with Blake."

He glanced over his shoulder at Blake who sat staring with his lips curved into a small smile, and then returned his gaze to Emma. "I've met him for drinks a few times. He seemed genuinely sorry about everything, and I'm all about second chances. Besides, I don't have many options these days."

She shrugged. "Who you spend your time with isn't my business. I just thought you'd have learned your lesson. The guy's a jerk."

Sally returned and set three tall mugs filled with beer in front of them. "Do you need help carrying them to the table?" As she asked, she stared at Antonio.

Emma rolled her eyes. "Thanks, but I can manage."

Antonio grabbed two of the mugs. "I'll carry these."

"Don't bother. Go back to your friend."

She spat out the words, and he jerked back his head as if she'd slapped him. "I'd rather spend time with you, if you'd let me." Her eyes remained cold as she held out her hand, waiting for him to give back her drinks. "But you're avoiding me, and Blake is the only person in this town who's actually talked to me."

Emma glanced behind her shoulder at Jonah and Meg, and the tight lines around the corners of her eyes relaxed a bit when she faced him again.

He set the beers back on the bar and lifted his palms in the air. "What am I supposed to do? Besides you, he's the only person I know. And you won't pick up the phone when I call. All I get are texts and emails about the house. Trust me. You're more fun and a lot nicer to look at, but that hasn't been an option."

A hint of a smile touched her lips. She again glanced over her shoulder.

He followed her line of vision. The back of Meg's head faced them, but Jonah's jaw tensed, and his entire face glowed red.

Emma sighed. "I'm sorry. I've spent a lot of time online searching for stuff for your house, and the rest of the time has been with the kids. Tonight is the first time I've been out with Meg and Jonah since I've been back. I didn't mean to avoid you."

Her words lacked sincerity, but he didn't want to dwell on it. She did have a lot on her plate right now, and he didn't need to behave like a neglected child. "I understand. Are you sure you don't want help with the drinks?" He nodded toward the two mugs he'd set on the bar.

She sunk her teeth in her bottom lip and scrunched her nose. "Do you want to sit with us?"

Indecision tore through him. He'd craved spending time with Emma over the last couple of weeks, but he wasn't ready to spend an evening with Jonah. "Are you sure? Jonah might not like me joining your fun."

"Jonah's opinion doesn't bother me if it doesn't bother you." Wrinkles creased her lifted brow.

Her tone issued a silent challenge he couldn't resist. "Lead the way." He picked up the mugs and watched the soft sway of her hips as he walked to the table. Her lack of awareness of her sexiness was much more alluring than Sally's blatant attempts at seduction. He set an ice-cold mug in front of Jonah and the other in front of Meg. He gave them each a brief nod, and then brushed Emma's elbow with his fingers. "I'll grab my drink and be right back." He hurried to the bar and picked up his half-empty glass of whiskey.

"Dude, what the hell?" Blake slapped his arm with the back of his hand. "I wanted you to meet some of my pals tonight."

Two guys sat on the other side of Blake with shots lined up in front of them. Neither one tore their gaze from Sally's breasts, her annoying laugh bubbling out and causing them to bounce gently in her too-small top. How old were these guys? Blake's demeanor earlier, and the idiots who sat beside him, had Antonio second guessing his interest in a friendship. He was thirty-one years old, not some young hotshot looking to score with the local bartender and get loaded in the middle of the week with his buddies. He patted Blake between his shoulder blades. "Sorry, man. We'll catch up later."

He walked back to the table to find Emma sitting across from Meg, forcing him to face Jonah. The intensity of Jonah's hard stare burned his face. The muscles in his face tensed, but when he glanced up he noticed Jonah's gaze aimed past him. He glanced over his shoulder. Blake sat directly behind him at the bar. He whipped his head around.

Jonah's scowl deepened. "I want to go up and put my fist in his face." He cracked his knuckles, and then cradled his frosted mug in his hands.

"He's not worth your time." Meg circled her hands

around the frosted glass.

"Maybe not, but Dylan beating the heck out of him instead of me isn't fair." Jonah huddled over his glass.

"Dylan beat up Blake?" Dylan was a big dude, but he was like a gentle giant. Antonio couldn't picture him hitting anyone.

Jonah scoffed. "Your buddy didn't tell you about that, huh? Shocking."

Antonio flicked his gaze from Jonah, to Meg, and back to Emma. No one would meet his gaze, spiking his interest in what happened.

Emma gave a slight shake of her head.

Something happened he wasn't aware of, but the fact nobody wanted talk about it was obvious. He cleared his throat to cut through the tension.

The screeching of barstools on the linoleum floor carried across the bar, and obnoxious laughter followed.

A low growl rumbled from Jonah.

Antonio turned around once more.

Blake lifted a hand to his forehead and gave them a salute, a wide grin on his face. "See ya later, Tony. Meg, always a pleasure."

Jonah stood.

Emma shoved him back to his seat.

Meg leaned forward and placed a hand on his arm. "Leave it, Jonah. I'm serious."

Her tone was low, yet sharp as a knife, piquing his curiosity. Antonio twisted his mouth to the side and tried to read between the lines.

Emma lifted a dark brow. "Tony?"

"Does anyone call you Tony?" Jonah leaned back in his seat.

"No, thank God." He'd always hated that

nickname, and luckily so had his parents.

"Good to know." Jonah smirked and cupped a palm around his mug. "I like it, though. I might have to use it from time to time."

He groaned. He'd just given Jonah ammo.

"Be careful, or we'll have to tell Antonio what the kids call you." She wagged a finger in Jonah's direction.

Jonah winced, then downed the rest of his beer. "Good point."

Meg blew out a small sigh and slid her full mug to the middle of the table. "I'm sorry, guys, but I'm not in the mood to be here. Seeing Blake always puts a sour taste in my mouth."

"We can go home." Emma rested a hand on Meg's.

His stomach dropped. Spending time with Emma was the best part of his week. He didn't want it to end so soon.

"You should have let me hit him, and we all would feel better." Jonah cracked his knuckles.

"You might be right." Meg pushed back her chair and stood. "Do you mind taking me home, Jonah?"

Jonah frowned and dipped his chin toward Emma's beer. "Not at all. We can do this another time. Do you want to finish your drink first, Emma?"

Emma glanced at her beer, and then her gaze met Antonio's. Her tongue moistened her bottom lip.

Lust spiked in his gut. "If you want to stay longer, I can take you home." The words were out of his mouth before he could stop himself.

Jonah tensed.

Meg's jaw dropped slightly, and she froze.

All gazes were on Emma. As he waited for her

answer, his pulse beat like a drum in his ears. A slow smile crept on her lips and a sexy, pink stain appeared on her cheeks.

"I'll stay for a little bit. Mom has the kids all night. I might as well take advantage."

"If you don't get her home safely, I'll kill you." Jonah stood and glared.

Meg slapped his arm. "Be nice. You guys have fun. Call me tomorrow, Emma."

"Yeah, call me too. See you around, Tony."

A cold, hard glint shaded Jonah's eyes, but Antonio smiled and waved without taking the bait. He lifted the glass and drained the cup. The whiskey entered his system, and his dancing nerves settled. He needed another drink. "Your drink is about half gone. Do you want me to grab you something from the bar?"

"I'll take another beer." She flashed a smile.

His heart threatened to stop. "I'll be right back." He bounced to the bar with a spring in his step. He'd missed her, and now he had her all to himself. At least for a little while.

Sally approached with a smirk. "I thought you weren't meeting anyone besides Blake tonight?"

"I got lucky. We'll each take a refill please." He glanced behind him while Sally filled his order. Emma sat alone, staring at her phone. God, she was so beautiful. He'd gotten lucky all right, and he planned on riding out his luck as long as he had it.

Chapter Nine

Emma's phone vibrated in her hand. A text from Meg. She swiped a finger along the screen to unlock it.

—*Jonah's mad.*—

Emma rolled her eyes and shook her head. Her brother was a pain in the butt sometimes.

—*He'll get over it*—

She raised her gaze until it locked on Antonio. He ordered them more drinks, and his forearms rested on the bar while he waited. He leaned forward, causing his shorts to tighten across his bottom. Her palms grew damp. Too bad her frosted mug had gone warm. The cold glass would have dropped her climbing temperature.

Another vibration in her hand had her lifting her phone.

—*I'm sure he will. Have fun tonight. Call me if you need me.*—

She slipped her phone in her purse and smiled. She loved her sister, but spending the evening with Antonio sent butterflies aflutter in the pit of her stomach. He'd called her out earlier, and he'd been right. She'd avoided him. She was ready to admit she had feelings for him. But she wasn't ready to do anything about them, so she'd stayed away like a coward.

Not seeing him was harder than she'd expected.

Antonio carried their drinks and weaved his way

through the growing crowd.

Sucking in a breath, she itched to run her fingers through his dark, wavy hair. She brushed her thumbs over the pads of her fingers to settle them.

He set a glass in front of her, and white foam trickled down the side. He nodded toward the half-full glass. "Will you finish your beer?"

She wrinkled her nose. "The beer's warm." His husky laugh skimmed over her like a lover's touch, and she shivered.

"You didn't drink it fast enough."

"Thanks for the explanation." She picked up the lukewarm mug, threw back her head, and drained the glass. The empty mug hit the table with a thud. "Happy?"

He held up his palms. "I never said you had to drink it. But you're impressive."

She beamed. Alcohol swam in her veins, and warmth flooded her body. She didn't drink often, and the beer she'd chugged already made her brain a little foggy. "Thanks. You better keep up with me, or I'll look like a lush."

He picked up his own glass, saluted her, and drained half of the dark liquid. He winced. "Not a good idea to drink whiskey fast."

Emma cradled her chin in her hands and rested her elbows on the table. She sighed. "Never in a million years did I think I'd end up here."

"I know what you mean." Antonio glanced around and swirled his glass.

She tilted her neck, her cheek resting in her palm. "I forgot you used to live here."

"Seems like a hundred years ago, and honestly I

wasn't around much. I worked all the time back then so I didn't have to be here." He lifted his drink to his mouth. A hint of moisture clung to his lips as he set his glass on the table and leaned back in his chair.

She tore her gaze from his lips and concentrated on his words. The fog closed around her and made her thoughts slow. "You didn't want to be home with Jillian and Sam?"

A beat of silence lingered, and he stared past her. "Being around her when she wasn't in love with me was hard. I didn't handle the rejection right. I left town as soon as I could, and I missed out on a lot of Sam's life. I moved back to make things right."

"Are you glad?"

His gaze found hers, and the corners of his mouth lifted. "I am now."

The front door swung open, and a large group entered, taking over the small space with their laughter and shouting.

Emma scooted her chair closer to Antonio so she wouldn't have to yell over the din. The side of her leg brushed against his hard calf and sent sparks of excitement through her. She nodded toward his drink. "How many have you had?"

"This is my third, and probably last. I don't need a hangover tomorrow. Sam's spending the day with me."

She moved her gaze from his chocolate eyes and down his hard chest. She bit down on her bottom lip and forced her gaze back to meet his. The little bit of alcohol gave her courage she didn't think she possessed. "What do you need tonight?"

Antonio's eyebrows arched high.

His eyes transformed into molten lava. Heat

scorched her cheeks, and she closed her eyes. Why did she ask that question? She blew out a long breath, opened her eyes, and reached for her beer. She gulped down the bitter liquid and prayed it would wash away her embarrassment.

He laid a hand on hers and guided her drink back to the table.

Her grip loosened on the glass, but Antonio didn't release his hold.

Holding her gaze, he laced his fingers with hers and squeezed.

She fought every instinct to turn away. Her rapid heartbeat pounded in her ears, and she sucked in a shaky breath.

"Tonight," he said, leaning forward. "I need you."

A lump lodged in her throat, and she swallowed hard. *Oh boy.* She widened her eyes, and her stomach muscles clenched. "You need me to what?" Her voice was small.

He leaned closer. "I need you to let loose with me tonight."

His hot breath skimmed her skin. Her brain wouldn't work. She needed to answer him, but her words were a jumbled mess. She nodded and then leaned closer as the intoxicating mix of whiskey and aftershave lured her in. The tip of her nose met his, and she closed her eyes and breathed him in.

"Emma." He placed his hands on either side of her face and lowered his lips.

Her heart leapt, and she deepened the kiss. His mouth parted, and the need to lose herself in him overwhelmed her. She broke away, gasping for air. "We can't do this."

His shoulders slumped, and he dropped his hands from her face.

Her cheeks cooled without his touch.

"I'm sorry, Emma. I shouldn't have kissed you." He rubbed a hand over his chin.

"I meant we can't do this here." She swept the room with her gaze. She'd be the talk of the town if she didn't get out of here. "Can we go to your place?"

His Adam's apple bobbed. "You want to go home with me?"

She again lifted her drink and downed the rest of her beer. She was attracted to him, and nothing was wrong with it. Moving on with her life was necessary. "I can't drive home. I could call Jonah to pick me up, but I'm not ready for the night to end. Are you?"

"No, but I don't want you to regret anything." He traced circles over the back of her hand with a finger.

Shivers raced down her spine. His words lowered her guard to the ground. Antonio wouldn't hurt her. If she could trust anyone to take this next step with, that man was him. She locked her gaze with his warm brown eyes, and her heartrate slowed. "The only regret I'd have is ending our night too early."

He stood and extended his hand.

Saliva filled her mouth, and she swallowed it back. She could do this. She wanted to go home with him. She lifted her gaze and stared into his eyes. With a deep breath, she accepted his offered hand. She followed him to the door with her hand linked in his. The burn of a dozen gazes followed her, but she didn't care. They didn't matter. Antonio was all that mattered right now, and she wouldn't waste her time on anything else.

Chapter Ten

The early morning sun streamed through the bedroom window and warmed Antonio's skin. He stretched his arms above his head, and then shielded his eyes to block out the glare. He needed to get some curtains. He curled onto his side, facing away from the window, and reached out to gather Emma in his arms. He roamed his palm over wrinkled sheets, and he snapped open his eyes.

"Emma?" He glanced around his bedroom, but no one else was there. Only his discarded clothes lay on the carpeted floor. "Emma!" Jumping out of the bed, he raced from his room in his boxers, and his pulse pounded in his ears.

Emma sat on the bottom step of the stairway and slid her sandals on her bare feet.

The tension in his gut loosened. She was still here. He flattened a palm on her back. "Are you okay? Do you need to leave, or can I cook you breakfast?"

She flinched. Moisture filled her eyes, and she secured her hair in a ponytail. "We need to forget we ever slept together."

A vise squeezed his heart. Last night was the best night of his life. No way could he just forget how holding her in his arms felt. He dropped to his knees, grabbed her hands, and placed them on her lap. "We both know what happened between us last night meant something. I haven't felt this way in a long time, and it scares the hell out of me. But we are great together. We can take a step back, slow down, and spend more time together. But please. Don't pull away."

She shook her head, and tears streamed down her face. "I can't. I need to forget about you and everything we did." She pulled her hands from his and wiped her eyes. Standing, she pushed past him and grabbed her purse from beside the door. She gripped the door handle and opened the door a crack. She froze, her back rigid and her face turned away. "I'm so sorry." Her voice cracked.

"Emma, please stay and talk to me." His heart lodged in his throat, and he grabbed the edge of the door. "We can figure this out." He couldn't lose her— not like this. Not after knocking down all of the walls and finding happiness together. Returning to his empty life on the outskirts without her by his side wasn't possible.

Pressure shot through the front of the door, forcing him backward. Jillian stood on the porch with wide eyes.

Sam ran into the house. "Hey, Dad, why aren't you wearing a shirt? Hi, Emma, what are you doing here?"

Antonio massaged his forehead and pinched shut his eyes. "Go take your stuff up to your room, buddy. Jillian, can you go in the kitchen for a second? I need to talk to Emma."

"You've said everything you need to say. I'm leaving." Emma pushed through the doorway.

An iron first slammed into his stomach.

Jillian stepped through the threshold and closed the door behind her. "Sam, do as your father said. Go to your room."

Yellow sparks ignited in her green eyes. Her jaw tightened, and her hard gaze never left his face, making Antonio's cheeks heat.

Sam's gaze traveled from Jillian, to him, and then he shrugged. He took the stairs two at time, dragging his backpack behind him.

"Grab me a T-shirt, Sam" He lowered his head and stormed into the kitchen. "I need coffee."

"What you need is to explain what happened." Jillian followed close and spoke through gritted teeth.

He grabbed a coffee pod and placed it in his coffee maker, along with the biggest mug he owned. He leaned against the counter and glared. "I'm a grown man. I don't need to explain anything."

She took three steps toward him with an index finger pointed at his chest. "I disagree. Emma looked awful, and she couldn't get out of here fast enough. What did you do?"

Anger tightened his chest. He needed to get his bearings and then go after Emma. Fighting with Jillian was a waste of time. "I didn't do anything."

"Is that why you're practically naked?" Her brows arched high, and she pursed her lips.

"I think you can put two and two together." He couldn't help but smirk. "Not like what happened is any of your business."

"I swear to God, Antonio, I could kill you. How could you take advantage of her? She's my sister-in-law, and Sam's new aunt. Luke's barely cold in the ground, and you go and sleep with her the first chance you get. And what about the flight attendant? Bethany…Brittany?" She snorted a breath through her nose. "You're unbelievable. Things are finally in a good place, and you're messing up everything."

He bit into the inside of his cheeks to rein in his temper. Leave it to Jillian to make his situation with Emma about her. "Don't you dare insinuate I took advantage of Emma. She's an amazing woman, and what happened last night was between two consenting adults. She was the one who suggested we come back here."

Jillian opened her mouth.

He held a hand in the air. "I'm not done. I'm falling hard for Emma, and I know she has feelings for me or last night wouldn't have happened. I didn't just sleep with her, and the fact you think so little of me is insulting."

Jillian threw her arms in the air. "What am I supposed to think? She was a mess."

"Yes, she was, and I wanted to help her. You're right, Luke hasn't been gone long, and thinking about moving on is hard." He rubbed the back of his neck. "But she's not a bad person for having feelings for someone else. We can't help who we fall for."

Jillian relaxed the muscles in her face. "I never said she was a bad person. I love Emma, and I can't even imagine how she's feeling right now. And you have to admit, you don't have the best track record with women."

He snorted and grabbed his mug. Steam billowed from the top, and he blew into the cup to cool the black coffee before taking a sip of the bitter liquid. "Thanks."

"Sorry, but you know I'm right. You haven't had one serious relationship since we split seven years ago." She brushed past him and grabbed a mug and another coffee pod.

He stepped over to the island and sat on a stool, the cold metal pressing against his bare legs.

The coffee machine chugged to life, and she faced him again. "Seriously, weren't you seeing some woman from work?"

His fling with Bridgette was nothing compared to his connection with Emma. He cradled his mug in his hands. "My relationship with Bridgette was a casual thing. We were over months ago."

Jillian grabbed a spoon from a drawer then milk from the refrigerator. She stood across from him and pointed the spoon in his direction. "See, casual. You can't get into something casual with Emma. She's too important to me and Sam. Not to mention Jonah would flip."

He took a sip from his mug. "The only person I care about is Emma. We need to clear up this situation."

Jillian sighed. "If you're serious about wanting to be with Emma, give her some space. She needs time to process everything, and having you hassling her won't help."

Disagreeing with Jillian's advice, he shook his head. "I can't let her think I don't want to be with her. She needs to know how I feel."

Jillian stirred a dollop of milk into her coffee. "Did you already tell her?"

A flash of Emma's sweet smile and rounded eyes filled his mind. She might have run away this morning, but last night she'd shown him exactly how she felt. "Yes."

"Then leave it alone—at least for a day or two."

Uneasiness burrowed into his gut. He didn't want

Emma to think sleeping with her was all he wanted. Because he wanted a lot more. In the last couple of months, she'd become his best friend, and he didn't want to lose her. But Jillian was right. Emma needed to wrap her mind around what happened.

Pounding footsteps drifted into the kitchen. Sam ran in and threw clothes across the room.

Antonio snatched them and placed them on his lap. "Thanks, buddy."

"No problem." Sam grabbed a banana from a bowl of fruit sitting on the island and peeled it. "So why was Emma here so early?"

Antonio met Jillian's gaze and watched a tight smile formed on her lips. He glanced at Sam and forced up the corners of his mouth. "She dropped off some stuff for the house but had to rush back home."

Sam took a bite of the banana and nodded.

Jillian sipped her coffee, and then set it down. "Please, tread lightly. Whatever happened between you two could end in disaster."

Sweat pooled in his palms, and he wiped his hands on his shirt before pulling it over his head. "Trust me, the last thing I want is to mess up things."

"What could be a disaster?" Sam tented his eyebrows.

Sam's words slurred around the banana packed in his mouth.

Jillian ruffled his hair. "This house, if your dad doesn't let Emma handle the details her way."

Antonio chuckled. "Message received. I'll give it a few days." He stood and slid his gym shorts over his hips. He'd take Jillian's advice and give Emma some space, but then it was game on. She needed to know he would fight for her. He'd made the mistake of running away once before and wouldn't let the woman he loved slip through his fingers again.

****

Bright fluorescent lights beat down from the ceiling in the airport terminal, highlighting the fast-paced travelers rushing to make their flights. Antonio searched his phone for signs Emma contacted him. Weeks had passed since the night she'd stayed with him, and still no word.

Nate, his friend and co-pilot, bumped a shoulder against Antonio. "What's up, man? We've only been off the plane for ten minutes, and you've checked your phone ten times."

Antonio put his phone back in his pocket. He'd flown with Nate for years, and he was one of Antonio's closest friends. He'd told him about Emma but didn't mention she hadn't responded to his texts or calls in two weeks. Heat crept up the back of his neck, and he wiped away the sweat that clung to his hair. "Nothing, just making sure Sam didn't call. He started school today, and I told him to call me when he got home."

"I can't believe the kids are back in school already. The summer flew by." Nate pulled his luggage behind him and dodged hurrying travelers.

Antonio's briefcase swung by his side. He grunted in agreement but didn't carry on the conversation. All he could think about was Emma. He'd sent a dozen texts since they'd slept together, and his angst to talk weighed heavy on his chest and scattered his brain. Not a minute passed she wasn't on his mind, and not hearing from her made his skin tighten with apprehension.

"Antonio, Nate! How was your flight?"

A velvety smooth voice broke into his train of thought, and he glanced up. A tall, raven-haired beauty with hazel eyes waved from the airport bar.

Nate stopped and lifted a hand to wave. "Hi, Bridgette. How are you? Haven't seen you in a while."

Bridgette approached, and her heels clicked against the tile floor. She leaned forward and hugged Nate, and then faced him. A smile took over her face, and she placed the palm of a hand on his chest. "I haven't seen you in too long, Antonio."

His body tensed. He cleared his throat and took a step backward. They hadn't flown together in months, which wasn't an accident. Once he'd met Emma, he hadn't been interested in Bridgette anymore, even as a casual fling. She had taken it as a challenge and acted aggressive any time their paths crossed. "It has been a while. Hope you're doing well."

She tilted her head to the side and ran a finger down his chest. "Do you want to get a drink? I hate drinking alone."

He grabbed her hand and stopped her fingers from dipping lower. "No thanks. I have to get home. Maybe Nate could join you?"

Brigette's face fell for a brief second, and then she beamed a smile. "Nate. What do you say? One drink with an old friend?"

Nate squeezed her shoulder. "Sure, Bridge. I got a few minutes."

"You two have fun. I'll see you later." He continued down the terminal. Thank God for Nate. He couldn't deal with her right now. His phone vibrated against his leg, and his heart stopped. He held his breath, pulled out his device and, glanced at the screen. His heart sank.

—Hey, Dad, I'm home from school. Had a good day.—

He battled back his disappointment. Sam was his priority, and he loved that Sam talked about the little things in his life now. He unlocked his screen and opened the text message so he could respond.

—Glad to hear it. I can't want to find out more tomorrow. Love you, buddy.—

Sighing, he slid the phone back in the front pocket of his trousers. What was he supposed to do now? As he walked to his car, he summoned his patience. He didn't care how long it took, he'd wait for Emma. Hopefully it wouldn't be much longer. His nerves couldn't take it.

Chapter Eleven

A soft breath tickled Emma's cheek. She lifted her eyelids and blinked to clear the sleep from her eyes. Exhaustion weighed down her limbs, but the wide crystal eyes of Sophie fastened on her. She swallowed a sigh. "Do you need something, honey?"

Sophie rested her chin on the side of the couch and leaned forward. Her nose was only inches away. "Will you ever wake up, Mommy?"

She forced herself into a sitting position. "What time is it?"

"I don't know, but Meg-Meg's been here forever, and my tummy's already hungry again."

She glanced at the clock on the living room wall and groaned. 12:30. She lifted Sophie onto her lap and wrapped her arms around her. "I'm sorry, sweet girl. I didn't mean to fall asleep."

"Could have fooled us, huh, Soph? You conked out as soon as you laid down Anderson," Meg said from across the room.

"Mommy's always sleeping." Sophie sunk into her.

Guilt clawed at her. Emma hugged her tighter. She nuzzled her neck and inhaled the scent of baby powder and lavender. She slept a lot lately. The black hole of depression surrounded her after her night with Antonio, and she couldn't escape it. Over a month passed since the night she spent with Antonio, and the depression grew heavier and lonelier every day. At least she was home with her family so they could help with the kids. She'd get through this dark time, but until then, the children were in good hands.

She lifted her chin and placed it on the top of Sophie's head. Wisps of golden hair brushed against her skin, but she didn't sweep them aside. She turned toward Meg. She hadn't seen her sister in the last couple of weeks. Gilbert Farms would have its grand opening, and a lot was on the line for her and Dylan. "What are you doing here? The farm opens next week. You must have a million things to do."

Meg settled back into the armchair and tucked her feet beneath her legs. "I do, but I need your help with something. I stopped by and figured you'd wake soon. Dylan's here, too. He's playing with Anderson in the backyard so Mom can get things ready for a guest coming in today."

A fresh wave of guilt rolled through her. Not only had she left the care of her kids to her family while she slept, but she hadn't helped her mom prepare the house. "Oh man, I forgot about the new guest. Does she need help?"

"She has everything under control, but I need to talk to you about something." Meg smiled at Sophie. "Do you want to go outside and play?"

Sophie cowered from Meg and pressed her body into Emma. "I want to stay with Mommy."

Meg twisted her lips to the side. "What if Mommy comes outside with us?"

Sophie tilted back her head to lock her gaze with Emma's.

Emma nodded. "I'll go with you, love. Let's get on

our shoes."

"Will you carry me?" Sophie's lips quivered in a small pout.

"Sure, baby." She stood and placed Sophie on her hip. At three years old, Sophie didn't need carried around. But the initial progress Sophie made once they moved was replaced by a clingy little girl who never ventured far from her side. The black cloud surrounding her seemed to cling to Sophie as well.

A soft knock sounded from the front door. The hinges creaked, and slow footsteps padded down the hall. Emma locked her gaze with Meg and arched her brows.

Meg shrugged. "Probably Mom's new guest."

A broad-shouldered man with honey colored hair and piercing gray eyes peeked around the corner and into the living room. "Hi. I'm sorry to intrude, but I'm looking for Annie Sheffield."

Sophie squeezed her arms around Emma's neck.

Emma coughed and loosened her small arms from her throat. "She's probably in the kitchen. If she's not in there, let us know, and we'll find her."

He flashed a grin. "Thanks." He passed the archway to the living room.

Meg whistled. "Well hello, Mr. Cutie Pants."

Emma laughed. "I'm sure Dylan would love to hear you call another man Cutie Pants."

Meg rolled her eyes. "Like he doesn't check out other women. And you'd have to be blind not to notice how cute he is."

"I didn't notice." She shrugged, and then shifted Sophie on her hip.

"I guess he doesn't have the same dark, brooding

good looks as Antonio. He was more of a young Brad Pitt." Meg wiggled her eyebrows.

Emma gritted her teeth, and a dull ache pulsed in her jaw. "I don't know what you're talking about. Come on. You wanted to meet Dylan outside." Meg's chuckle grated on her nerves from behind as she stepped into the kitchen.

Annie sat at the table with a cup of tea in her hands and glanced up with a smile pasted on her lips. Her guest sat beside her. "How was your nap, Emma?"

Heat flushed her cheeks. She didn't need everyone in town to know she was too depressed to keep her eyes open throughout the day. She shifted her gaze to meet the kind, gray ones beside her mom, and then back to Annie. "My nap was good. Thanks for watching Sophie."

Annie set her cup on the table and dabbed a lace napkin at the side of her mouth. "I didn't do much. She wouldn't leave your side until Meg got here and read her a story."

Emma set down Sophie and ran a hand over her hair. She wished Sophie would run and play the way she used to. "What can I say? She loves her mama. Sophie, get on your shoes so we can go play in the backyard."

Sophie kept her head down and climbed on the bench beside the back door.

Meg took a seat beside her, handing her one shoe and then the other.

"I'd like you both to meet Travis. He's in town for a few weeks for work. His mother and I used to be friends a long time ago." Annie nodded in their direction. "These are my daughters, Meg and Emma.

Emma and her children live here as well. I'm sure you will see each other from time to time."

Travis raised a hand and waved. "Nice to meet you both."

"Nice to meet you, too." Meg peered around Sophie through the kitchen window. "Dylan's out there with the other little rug rat. If you need anything, let us know."

"I appreciate the hospitality. I'll be working most of the time, but I'm sure I'll be around town."

Annie placed a hand on his forearm. "You'll have to go to Gilbert Farms while you're here. Meg and Dylan are busting their butts getting the place ready, and the big opening is next week."

Travis smiled. "I'll check that out if I have the time."

Annie clapped together her hands. "Emma could take you. She could give you the insider's tour." She winked at Travis, and then grinned at Emma.

Irritation burned in her gut. Emma tucked in her lips and slid on her sandals. She leaned one arm against the doorframe to brace herself. She had no desire to spend time with a strange guy. "Yeah, maybe. I'm not sure what I have going on."

"You'll have to take the kids, why not Travis as well?" Meg shrugged and quirked her lips to the side. "Making him go alone wouldn't be right."

The tight smile Emma forced made her cheeks hurt. "We'll talk about it later, Mom. We promised Sophie she could play outside, so we need to step out. I'll see you around, Travis." She turned the doorknob and swung open the back door. The hot sun streamed down on her face as soon as she stepped on the deck.

Tilting her chin, she relished the warmth on her skin. She hadn't been outside much the last month. The cheerful sky and joyful song of the robins boosted her spirits.

Sophie wrapped an arm around her leg.

She smiled down at Sophie. "Why don't you go play with Dylan?"

Sophie glanced up. "Will you stay right here?"

Her heart lurched. "Yes, baby. Meg-Meg and I will be right here the whole time."

Baby giggles filled the air. Anderson toddled around a tree in search of Dylan, who peeked around the side to surprise him. Anderson burst into laughter and grabbed Dylan's beard.

Dylan scooped Anderson into his arms. "Easy, little man. Look, there's sissy. Should she come chase us?"

Sophie unwrapped her arm from Emma's leg and took one step forward. She glanced over her shoulder, her top lip tucked and eyes wide.

"Go on, honey. Go have fun." Her heart lurched. Gone was the carefree little girl who loved to laugh and play. She'd do anything for a glimpse of the old Sophie.

"Come on, Soph. I bet you aren't fast enough to catch us." Dylan took off in a slow jog.

Sophie shot down the stairs and ran after him. Her giggles trailed behind her.

Emma sighed, and she hitched up one corner of her mouth. "Hearing her laugh is the most beautiful sound in the world."

Meg rested her hand on a shoulder and squeezed. "I agree. Let's sit for a minute."

Sophie squealed and chased Dylan and Anderson.

She took a seat on the white Adirondack chair that overlooked the backyard. She trained her gaze on Sophie and relaxed in her chair. Her life should be like this all the time—relaxing with her sister on the deck in the sunshine, while her kids played happily in the yard. How had enjoying her family become a rarity instead of the norm?

"Do you think you'll accompany Travis to the farm next week?"

Meg's voice dripped with amusement. She groaned. "Was Mom seriously fixing me up?"

"I doubt she's suggesting you go on a date. Probably just a way to get you out of the house for a little bit."

A knot formed in her stomach. "I get out of the house."

Meg arched her eyebrows. "Really?"

Irritation made her skin tingle. "Yes, really. Besides, getting two kids ready isn't easy, and I've been busy decorating Antonio's house."

"Really?" Meg's brows arched higher.

"Stop saying really." Emma swatted a hand through the air. "I've bought stuff and sent it over. I don't have to leave the house to do my job."

"Doesn't a decorator usually help put things in place? You're always so particular about where stuff goes."

She focused on the white clouds overhead. The warm weather of early September would soon fade into the bitter chill of fall. The clouds shifted, and she shielded her eyes from the glare of the sun. "I've sent emails. I'm sure he can follow simple instructions."

Meg was silent for a beat. "Did something happen

between you two? You enjoyed spending time with him, and all of a sudden he's never around, and you're hiding here."

"I'm not hiding." Fisting her hands on her lap, she took a breath and steadied her nerves. She loved Meg, but sometimes she hated how well her sister knew her. "Antonio is a client and nothing more. I enjoyed spending some time with him, but I have no reason to see him now."

"Okay, sorry I brought it up." Meg took a deep breath. "I wanted to talk about something else, anyway."

Emma straightened and turned in her chair to face Meg. Something in Meg's tone had her hairs standing on end. "Is everything all right?"

Meg clasped her hands in front of her and roamed the tips of her thumbs over her skin. "I need your help with something. Can you help plan a wedding reception at the farm? It will be our first big event, and I'm not good with this stuff. I thought you'd like to have a hand in the planning."

Emma cocked her head to the side. Something was off. "Why did you agree to host such a big event right when you're opening if you're not comfortable handling it yourself?"

Meg skimmed the toe of her shoe against the floor but couldn't hide the grin splitting her face. "I didn't have much of a choice. Dylan insisted we celebrate our marriage at the farm."

Shooting to her feet, Emma dropped her gaze to the diamond ring on Meg's finger. "What?"

"Be quiet, and sit down." Meg grabbed her arm and pushed her back to her seat. She glanced over her shoulder and giggled. "Dylan and I got married over the weekend. I didn't want to make a big deal out of it, so we eloped to the courthouse."

"Why didn't you say something? Didn't you want us there?" Leaning forward, she kept her voice soft and low. Excitement fluttered up her throat, beating down the edge of disappointment at not witnessing her baby sister getting married.

"I've never wanted the big wedding thing. If I had said something to Mom, she would have talked me into doing something. I'd feel guilty for not doing what she wanted, and then no one would be happy." Meg shrugged. "This way was easier."

Tears gathered at the corners of Emma's eyes. Her sister was married. She leaned forward and gathered Meg in her arms. "I'm so happy for you. I love Dylan, and I love you two together."

"Thanks." Meg smiled. "I hope Mom and Jonah are as cool about our elopement. I wanted to tell you first so you could help smooth the way."

Emma laughed. She should have recognized Meg's ploy. "I'll see what I can do. When do you want to have the reception?"

Meg winced. "I don't know when we can fit it in. We're so busy with the impending opening, and once the farm is open, we'll be working like dogs every day."

"Do you want to put it off for a while? We could wait until the fall is over and things slow down. You want to enjoy your special day, not rush through it." Emma settled back in her chair and tucked her feet beneath her.

"I don't really care to have a reception at all.

Dylan's the one who thinks we should do something our families can be a part of." Meg shrugged and twisted her lips. "I don't see what the big deal is."

Memories of her own wedding flickered through her mind and brought tears to her eyes. "Having the family witness Luke and me pledging our lives together is a memory I will always hold dear. We'd all like to celebrate with you, too. I understand you didn't want a big wedding, but please let me help give you the best wedding reception this town's ever seen. A big family celebration will soften the blow to Mom."

Meg chuckled. "Calming down Mom is a good point."

"Why don't we wait until spring? Give me plenty of time to plan everything, and you don't have to worry about it interfering with your schedule at the farm.

"Spring won't work." Meg shook her head and bit into her bottom lip.

"Why not?"

Meg's gaze locked on hers. Tears filled her eyes, and a large smile lifted her lips. She set a palm on her stomach. "I'm pregnant."

Emma let her mouth fall open, and she shot up again. "What?"

"Shut up, and sit down. Mom's in the kitchen, and I can't deal with her right now." Meg widened her eyes.

Meg's voice was stern, but a brilliant smile took over her face. "Okay. I'm sorry." Emma sat on the edge of her chair and smiled. Joy warmed her to her toes. "You need to learn some tact. You can't drop these bombs and not expect a reaction."

"You're right. But have you ever known me to be tactful?"

"Good point." Emma grabbed Meg's hand. "How far along are you?"

"Two months. The pregnancy is why we decided to get married so quickly. We talked about getting engaged, and we knew Dylan would propose eventually." Meg cleared her throat, and her voice shook. "Everything's coming together, Emma. I'm so happy."

Joy radiated through her. She would be an aunt. Soon she would hold a new baby. She could almost smell the top of the baby's head and hear the soft coos of a newborn. Ice filled her veins, and she froze. Her stomach dropped, and her heart pounded. She tightened her grip on Meg's arm. Oh God, how could she have been so stupid?

Chapter Twelve

Ding-Dong

Antonio pinched the bridge of his nose and groaned. Sweat dripped from his brow, and he wiped it off with the back of his hand. He'd fought every instinct to crawl into bed and sleep after he got home from work that morning. Instead, he'd jumped on the treadmill to get in his cardio for the day. He placed his empty water bottle on the island as he passed through the kitchen, down the hall, and to the front door.

He opened the door and frowned. "Can I help you?" The soft breeze carried droplets of rain into the house.

"Mr. Mendez? I have some packages you need to sign for." The brown-and-tan uniformed man held out a stylus and electronic signature box.

He grabbed them, signed his name on the dotted line, and cursed Emma for sending more stuff to his house. What was he supposed to do with everything? Oh, she sent emails describing where she thought everything should go, but he could care less about the furnishings. He wanted her…not a newly decorated house. "Thanks. Can you carry them into the living room?" He handed back the pen, and then propped open the door. He turned his face as water splattered on him.

"Where do you want them?" The man nodded toward the two soggy boxes weighing down his arms.

Antonio gestured toward the corner of the living room. "Over there's fine."

"You have a lot of unopened boxes. Are you moving in or moving out?"

"Neither." His tone was hard, and he clenched together his lips. No way was he having this conversation with the deliveryman.

"Okay." The man placed the packages on the floor, and then offered a half-hearted smile. "Have a nice day."

"You, too. Thanks." Antonio followed him to the door and closed it behind him. Water pooled on the floor, but he'd deal with it later. He climbed the stairs. Sweat clung to his body, and he needed a shower. He made his way back down the hall toward his bathroom.

Ding-Dong

"You've got to be kidding me," he mumbled under his breath. The guy must have forgotten another package in his truck. He bounded down the hall and opened the front door. Irritation simmered in his blood, and he yanked open the door. "Did you forget something?" His words came out harsher than he intended. Recognition punched him in the stomach, and his heart stopped beating.

"Hi. Can I come inside?" Emma stood on the porch with her hands clasped in front of her body.

Her damp strands curled over her cheek, and her blue eyes were as dark and stormy as the sky behind her. "Of course." He opened the door wider.

Emma brushed past him and stepped into the house. She stopped in the middle of the living room and pointed at the dozen boxes sitting in the corner. "You haven't opened them?"

He took a step toward her, and his heart started beating again. His pulse raced, and he moistened his dry, cracked lips. The need to touch her was overwhelming, but he curled his thumbs into his hands and kept them at his sides. "Are you okay?" Her wavy, light brown hair hung limply on her shoulders. Her red-rimmed eyes were too big on her face, and her petite frame drowned in a gray T-shirt and jeans.

She opened her mouth, but nothing came out. She faced the boxes. "I don't understand. I sent you emails so you'd know where to put everything. Didn't you read them?"

He raked a hand through his sweat-slicked hair, and then wiped his palm on his shorts. "I read all of them, but none of them told me what I wanted to know. I wanted to hear about you."

She wrung her hands. "But I gave very specific instructions."

"Would you shut up about the boxes and look at me?" His long strides closed the distance between them. He grasped her shoulders and spun her to face him. He took in the dark circles under her eyes and the wary lines of her mouth. "Is everything okay?"

Her gaze dropped to the floor, and she breathed in a shaky breath. "Antonio, I'm pregnant."

His mouth went dry, and he swallowed hard. His heart lodged in his throat, and joy erupted in his gut. He tightened his grip on her shoulders, and then he gathered her in his arms. He tucked her head under his chin. "Pregnant? We're having a baby? Emma, that's wonderful news."

Her body stiffened, and she pressed her hands against his chest. She stepped away and dropped her gaze to the floor. "How can you say a pregnancy is wonderful? This is a nightmare. I can't believe we were so reckless."

He folded her hand in his. "I know the timing's not ideal, but Emma, a baby is a blessing." Tears threatened to fill his eyes. He was to be a father again and have the home and the family he always wanted.

A sob broke from Emma, and she closed her eyes and took deep breaths. "A baby is a blessing under the right circumstances. Our situation is not the right circumstance."

He dropped her hand, and panic filled his veins. "What are you saying? You don't want to have this baby?"

Her eyes snapped open. "I'll have this baby, and I'll love it with my entire being. But getting pregnant right now is not a blessing. This baby should have a mother and father to love it and spend every day with it." Her voice broke, and she covered her mouth to stifle another sob.

He planted his feet on the floor. "This baby will have a mother and father to love it every single day. I want to be here for both of you. I've always wanted that. You're the one who's kept your distance. But now…now we can be together. We can start a family."

Her eyes bore into his, and she sneered. "I won't be with you just because I'm pregnant. I'm not your second chance to actually be around for your child as it grows up. Having a child together isn't an opportunity for redemption to soothe your guilt over not being around for Jillian and Sam."

Her words attacked him like a punch to the gut. Each word hitting harder—each punch more painful.

Anger threatened to seize him, but he wouldn't lash out. Harsh words wouldn't help anything. He drew in a deep breath, and then slowly released it through pursed lips. "I've been clear about my feelings for you. The night we spent together was one of the best of my life, and I tried so hard to talk to you. I want to be with you, Emma. Now more than ever. We owe it to the life we made to see if what we have is real."

She shook her head. "We don't have anything. I've already had the love of my life, and he's gone. I'm not getting a second one. You need to set aside whatever fantasies you have stewing around in your mind right now, because it will never happen." She stepped around him.

He grabbed her arm as she passed by. She faced him with steel in her eyes and yanked away her arm.

"We'll talk more later. I have to go." She strode to the door.

Numbness crept into his limbs, and he stood rooted to the spot. "Don't go, Emma," he said in a whisper.

She didn't turn around as she opened the door and stepped into the rain.

He searched for something to brace himself, but the room was bare. He stumbled backward to the stairs, dropped down on a step, and hung his head in his hands. Heaviness weighed down his heart. Having another child should be something to celebrate, not cause problems between him and Emma. He loved her. They should be together, doing this as a team. Instead, she'd marched into his house, dropped a bomb, and attacked his character. Anger boiled in his blood. This bomb was too much to handle alone.

He scrambled to his feet and darted his gaze around

the house. He had to get out of here and talk to someone. Stalking into the kitchen, he grabbed his keys off the counter then left the empty house behind him. The rain fell harder as he walked the few blocks to Jillian's house, but he didn't care. He was oblivious to the drips of water, except for when it splashed up from the sidewalk and soaked his shoes. The autumn breeze combined with the drizzle caused goose bumps to take over his skin, but his anger burned hot.

Sam's bike lay sprawled across the sidewalk, and he stepped over it as he leapt on to the front porch. He yanked open the screen door and pounded on the red door. Seconds later Jillian opened the door, breathless and wide-eyed.

"What in the world is going on?"

Raindrops splattered above them on the porch roof, and he wiped droplets of water from his face. "Can I come in? I really need somebody to talk to."

"Sure. I was making some coffee. Do you want a cup?" Jillian padded barefoot toward the kitchen. Her blonde hair piled high on her head in a messy bun, and her reading glasses perched above her forehead.

"Caffeine and I wouldn't mix well right now." He swept his gaze around the room. "Where's Sam?"

"Jonah took him to the farm to help. The festival opens in a few days, and we still have a lot of work. Meg and Dylan are getting pretty stressed, and Sam's dying to be put to help." Jillian stopped in front of the coffee pot and poured the brown liquid into a mug, steam billowing from the top. She eyed him with slitted eyes over the top of her mug. "What's wrong?"

He sank into a chair at the table and braced his elbows on his knees. "Emma's pregnant. She came over

119

to tell me, and then left before we could figure out anything."

"Holy cow." Jillian sat across from him. "Does Jonah know?"

"I don't really care what Jonah knows right now." He raised his voice and narrowed his eyes. "What I'm dealing with isn't about him, Jillian. Can you please be my friend right now and not worry about your husband? I need someone in my corner, and I have nowhere else to turn."

Jillian's shoulders rose on a sigh, and she set her mug in front of her. "I'm sorry, but your news is a lot to process. You're right. This situation is about you and Emma. What can I do to help?"

He shook his head, and water spattered from his hair and landed on the table. Anger and pain jostled in the pit of stomach. Bile slid up the back of his throat, and he willed himself to keep it down. He needed to focus. "I don't know what to do."

"What do you want to do? How do you feel about having a baby with Emma?"

Her voice was tender, and her kindness almost broke him. He sat up and leaned against the back of his chair. "I had feelings for her before we spent the night together, and they only grew afterward." He shrugged. "I fell in love."

The corners of Jillian's eyes crinkled. "Then what's the problem?"

"She doesn't want anything to do with me." He rubbed the back of his neck and snorted. "I don't even know if she wants me involved with the baby."

Jillian grimaced then curved her lips into a small smile. "Do you want to be involved with the baby?"

He pushed up from his chair and paced across the small kitchen. "Of course I do. I missed so much with Sam, and I don't want to make the same mistakes. I want to be there for everything."

"Okay, so be there."

He stopped pacing and met her unwavering gaze. "You make it sound so easy."

She placed her elbow on the table and rested her chin in her hand. "It is. Would it be great if you and Emma decided to raise this baby together? Absolutely. But if Emma doesn't want to be in a relationship, she can't take away your rights as the baby's father. You can still be a very big part of the baby's life."

"I didn't think about my rights." He squeezed his hands on the back of the chair. "I don't understand why she won't make things work. She has feelings for me. I know she does. Even if she denies it."

"Give her some time." Jillian rested a hand on his. "You've always been someone who knows what he wants and goes after it full speed ahead. You and Emma don't have to have all of the answers right now. You both need to take a breath and see how you feel in a few weeks."

"A few weeks?" His stomach dropped. Time away from Emma was hard enough, but keeping his distance now that he knew she carried his child would be impossible.

She laughed. "Three weeks isn't that long. Use the time to think about what you want and how to work it out with Emma if she is adamant about not being together. Trust me, she'll appreciate you having a plan, not just spouting out emotions and ideas about what you think is the ideal situation. She needs you to be calm and levelheaded. She's been dealt some tough blows over the last seven months, and getting pregnant right now has to be difficult."

"What did you say?"

The hard edge in Jonah's voice made Antonio wince.

Jillian jumped up and widened her eyes. "I didn't know you were back. I thought you and Sam were helping at the farm all afternoon."

Jonah's nostrils flared. "You got Emma pregnant?"

Antonio stiffened his back, and he tightened his jaw. "I'm sure Emma would rather discuss what happened with you."

"I don't care what Emma wants right now." He glared and fisted his hands at his sides. "I want you to tell me what the hell is going on?"

Jillian rested a hand on Jonah's shoulder. "Jonah, calm down. Antonio just found out, and he needed someone to talk to."

He brushed her aside. "Coming to Emma's brother's house and speaking with her sister-in-law was the best place to go? You've got to be freaking kidding me right now."

He clenched his teeth and fisted his hands at his sides. "I don't need to explain anything."

Jonah stepped in front of him, their faces inches apart. "I beg to differ."

The heat of Jonah's breath on his face matched the heat igniting through his veins. "Get out of my way."

Jonah grabbed the front of his shirt. "I'm not going anywhere."

"Let go of him, you idiot." Jillian stomped over and grabbed Jonah's arm. She yanked on his bicep, straining against his weight.

Jonah tightened his grip.

"I've dealt with one stubborn Sheffield today. I don't need to deal with another." He jerked away, tearing his shirt form Jonah's grasp. "I'll say it one more time…get the hell out of my way."

Jonah pressed in closer.

The tip of his nose brushed against Jonah's. Adrenaline pumped through his body. He pulled back his fist and slammed it into Jonah's face.

Jonah grabbed his nose, and the red stain of blood coated his hands. He lunged forward.

Jillian wrapped her arms around his waist and tugged him back. "Enough! Both of you stop acting like children. Jonah, get in the bathroom and get yourself cleaned up before you get bloodstains all over the house." She shoved Jonah toward the bathroom and pointed a finger. "Antonio, step outside and cool off. Fighting won't solve anything."

Jonah stood rooted to the spot and shot daggers with his cold, blue eyes. Antonio curled his fingers and winced. He needed ice. He cradled his injured hand and shoved past Jonah and Jillian. Opening the door, he stalked into the rain. Stopping on the sidewalk in front of the house, he lifted his head to the sky. His chest tightened and his lungs burned as he struggled to take in air. Falling in love with a woman whose heart belonged to someone else was painful, and he'd gone and made the same mistake again. At his own stupidity, he shook his head and walked toward his empty home.

Chapter Thirteen

"Do you want mums on every table?" Emma picked at the brilliant orange petals poking out of the terra cotta pot. The farm was the last place she wanted to be, but Meg needed her. Her heart ached over her conversation with Antonio, but starting a relationship right now would end in a disaster. No matter how strong her feelings were.

"Yes. We have more than enough pots." Meg carried over two more pots filled with flowers, her dog, Nora, glued to her side. "Are you sure you're okay? You look awful."

"Gee, thanks." She swallowed a groan and compared herself to Meg. Meg's thick, golden hair trailed down her back in a simple braid, and a healthy glow touched her cheeks. Emma pushed an unruly wave behind her ear and rested a hand on her stomach. Any glow on her cheeks was from her rising body temperature every time she fought down nausea.

Meg set down the pot on the circular table and grabbed Emma's hand. "I'm sorry. I appreciate your help, but today was tough. Do you want to lie down inside for a minute?"

The barn door slid open, and the howling wind echoed around the large, open space.

Jonah stormed inside, slammed the door closed, and marched toward them. A trail of mud and water stained the floor behind him. "Emma, we need to talk. Now."

Nora crouched in front of Meg and bared her teeth.

A lead ball settled in the pit of Emma's stomach.

Nora took a step toward Jonah, and a low growl hummed in her throat.

Meg held up a hand. "What's your problem? I've been cleaning for days, and you storm in here and get mud all over the floors. I hope you plan on cleaning up your mess." She jabbed a finger in his chest.

"Cleaning your floor is the last thing on my mind right now." He huffed out a breath and glared.

"What did you do to your face?" Emma leaned forward and narrowed her eyes. Purple bruises spread out on either side of his nose, and a bandage covered with cartoon turtles stretched across the center. The lead ball in her stomach bounced around. Whatever happened to Jonah couldn't be good.

Jonah bounced his hard glare from Meg to Emma. "Antonio sucker punched me."

Emma covered her mouth with a trembling hand. Bile formed in her stomach and slid up her throat. The tinny taste of fear mingled with the acidic bile, and she gagged as she swallowed it down. "Why would he hit you?"

He snorted. "Maybe because you were stupid enough to let him get you pregnant."

"Excuse me?" Her blood boiled with anger. "You need to watch yourself."

Jonah snorted. "What were you thinking? How could you sleep with him? And how careless do you have to be to get pregnant?"

Emma raised an eyebrow and cocked her head to

the side. "Didn't you get Jillian pregnant on accident?"

He worked his jaw back and forth. "What happened with Jillian is different. We were kids. Adults should know better."

"Oh really?" Meg linked her arm through Emma's.

Emma gave a slight shake of her head. Meg's intentions were written clearly across her face. She didn't have to do this.

Meg ignored her. "Maybe I need this lecture, too, since I was stupid enough to get pregnant as well."

Jonah's jaw dropped, and his eyes bulged. "Are you serious?"

"Is she serious about what?" Dylan stepped through the doorway and made his way to Meg's side. "You guys are so loud. I heard you all the way in the stable."

"You knocked up my baby sister?" Jonah balled his hands into fists.

"Jonah." Emma silenced her brother before he said something he'd regret. "Enough. You need to calm down."

"You better listen to Emma." Dylan snaked an arm around Meg's waist. "I won't let you upset my wife, especially in her condition."

A small gasp sounded behind her, and Emma glanced over her shoulder. Her stomach dropped to the floor.

With a hand covering her heart, Annie stood surrounded by the children.

"Mommy!" Sophie ran across the floor and threw herself into Emma's arms.

Emma squeezed her, and then set her on ground. "Hi, sweet girl. Were you a big help while I was gone?"

Sophie nodded. "Sam and I both were, but Anderson got in the way a lot."

"I think you all have a lot of explaining to do." Annie cleared her throat. "Let's head into the house for some tea, and we can figure out what is going on."

Emma nudged Sophie toward Annie. "Go with Grandma, honey. Make sure to use your umbrella so you don't get soaked."

"I want to go with you, Mommy." Sophie's eyes widened, and her bottom lip trembled.

"Mommy needs to talk to Uncle Jonah for a second. I'll meet you in the house, and then we'll make some popcorn and hot chocolate. How does that sound?" Her heart twisted. She'd have to have a similar conversation with Sophie soon, and she had no idea what to say.

"Come on, Soph." Sam grabbed her hand. "I'll help you with your coat. Maybe we can watch a movie while we eat our popcorn. I'll even let you watch a princess movie if you want."

Emma crouched and whispered in her ear, "Go with Sam. I'll meet you inside."

Sophie sighed, and then ran to Sam.

Sam put his arm around Sophie, and they followed Annie and Anderson.

A flutter of warmth burst in the corner of her chest. She dropped her hand and rested it on her stomach. Sam was so good to Sophie. He would be a wonderful big brother to the child she carried.

When Annie and the kids were out of sight, Meg stared at Jonah with narrowed eyes. "Way to go, jerk. You barged in, demanding answers to questions you had no right to ask. You've made a mess of everything." She turned on her heel and followed after Annie with Dylan and Nora on either side of her.

Emma's pulse thundered in her ears. "You better pray the kids didn't hear I'm pregnant. Sam deserves to be told by Antonio—not by you. Sophie will have a hard enough time understanding what's going on without wondering why you're acting like a jerk. Pull yourself together before you step inside. Nobody wants to deal with you when you're all worked up."

She grabbed her jacket off the back of the chair and yanked it on before turning away. She slid open the barn door and flipped her hood over her head. Rain poured down in sheets. She should follow the others to the tack room and get an umbrella, but she couldn't face them right now. A few minutes alone to gather her nerve was what she needed. Lowering her head, she stepped into the rain and ran toward the house.

Tears streamed over her cheeks and mingled with the rain as it pelted her skin. Pressure weighed down her heart. She wasn't ready to deal with telling her family about her pregnancy yet, and now she didn't have a choice. She let the tears fall, at least for a minute. No one would see them, and they'd be gone by the time anyone else stepped foot in the house. Her heart was torn in two, but she couldn't let it show. Her family needed to see her strong and in charge of her decisions, not pity the mistake she'd made. She'd had enough pity to last her a lifetime.

She charged up the back steps to the kitchen door and let herself in to Meg and Dylan's house. Betsy, Dylan's Golden Retriever, rounded the corner and jumped on her chest. She smiled and pushed down the dog.

Betsy's tail thumped against the floor as she waited for attention.

Emma tore off her jacket and hung it on the hook by the door, and then peeled off her rain boots. "Okay, girl. Come here." She knelt to the floor and opened her arms. Betsy wiggled and covered her face with kisses.

The door opened behind her, and rain sputtered in and clung to the back of her shirt.

"She'll never leave you alone if you let her love on you like that." Jonah kicked out of his boots.

Anger pulsed through her, and she straightened her back as she stood. She reached into the cabinet for oil and popcorn kernels, and then grabbed a pot to place on the stove. "What happened between you and Antonio?"

Jonah sighed and took a seat at the table. "I walked in on him and Jillian talking. The news took me by surprise, and I didn't react well."

She leaned against the counter. "What a shock."

"You have to admit, you being pregnant is unexpected." He ran a hand over his chin, and then snaked it around to rub the back of his neck. "And now Meg…geez. Something must be in the water."

"Trust me, water had nothing to do with it." She turned back to the stove, covered the bottom of the pot with oil, and filled it with popcorn kernels. She placed the lid on the top, and then faced Jonah, crossing her arms over her chest.

"Did he take advantage, Emma?"

His voice was thick, and his eyes darkened to cobalt. Heat flooded her. "Are you out of your mind?"

"What am I supposed to think? You've only been here for three months. Luke hasn't been…" His voice trailed off, and he dropped his gaze to the table.

Crushing pain swooped in and squeezed her throat. Jonah hadn't said anything she hadn't already told herself, but hearing his words out loud threatened to bring her to her knees. She closed her eyes and took a deep breath.

"I'm sorry, Emma."

She shook her head and opened her eyes. Moisture gathered at the corners, and she bit her lip to keep the tears from falling. "I know what you think. I can't wrap my own mind around what happened."

"Help me understand. Were you drunk? Did he pressure you at all? Because if he did, I'll handle it."

"Because you did so well handling yourself earlier?" She raised her brows and hitched up the corner of her mouth. She sat across from him and cradled her head in her hands. "I'd had a few drinks, but not much. Antonio did absolutely nothing to pressure me, so back off, okay?"

He nodded. "Okay."

She lifted a shoulder, and a vise squeezed her heart. "As crazy as it sounds, I thought I was ready. Feelings had built since I moved here, and I fought them. I didn't want to deny my feelings anymore. I wanted to see if we could make something work." She sighed and wiped the corners of her eyes. "It was too soon, and now I'm being punished for being the worst widow in the world."

Jonah squeezed her hand. "You're doing the best you can. No one would judge you for wanting to start a relationship with someone else."

She pursed her lips. "In this town?"

"Okay, maybe some people in town would. But no one who matters." He chuckled. "Out of all the men in the world, why did you have to fall for Antonio?"

She straightened her spine. She needed to be clear about her intentions. "Acting on my feelings was a mistake, and one I don't intend on making again."

"But you said—"

The door swung open and banged hard against the wall. Dylan entered with Sophie in his arms, followed by Meg and Sam, and Annie carrying Anderson. Nora ran into the kitchen, barking and jumping with Betsy.

Mud caked the floor, and Emma jumped up to grab a towel.

"This rain better stop soon, or the yard will be a wreck for the opening." Dylan placed Sophie on the ground and peeled off her coat.

"You'll make everything sparkle like new, no matter the weather." Annie turned toward Meg. "Do you have decaffeinated tea in the house?"

"Yeah, but I want coffee." Meg shrugged out of her raincoat.

Annie arched her brows and shifted Anderson on her hip. "How many cups of coffee have you had today?"

Dylan choked back a laugh.

Meg glared and swatted his arm.

"Sorry, but now that the cat's out of the bag, you have more people to make sure you're eating healthy. You've had two cups too many today, Meg." Dylan hung up Sophie's coat then placed her boots on the welcome mat by the door.

Meg grabbed the towel from Emma and wiped down Nora. "Fine, I'll have tea. But you can make your own damn coffee from now on."

Dylan kissed Meg on the top of the head. "Yes,

dear. I also need to make some hot chocolate."

"I can help." Sam raced to the cabinet and grabbed two mugs. "Emma, will you make it?"

She smiled at Sam, and warmth spread to her toes. Sam would be a great big brother. "Sure. Why don't you and Sophie pick out a movie?"

"Okay, come on, Sophie." Sam grabbed Sophie's hand, and they ran into the living room.

Kernels of popcorn exploded and slammed against the lid. Emma retrieved packets of hot chocolate mix from the counter, and then crossed paths with Meg when she walked to the fridge for milk.

Meg grabbed the kettle from the stove and filled it with water. "How big of a jerk was Jonah while we were gone?" She turned on the stove, and then sat at the table.

A low growl sounded from Jonah.

Meg chuckled.

"Don't start, Meg." Annie pulled out the chair across from Meg and sat with Anderson in her lap. "First things first. How long have you and Dylan been married?"

Meg squirmed in her seat and locked her gaze with Dylan.

A stab of jealousy pierced through Emma. She wished she had a partner to lean on right now.

Meg glanced back to Annie. "We got married last week. I'm sorry we didn't tell you, but I didn't want to do the whole big wedding thing. I also didn't want to feel pressured into it or guilty for getting married my way."

Annie's mouth rested in a firm line. "Is it true you're pregnant?"

"Yes, and we couldn't be happier." Dylan stood behind Meg and rested his hands on her shoulders. "A family of my own is what I've always wanted out of life."

Annie skirted around the table. She wrapped one arm around Meg's shoulder, while Anderson tugged her braid and laughed. "Then I'm happy for you. My dear girl, it's your life. You need to live it the way you want, and to hell with everyone else."

Meg's mouth dropped. "You aren't mad?"

Annie waved a hand in front of her. "Of course not. I'm a little disappointed I didn't see you and Dylan get married, but I understand why you did it this way."

Emma turned her back to them, busying herself with getting the popcorn off the stove and into a bowl. A hand squeezed her shoulder, and she closed her eyes. She inhaled through her nose slowly to drop her heartrate.

"Did you hear what I said to your sister?"

Annie's voice was quiet, and her touch was reassuring. Tears clogged Emma's throat, so she nodded. She couldn't lose it now.

"The same goes for you. Don't waste your time worrying about what your choices mean to other people. They don't matter. What does matters is this baby." Annie's voice cracked.

A shrill whistle sounded from the teakettle, and Emma grabbed the handle and took it off the burner. A small piece of the fear that encased her heart fell away. She'd figure out this mess. She had her family, and they would always stand with her. Taking a deep breath, she squared her shoulders and turned around finally ready to face them all. "Who wants some tea?"

Chapter Fourteen

The smell of marinara sauce hung heavy in the pizza shop. Red-and-white checked tablecloths covered the full tables, and a constant hum of chatter beat against the music blaring from the jukebox. A low growl grumbled in the pit of Antonio's stomach. He hadn't had much of an appetite in the last couple of days, but it returned in full force this evening. He tapped his knuckles against the wooden counter and waited for the server to take his order. The bell above the door chimed, and he glanced over his shoulder.

"Are you freaking kidding me?" Jonah stopped in the doorway.

Antonio's blood turned cold. Jonah had been a thorn in his side since the day he'd moved back to Smithview. The thorn had burrowed itself into his ribcage at this point. The waitress needed to hurry up so he could get out of here.

"Dad! What are you doing here?" Sam ran around Jonah to get to Antonio.

He bent forward and wrapped his arms around Sam. "Hi, buddy."

Jillian stepped up behind Sam. "Hey, how are you?"

He flicked his gaze from Jonah to Jillian. "I'm okay. I'm still processing everything." He straightened and flexed his hand at his side. The pain in his hand had subsided, and he bit into his cheeks to keep from smiling. The bruising around Jonah's nose was now a nasty shade of green.

"Are you putting in an order?" Jillian asked.

"If the server ever shows up." He glanced around and held up a finger.

She nodded, and then turned away.

Her soft red curls swayed as she hurried from table to table. Getting his food was taking forever.

Jillian grabbed Sam's arm and pulled him to her side. "Perfect. You and Jonah can talk about your issues while you wait. Sam and I will be in the back playing the claw game."

"Wait, what?" Jonah took a step forward.

Dread curdled in Antonio's stomach and threatened to steal his appetite. "You and Sam leaving isn't necessary. We don't have anything more to—"

"I'm so sorry for your wait. We're swamped tonight, and the other server called off. Do you know what you want?" The server tucked her hair behind her ear and posed a pen above a notebook.

Antonio shifted his focus. "I'll take a large pizza with pepperoni and ham."

"Anything else?"

"Nope."

"All right. Give us twenty minutes." She hurried off in the direction of the kitchen.

"Perfect, you two have twenty minutes to figure out how to get along." Grinning, Jillian winked. "Sam, tell your dad bye."

"Bye, Dad. I'll see you on Thursday."

Antonio hugged him tight. "Be good. I love you."

Sam ran back toward the video games.

Jillian followed. She turned, walking backward, and mouthed, *Be nice*.

Antonio shoved his hands into the pockets of his jeans and rocked back on his heels. He fixed his gaze past Jonah's shoulder. "Talking is pointless."

"I agree, but Jillian's watching, and she'll be mad if I go back there now."

He slid his lips to the side. "Sorry, man. Not my problem."

Jonah lifted his eyebrows. "Do you really believe Jillian being upset doesn't affect you?"

Jonah had a point. Jillian would be a pain in his butt if he didn't at least pretend to talk to Jonah. "Fine, but let's step outside."

His shoulder bounced off Jonah's as he passed him and exited the restaurant. The slight breeze kept the late September air pleasant, and the sun hung low. The days grew shorter this time of year, and before long, darkness would beat back the blue sky. He stopped in front of the large picture window that displayed the pizzeria and batted a stone around with the toe of his sneaker.

Jonah leaned against the window and pulled his baseball cap low over his eyes. "Have you talked to Emma?"

"I don't want to talk to you about Emma." Blood pounded in his ears. They wouldn't accomplish anything. He glanced down at his watch…eighteen minutes before he could get his pizza and get out of here.

"Standing here having a conversation is a waste of time." Jonah glanced behind him and into the pizzeria.

Jillian waved and smiled.

Jonah chuckled. "She's too stubborn."

"Now that's one thing we can agree on." Antonio took a deep breath and ignored the annoyance coursing through him. "Listen, you and I will have to deal with each other even more now. We've been civil so far, and I don't see why we can't keep it at that."

Jonah shrugged. "I guess. I needed to hear from Emma what happened. I overreacted the other day."

Heat spread up his back and poured into his cheeks. "Why is what happened between me and Emma any of your business?"

"Because she's my sister, and she's been hurt enough." Jonah's voice raised an octave, and he took a step toward him. "I couldn't do anything to protect her from what happened with Luke, but if I can help her with some guy taking advantage, you better believe I will."

"I would never take advantage of a woman." He fisted his hands in his hair, and a growl of frustration ripped from his throat. Why was everyone making him out to be the bad guy when all he wanted was to be with Emma? He didn't need to keep explaining himself to this jerk.

Jonah held up his hands. "I know, man. I'm sorry. But I know your history, and I, damnit... I don't like you."

Antonio laughed and put his hands back in his pockets. "I don't like you much either."

"Look at that, we have something else in common." Jonah met his gaze, and the lines in his face tensed. "I don't like seeing her hurt."

"I don't want to hurt her." A tiny crack of resistance broke though the resentment he held against

Jonah. He hated to admit it, but he admired the guy for loving his family so much.

"Do you have a plan?" Jonah's gaze shifted, and he frowned. "You've got to be kidding me."

The scuff of footsteps fell behind Antonio. Blake's hazy reflection stared from the window.

"You're spending all sorts of time with the Sheffields, buddy."

Blake's hand landed with a thud between his shoulder blades.

Blake swayed toward the pavement between them.

Antonio caught his shoulder, steadying him. He wrinkled his nose and swallowed a gag. Alcohol oozed from Blake's pores, mixing with what had to be two days' worth of body odor. Wrinkles creased his clothes, and red veins covered the white of his eyes.

"Geez, Blake. You reek." Jonah turned his face to the side.

"Yeah, well, your sister never thought so. The slut." His words slurred, and he leaned forward, invading Jonah's personal space.

The hairs on the back of Antonio's neck stood. He grabbed Blake by the back of his shirt and pulled him away. "Watch yourself."

Blake sneered and shoved away his hand. "Or what?" His eyes lit up. "You probably don't know the story about Meg. Do you?"

He fisted his hand around the collar of Blake's shirt and brought Blake's face inches from his own. Antonio cringed as his hot breath slid across his face. "Go home and sleep it off. No one wants to hear your lies." He tossed him to the side.

Blake stumbled back a few feet. "Screw you both."

He spat on the ground, and then stumbled down the sidewalk.

Antonio rubbed a hand through the stubble on his chin. "He's an idiot."

Jonah snorted and paced in front of the window. "Did Emma tell you what he did to Meg?"

He shook his head. "She said the story was Meg's to tell."

"Yeah, Meg doesn't like her business being talked about." Jonah's cheeks filled with air, and then he blew it out slowly through parted lips. "Why did you stick up for her?"

He shrugged and kicked another stone in front of him. He watched as it skittered down the curb. "I don't know Meg very well, but she's always been nice to me. I don't need to know the details to know Blake's full of bull."

A moment of silence passed. Jonah shifted his weight and yanked at the bill of his hat. "Emma will be mad I'm telling you this, but she has a doctor's appointment tomorrow. We all offered to go, but she said she could do it alone. You should go."

A stab of disappointment pierced his gut that she hadn't told him. "Why are you telling me?"

"Listen, dude, we need to get along. You're Sam's dad, and I'm your new baby's uncle." Jonah shook his head. "This situation is messed up, isn't it?"

Antonio chuckled. "Very."

"Every time I see you, it's awkward, and it'd be nice to get past any hard feelings."

The crack of resistance splintered even more. Jonah was right. Life would be easier if he wasn't filled with annoyance every time they set eyes on each other.

They might never be great friends, but they could at least get along. "Do you know what time her appointment is?"

He cut his gaze to the window and grimaced. "No, but I'm sure Jilly does. I'll have her text you the information. Do you work tomorrow?"

"It doesn't matter. I'll make it work." Wednesdays were usually busy flying days, but he'd call in every favor he was owed to make the time to be with Emma. She needed to know he intended to be there for the baby from the beginning.

The door to the pizzeria cracked open, and the server peeked out her head. "Your order's ready."

"Thanks. I'll be inside in a second." He glanced at Jonah. "Thanks for letting me know about Emma. Tell Jillian to text me soon so I can figure out my schedule."

Jonah nodded.

Antonio walked to the door. He grabbed the handle, tugged, and inhaled deeply as he stepped inside. The intoxicating scent of garlic and oregano smacked him in the face, and his stomach growled. Emma would be upset to see him tomorrow, but he didn't care. He had every right to be there.

He paid for his pizza, waved goodbye to Jillian and Sam, and stepped back outside. The bottom of the pizza box warmed his hand.

Jonah still stood by the window, staring out into the distance.

He walked by with a tight smile and a brief nod. He was in a better spot with Jonah than with Emma right now. Who would have thought?

****

Antonio sat in the waiting room, and his heart

pounded. He kept his gaze fixed on the mess of magazines spread across the narrow coffee table, not wanting to make eye contact with the few women waiting their turn to see the doctor. He wiped off his palms on the thighs of his jeans. Nervous energy ricocheted in every corner of his body, and the friction of his jeans against his legs made his thighs burn. But he couldn't stop. A pit opened in the bottom of his stomach, and nervousness bubbled inside him. He tapped a foot against the linoleum floor and kept his gaze glued to the door. Emma would be here any minute.

A glance at his phone showed her appointment began in ten minutes. He swiped the screen and opened his email. One from Brigette caught his eye.

Hey, Stanger. I'm on your flight on Friday. Do you want to get a drink afterward? It'd be nice to catch up.

The woman couldn't take a hint. He'd been upfront about not wanting to see her anymore. He needed to tell her again where things stood.

"What are you doing here?"

He glanced up from his phone, and Emma stood in front of him. Her words came out clipped, and her tone was harsh. His heart stopped beating. He shot to his feet and tried to usher her to the chair.

She pulled away and planted her feet to the ground.

He cleared the nervousness from his throat. "I found out about your appointment, and I wanted to be here."

She dropped her gaze to the floor. "This is a quick appointment. I'll pee in a cup, they'll take my vitals, and then tell me the due date. If it had been an important visit, I would have told you."

"They're all important to me."

"Emma, we need you to sign in," the receptionist said.

"I'll be right back." She hurried to the sign-in desk.

He fell back to his chair and exhaled a pent-up breath. She was so cold. How could he break through? Her back was ramrod straight, and she clasped her hand around the strap of her purse. She was so different now. Not at all like the warm, open Emma he had always been drawn to.

She took a seat beside him.

He folded his hands in his lap. "How've you been feeling?"

Sighing, she slumped in her chair. "Tired."

The air crackled with tension, and he searched his brain for something else to say. "I wanted to call but thought you might need some space."

"I only found out about the pregnancy a week ago. Space is good, thanks." She shifted her purse from her shoulder to the floor.

"I've thought a lot over the last few days, and when you're ready, I'd like to sit down and talk."

She turned to face him. "Okay, but not now."

"Emma, we're ready for you." A nurse stood in the doorway holding a clipboard and a plastic cup. "Are you able to give us a sample?"

Emma's hand shot out and grabbed the cup, and red stained her cheeks.

He'd forgotten what these appointments entailed, and he glanced toward the exit. No wonder Emma hadn't wanted him here. He might be in love with her, but they hadn't experienced all the intimacies most couples shared before heading to the obstetrician's office together. He pointed toward a chair at the end of the hall. "I'll wait over there."

The clock on the wall ticked off the seconds as he waited for her return. He stared at the hands as they moved along, willing them to speed up.

Emma and the nurse approached him.

The nurse gestured toward the empty exam room across from them. "We can head in here."

Emma sat on the exam table and folded her hands on her lap.

He leaned against the wall to give her the space she deserved. He swept his gaze over the room, unsure of where he was supposed to look. The last time he'd been in this position, he'd accompanied his wife. With Emma, he didn't know what he should do.

After jotting down Emma's heart rate and blood pressure, the nurse looped her stethoscope around her neck. "The doctor will be right in."

"Thank you." Emma sighed and leaned back on the table.

He stood beside her. A sheen of sweat coated the back of his neck, and nerves danced in the pit of his stomach. "Have you seen this doctor before?"

"No, but Meg sees him. I've heard good things." Emma kept her focus ahead of her and the muscles of her face tight.

The door swung open, and a middle-aged man in a white coat stepped inside, closing the door behind him. He glanced at the chart in his hand and smiled. "Hello, I'm Dr. Dressler. Congratulations Mr. and Mrs. Harris, you're having a baby."

Emma sat and twirled the gold band she still wore on her left hand. "Thank you, but we aren't married.

I'm Emma Harris, and this is Antonio Mendez."

Antonio leaned forward and shook the doctor's hand. Flames heated his face, and he wanted to crawl into a hole and hide somewhere. Not only was he not Emma's husband, but she still wore another man's ring.

"My apologies. Nice to meet you both." He set down his chart and clapped his hands once. "Go ahead and get undressed, and then we can start your internal exam."

Emma's eyes widened, and she locked gazes.

His pulse pounded in his ears, and he braced himself on the wall as dizziness swam in his head. Forget finding a hole to hide in. He wanted one to open and swallow him whole instead.

Chapter Fifteen

Emma lay down on the exam table and covered her face with her hands. Yellow lights beat down on her, highlighting her mortification to everyone in the small room. Of course the doctor would want to do an internal exam right away. She sent over her history from her previous doctor, and after the complications she'd experienced with Anderson, they'd want to do more than a simple urine test today. No way could she let Antonio stay in the room for an internal exam.

But she couldn't kick him out. Not after he showed up and told her how important the appointments were. She'd been horrible over the past month, and he'd been nothing but kind. To make him leave now would be a slap in the face.

Antonio coughed.

She peeked through the slits in her fingers. She hadn't stolen a glance since he'd turned his back so she could undress. Now, he stood facing her.

The doctor laid his instruments on the silver tray beside the exam table.

She groaned.

Antonio's wide eyes turned toward the instruments then refocused on her, and his Adam's apple bobbed up and down. "Umm…Emma? Do you want me to be in here?"

She dropped her hands and balled up the white

paper underneath her. The crackling sliced through the tense silence.

The doctor faced her with raised brows.

She licked her cracked lips. "If you're uncomfortable, you don't need to stay. We can call you in when this part's done."

The doctor chuckled. "If you plan on being in the room for the birth, you'll have to toughen up, son."

If a bolt of lightning struck her right now, it wouldn't take her out of her misery soon enough.

Antonio's shoulders slumped forward. "I'll stay." He took two steps backward toward the wall and leaned into the corner.

"All right, let's get started. Emma, can you put your feet in the stirrups, please?" The doctor approached her with a smile.

She settled her heels against the cold metal and an icy blast shot up her legs, but it couldn't dampen the heat that enflamed her cheeks. Every muscle in her body tensed, and she mentally sang the words to Sophie's favorite nursery rhyme in her head until the exam was over.

"We're all done. You can relax now." Dr. Dressler washed his hands. "I'll let you get yourself together, and then meet you both in my office across the hall."

Her muscles relaxed, and she removed her heels from the stirrups and sat up on the table. A waft of air tickled her spine, and she reached around to close the flaps of her gown. "Can you wait for me in the hall while I get dressed?" Antonio's pale face made his chocolate eyes as black as coal.

He bobbed his head up and down, and then followed the doctor out of the room.

She hung her head in her hands. Tears sat heavy in her throat. She sucked in a shaky breath, jumped off the table, and dressed. The rest of the appointment would be a cakewalk, and then she could get out of here—hopefully without saying much to Antonio. She was hanging on by a thread, and his kind eyes and constant reassurance they could make a relationship work would snip that thread in half.

Emma pushed open the door, and it squeaked on its hinges. She rested a hand heavily on the doorknob and squeezed it in her palm, releasing her pent-up energy before stepping into the hall. "All right. Let's head in." She forced cheerfulness in her voice and stepped into the doctor's office.

Antonio followed.

Dr. Dressler sat behind a large, oak desk.

Pictures of his family covered the walls, and framed diplomas hung prominently behind him. Two tufted armchairs sat in front of the desk, adding a homey feel to the business space that put her at ease. She sank into the beige chair and relaxed into its comfort.

Dr. Dressler cleared his throat and flipped open the file in front of him. "So, everything looked good, but I'll let you know what the swabs show when they come back. Those are mostly for precaution since you're a new patient. Now, I'd like to talk a little about your previous pregnancy. I see your son is a little over a year old, and he was born early."

"Yes, he was close to two months early." Antonio's gaze burned a hole in her cheek, but she kept her gaze fixed on the doctor.

The doctor scribbled something on a piece of

paper. "And you had no issues during your pregnancy, other than what ultimately led to his birth?"

"I suffered sudden pain that led my husband to take me to the hospital. They couldn't figure out what was wrong and chalked it up to normal pregnancy pain. After being discharged, and then returning the next day, I was told the baby was resting on my kidney, which blocked my bladder. They planned on putting in a stint in my bladder to relieve the pain, but Anderson decided to come out instead." At the memory, a phantom pain pulsed against her back. Anderson's birth had been traumatic, but Luke had been by her side the entire time.

The doctor's gaze shifted from Antonio, to her, and then to her wedding ring.

From the doctor's simple glance, guilt burned her gut like acid. She covered her left hand with her right and pinched together her lips. To keep from bursting out the reality of their situation, she bit the tip of her tongue. She didn't need to explain herself.

"Probably what happened was a one-in-a-million complication, but I'd like to keep a close eye on you just in case. For now, plan on extra sonograms to check the position of the baby, as well as to measure the length of your cervix. If everything continues to progress as expected, we won't worry about anything else." He closed the file, and his hazel eyes softened at the corners. "But, if we do see anything of concern, we can handle it in a timely manner so we can keep the baby inside as long as possible."

"Sounds reasonable." She'd do whatever she could to make sure this baby wasn't as early as Anderson. Seeing her tiny baby in an incubator for the first three weeks of his life had been a nightmare.

"We'll need to see you again in a month, and at that time, you will also schedule your first sonogram. Do you have any questions?"

Her mind went blank.

Antonio shifted in his seat. "When is the due date?"

"Going off the first day of Emma's last period, April twenty-second. A beautiful time of year to have a baby. Don't you agree?"

She forced a tight smile and nodded. "Absolutely. Is there anything else?"

"No, that's it for today. You can schedule your next appointment when you check out."

"Thank you, Doctor." She pushed up from the chair and extended her hand. He placed his large, warm hand in hers and shook it gently.

"It was my pleasure. I'll see you next month." He shifted his attention to Antonio and gave a quick nod. "Same to you, Mr. Mendez."

Antonio fell into step beside her as she strolled toward the exit and approached the checkout counter.

The receptionist glanced up from her computer screen with a wide smile. "Would you like to schedule your next appointment now?"

Emma forced a smile. "Yes, please."

"Do certain days work better?"

The perky blonde cocked her head to the side, and her perfectly coiled curls bounced. Emma'd been too tired to add any curls to her naturally wavy hair and looked like a drown rat. "Any day's fine." She glanced up at Antonio. "What about you?"

The corners of his mouth hitched up in a smile. "I

can make anything work, as long as I have enough time to figure it out."

His meaning was clear. He wasn't just talking about a day for an appointment. He was referencing their relationship. Her stomach flipped, and she broke the eye contact before she did something stupid.

"Well aren't you two the cutest?" The receptionist beamed and wrote on a white appointment card.

"Thanks." Emma grabbed the card and threw it in her purse. She strode toward the door and pushed it open, shielding her eyes against a harsh glare.

Antonio accompanied her and grabbed the handle on the driver's side door. "Do you want to get a cup of coffee or something?"

She shifted the purse strap on her shoulder and fixed her gaze on a spot of dried bird poop on the side of her car. "I don't know."

"Please, Emma, we need to talk. Just ten minutes."

He was right. She at least needed to open the line of communication. She'd shut him out, and she couldn't do that anymore. Not only because they were having a baby together, but because her heart ached with longing for him. "Okay, one cup."

He flashed a smile, and his dimples deepened as he opened the car door.

She pressed together her lips but couldn't hide the whisper of a smile those damn dimples caused. They made her knees wobble like jelly, and her pulse jump every time they deepened his cheeks. "I'll meet you at Average Joe's." She climbed into the car and flashed him a smile.

He nodded and closed the door after she climbed in.

She watched his long legs cross the parking lot and climbed into his car. He flashed a thumbs-up, and she laughed. She turned the key, and the SUV roared to life. The radio blasted the same stupid nursery rhymes that had been stuck in her head during her exam. She plugged in her phone, turned on 90s country music, and sang along while she drove to Average Joe's. Her voice screeched, but her mind was empty of everything but the lyrics. A soft breeze floated through the small crack in the driver's side window and whipped her hair across her face.

She slid into a parking spot in front of the coffee shop and cut the engine. She stole a quick peek in the rearview mirror. Her hair was a mess. She worked her fingers through the tangles and corrected her part before Antonio parked beside her. Dropping her hands, she scrambled out of the car. The sun beat down, kissing her cheeks. Birds sang in a tree overhead and made her wince at the pitch in her own singing voice. If the weather stayed the same, the opening of the farm would be perfect tomorrow.

A shadow fell over her, and the lack of warmth from the sun cooled her skin. Antonio stood in front of her. His gaze landed on the tree she'd been staring at, and a smile lit his face.

"Today's a beautiful day, isn't it?" Antonio lifted his gaze to the sky.

"I thought the same thing. Meg and Dylan will be happy if it stays like this."

"Oh right, the opening is tomorrow. Sam and I are going after school." He caressed her shoulder, and then walked toward the coffee shop. He swung open the door and gestured toward the interior.

"Thanks." She brushed past him and inhaled a deep breath…he was so close. The familiar aftershave clung to his skin, and her heart trembled. She stepped farther into the shop and took in a deeper breath to force the smell of him from her mind. Vanilla and cinnamon mixed gloriously with coffee and mocha. Her stomach growled, and she pressed a hand firmly against it.

"Are you hungry?" Lines etched in the corners of his mouth.

She laughed and peered into the display case. Muffins, cookies, and brownies all clamored for her attention. "I'm always hungry."

"Tell me what you want, and I'll order while you find a table."

She studied the pastries, and her mouth watered. She should grab an apple and call it a day, but how could she resist Joe's giant monster cookies? She bit her lower lip. "If I get a cookie, will you split it?"

Antonio leaned forward and studied the cookies. "How about I get a cookie and a brownie, and we can snack on both?"

She bit harder on her lip to suppress a groan. If he was hard to resist before, offering her an excuse to be a glutton with sweets made him ten times sexier. "Deal, but skip the coffee. I'll take a bottle of water."

"Okay. I'll meet you at a table."

"Wait. I'll give you some cash." She fished inside her purse to search for her wallet.

He covered her hand with his.

His touch singed her skin. The heat traveled up her arm and settled in the pit of her stomach.

"Don't be silly. I've got this."

She swallowed hard and dropped her hand. She

searched for a seat. Most of the tables were open, which wasn't a surprise for a Wednesday afternoon. They'd missed the lunch rush, and the late-afternoon crash hadn't yet hit most people. She ducked her head, walked to a table for two at the back of the shop, and sat.

As she waited, she tapped the tips of her fingers against the wooden table, and the sound echoed through the room. A previous teacher waved from a nearby table, and she lifted her hand in greeting before dropping her gaze to the floor.

"Making friends?"

Antonio's sneakers floated in her line of sight, and she lifted her gaze.

He nodded toward the older woman by the window.

"She was my high school English teacher." Emma shrugged. "Gotta love small towns."

Antonio pulled out the chair across from her and sat. He set a bag and a bottle of water in front of her, and a cup of coffee in front of him.

She grabbed the bag, pinched off a piece of the cookie, and placed it on the tip of her tongue. Sweet chocolate coated her tongue, and she closed her eyes on a moan.

Antonio laughed.

His throaty chuckle coated her skin like honey. A shiver ran down her spine. "Thank you."

He took a sip of his coffee, and then set it in front of him. "You're welcome." He drew in a large breath and drew circles on the top of his plastic lid with a finger. "I know you don't have a lot of time, so I'll get right to it. I've thought a lot the last couple of days, and

I want you to know the baby is my number one priority."

She put another bite in her mouth. "I've never doubted your commitment to the baby."

"I also don't want you to feel pressured be with me." He held up a hand. "I still think we would be great together, but we don't have to decide our relationship right away. We have plenty of time to think about what we want. I just need to know if you have feelings for me."

She slumped back in her seat. For once, his bluntness wasn't what she wanted. But she owed him honesty. Her heart tightened, and a thin film of sweat covered her hands. "Of course I have feelings for you, but I'm still not ready to start a relationship. Hell, I haven't even talked to Sophie about the baby. She'll be confused, and I need to be available whenever she needs me. This isn't the right time to bring another man into my life, no matter how I feel. Can you understand?"

"I understand. I haven't told Sam yet, either, and I'm scared to death." He chuckled and cradled his cup with his hands as he leaned forward. "Even though I'm sure he'll be thrilled."

"He'll be a great big brother."

The planes of Antonio's face flattened. "Can we agree we might have a future—someday?"

The intensity of his gaze stole her breath, and her lungs burned for air. She glanced away. "I don't want to give you false hope. I have no idea what the future holds, and asking you to put part of your life on hold while I figure out what my future holds isn't fair."

He laced his fingers with hers. "You're not asking

me to do anything."

The warmth of his hand shot to her toes, and she curled them in her shoes. "But what if…"

"I don't want anyone else but you. I don't want to pressure you or scare you, but my feelings won't change for a very long time…if ever. The way I feel for you goes beyond anything I've ever felt before. When you decide the time is right to let in someone, I'll be around."

She slid her hand from his and wrapped it around her water bottle. The coolness seeped through her skin, and the condensation washed away her sweat. Her heart hammered in her chest, and confusion continued to cloud her mind. She couldn't deny her attraction to Antonio, but a relationship needed more. A relationship needed soul-crushing, all-consuming love. She'd had a storybook romance with Luke, and he was gone. She couldn't be lucky enough to have such a wonderful love twice in one lifetime—even if one glance at Antonio could reduce her to a puddle of mush. "As long as you're around to help with this baby, that's all I need."

"For now?"

She shook her head and laughed. He was relentless. "Fine, for now."

He leaned back in his chair and grinned. "Can you do me one more favor?"

She narrowed her eyes and rested her chin in a hand. "What?"

"Will you come to my house and unpack those stupid boxes? They're driving me crazy."

She lifted her water bottle and let the cold liquid pour down her throat. Her thirst was quenched, but she kept the bottle lifted to hide the smile she couldn't suppress. She'd be seeing more of him, and pleasure spread through her. She set down the bottle and locked her gaze with his. "Just tell me when."

Chapter Sixteen

Cars lined the road leading to Gilbert Farms. Meg and Dylan hadn't put enough thought into where everyone would park. Maybe they hadn't expected such a big turnout. Antonio steered his car to the side of the road, and the tires sank into the soft, spongey grass.

"Wow, look how many people are here." Sam stuck his head out the window and turned his neck from side to side. "I can't believe you made me go to school today. I should have been here when they opened."

Antonio rolled his eyes. "School's more important than a few extra hours at a farm."

Sam pulled back his head in the car and unhooked his seatbelt. "Whatever you say, Dad."

"Wait until the engine's off to unhook your seatbelt, kiddo." Antonio chuckled and tousled Sam's mop of jet-black hair. It curled around his ears and brushed the top of his neck. His chest tightened. Sam was the spitting image of him. Would the new baby look like him, too?

"Why is your face weird?" Sam crinkled his nose.

"Sorry." He shook his head to clear the new baby from his mind. He still needed to tell Sam he would be a big brother soon. "Did I mention Grandma and Grandpa are coming to visit Sunday?"

"Cool." A smile beamed from Sam, and he widened his eyes. "I haven't seen them in forever."

Danielle M Haas

Antonio put the car in Park and cut the ignition. He stepped out and right into a mud puddle. He shook his leg, and muck flew from his pant leg, but the motion didn't make much of a difference. Mud clung to the bottom of his sneaker, and he wiped his foot along the long grass on the side of the road. "You saw them at Thanksgiving."

"Thanksgiving was almost a year ago." Sam rounded the car and stood on his tiptoes to peer over the front end.

Wow, a year had almost passed since they'd seen them. His parents hadn't visited Smithview since he'd returned, even though they only lived a couple hours away. Hell, they didn't visit anything. They hated leaving their house, and he despised visiting theirs. He loved them, but being in the smoke-filled house with his mother's stuff crowded around depressed him. He usually left annoyed with his mother's constant negativity and his father's lack of interest in anything but his newest cigar.

"Dad, what did you do?" Giggles burst from Sam, and he doubled over, clutching his stomach in his hands.

His soggy sock bunched in his shoe, and he met Sam at the front of the car. "I stepped in a puddle."

"Yeah, no kidding."

"Want me to throw you in the puddle, too?" Antonio squeezed his hands around Sam's slight shoulders and steered him toward the side of the road.

"No! Please, don't!" Sam dug his heels into the pavement and gasped through his laughter.

Antonio aimed him in the opposite direction. "Then don't give me a hard time." He chuckled. Dried-out corn husks filled his view for miles on either side of the road, creating golden fields of splendor. The sky overhead was a brilliant blue, and the caw of a crow drifted along with the slight breeze.

The hair on his arms stood on ends. Being in the middle of nowhere gave him the creeps, and he hurried his pace to get to the entrance of the farm. He wouldn't be surprised if one of the scarecrows that dotted the landscape sprang to life and waved in greeting.

A wooden sign that read Gilbert Farms hung above the gravel entrance to the farm, supported by wooden beams on either side of the drive. People milled about carrying pumpkins and planters of colorful mums. A line of parents stood calming their bouncing children while they waited to get in the main barn at the front of the property.

"What's in there?" Antonio nodded toward the large, red barn.

"We have to pay in there, but Meg won't make us pay. Let's go find her. I bet she's in with the horses."

"Think again, buddy. We won't take advantage of Meg by sneaking in for free. We'll wait in line like everybody else."

Sam crossed his arms over his chest. "Seriously, Dad? She's my aunt now. Family doesn't pay."

"But I'm not family, so I need to wait in line. Come on. I need you to show me around. The line won't take long." A twinge jolted his heart. Family. His stomach twisted in knots, and the ache in his heart spread through his chest. He wanted a family of his own, and if he got his way, Emma would be a part of his family. The Sheffields had grown on him since he'd met Emma, and having them in his life wouldn't be as big of a pain as he'd expected.

The line moved along, and when they stood at the front, Annie sat inside the door at a makeshift counter. Her blue eyes turned sapphire with warmth, and a giant smile curved on her lips. In her face, Antonio saw what Emma would look like in thirty years. It stole his breath.

"What are you two doing in line?" Annie leaned over the counter and planted a kiss on Sam's forehead.

Sam wrinkled his nose. "Dad said we have to pay like everyone else, even if I'm family."

Annie waved a hand. "You're both family. Now get on in there. Meg and Dylan will be delighted to see you." She held Antonio's gaze. "Emma and the kids are here, too. Make sure you find them and say hello."

"Is Meg with the horses?" Sam lifted onto his tiptoes, craning his neck to take in the sights of the room behind Annie.

"She's giving pony rides in the corral outside. I'm sure she'll let you ride."

Antonio grabbed his wallet from his back pocket and found some bills. He extended a hand toward Annie and offered her the money.

Annie's eyes narrowed. "What did I just say? Family doesn't pay. Now, my line's getting longer, and you're taking up my time." She winked at Sam. "Have fun."

He tucked in his lips, and a wave of gratitude washed over him. "Thanks, Annie."

Sam grabbed his hand and tugged. "Come on, Dad. I'll show you where the horses are."

The main room was packed, and he weaved in among the crowd toward the back of barn. He darted his gaze around the large, open space, but Sam dragged him along. An old-fashioned wagon had been converted into a serving cart for caramel apples and hot cider, and his mouth watered as they hurried past.

"Slow down, Sam. Don't you want something to eat? Those apples smell amazing. And is that caramel corn over there?" He nodded toward the opposite corner where popcorn spilled out of an iron kettle.

"We can eat later. I want to see Meg."

He sighed. Sam had a one-track mind. "All right, but after we see her, we're coming right back here, and I'm stuffing my face."

A squeal of laughter broke through the commotion, and Antonio turned his head to find the source. The laugh belonged to Sophie. He whipped his head from side to side, searching for her. His heart stopped beating, and his feet morphed to lead. She sat on the shoulders of a man he didn't recognize. A man with sandy blond hair and a pretty-boy smile. Emma stood next to him with Anderson in her arms. Her chin tilted up, and she smiled broadly. Jealously, hot and raw, swam in his veins.

"Dad, come on." Sam tugged on his hand.

He shook the image from his mind and followed Sam to the doorway that led to the stable. The man was probably a friend from high school. Smithview was a small town, and she was bound to run into people she knew. He stepped into the stable, and the musty scent of hay, dirt, and manure engulfed him. He covered his nose with his hand, but it didn't help. Life on a farm wasn't for him.

A soft whiney sounded from the far end of the aisle. Sunlight spilled through the open door at the end of the aisle, sending shafts of soft light down to the floor.

Sam ran past the empty stalls, his fingers grazing the wooden doors.

Antonio followed. Fresh air beckoned. He stepped outside and filled his lungs.

"Hi, Meg." Sam ran to the gated corral located outside the barn.

Meg stood in the middle of the corral, leading a pony in a small circle with the rope in her hand. Dust flew behind the pony, and a child swayed from side to side as he clung to the saddle horn and giggled. "Hey, I wondered when you'd get here. How was school?"

Sam sighed. "Long and boring."

"Poor kid. Hi, Antonio. How are you?" She applied pressure to the lead and brought the pony to a stop.

"Good, thanks. You have quite a crowd today."

"I know. I can't believe it." She helped the child off the pony. "Sam, do you want a ride?"

Sam placed his feet on the edge off the gate. "Nah, only babies ride ponies. I want to ride Snowball."

"Snowball's in the pasture with the other horses. You can go say hi, but you can't ride her now. Maybe if it slows down a little, I'll let you get on." Meg wrapped her hands around a little girl's waist and lifted her on the black-and-white pony. "Dylan's giving hayrides through the fields. Or you can show your dad the corn maze you helped with."

"Or we could go back for those snacks that smelled so good." Antonio's wet sock still clung awkwardly to his foot. He'd rather skip activities where more puddles might find him.

Sam shrugged and hopped off the gate. "Sure.

Let's get something to eat."

He led Sam back through the musty stable and into the main room of the barn. Scanning the crowd, he searched for Emma. He spotted her sitting at a table with Sophie beside her and Anderson in her lap. Relief flooded him, and he took a step in her direction.

The man from earlier stepped behind her chair with a bag of caramel corn in his hands. He set the bag in front of Sophie, and then placed his hands on Emma's shoulders.

Antonio stopped, and every muscle in his body tensed. "Sam, do you know who the man is with Emma and the kids?" He pulled Sam in front of him and pointed at Emma.

"Travis. He's been at the inn all week. He was here with Emma one day laying hay on the mud on the paths, too."

Who the hell was Travis? Emma smiled, and her white teeth flashed across the room. She placed a hand over the man's, and then pulled out the chair beside her.

Travis sat, his hand lingering on Emma's shoulder.

Antonio's blood simmered.

Sam widened his eyes. "What's wrong, Dad?"

He was an idiot. He had actually believed the crap she'd spouted yesterday about not being ready for a relationship with anyone. But now she sat with another man, who apparently had been around for a while, with his hands all over her. Even Sophie was full of smiles and giggles. "Nothing, buddy. Let's get some food."

"Can we go say hi to Sophie and Emma?"

He flicked his gaze to their table again. Travis's hand lingered at the back of Emma's chair, and the four of them sat together like a picture-perfect family. His heart shattered. "Not right now. I want to see what else this place has." He swiveled Sam in the opposite direction of the woman who was carrying his child and smashed his illusion of a future together. Pain pierced every inch of his body, but it was better to know the truth. He'd waste no more time pining for a future he'd never have.

****

The next night, Antonio swirled his glass, and ice clinked together. His forearms rested on the gleaming bar of the hotel, and he lifted the glass to his lips. The smooth bourbon burned his throat as it slid down, and he closed his eyes on a sigh as it warmed his blood. He signaled the bartender for another.

"There you are. I wondered where you took off to so fast after we landed. Do you mind if I sit?" Bridgette traced a finger along the nape of his neck and down his arm. She sat and leaned against him.

He rolled his neck to the side and lifted his glass in greeting. The drink was his second, and the liquor hummed in his veins. After seeing Emma with another man yesterday, he'd wanted nothing more than to drown his misery in a glass of Blanton's. But Sam had been with him all night, and he'd had a long flight to get through today. He had to wait until tonight, sitting alone in a hotel bar, to get drunk.

A fresh-faced bartender with a crisp white shirt carried over another bourbon. She slid a napkin in front of Bridgette and placed a bowl of peanuts between them. "Can I get you anything?"

"A glass of merlot, please." Bridgette turned toward him while the bartender grabbed a large glass and filled it half-full with the dark burgundy liquid.

Bridgette took a small sip and set the glass in front of her. She tilted her cheek to the side, and her lips curved up. "I didn't think we'd get a chance to catch up. You never emailed me back."

He lifted a shoulder. "I've had a lot on my mind."

She stroked her fingers up and down the stem of her glass. "I've missed you."

Instead of answering, he picked up his bourbon and downed half of it.

"You might want to slow down. Don't you fly home in the morning?"

Bridgette's hazel eyes burned hot, and her voice dipped low. "No, I'm not flying back until the evening. Trust me. I've got plenty of time to kill. But thanks for the concern."

A soft melody drifted through the air from the piano in the corner of the room. The gentle lull grated on his nerves, and he hunched over his drink as a dull ache throbbed at his temples.

"Are you okay? You seem a little down." She covered his hand with hers.

Her warmth penetrated his skin, but it did nothing to stir him. He swiped his tongue over his teeth and bit back a sigh. "I'm fine." He glanced at the bartender and gave a brief nod.

"Did you need something else?" She stopped in front of him.

"My check, please." He wasn't in the mood for small talk, and Bridgette wouldn't let up.

"And you, Miss?"

Bridgette took a long drink of wine, and then sighed. "I guess I'll take my check, too. I don't want to drink alone."

"Put her drink on my tab." He leaned forward and grabbed his wallet from his pocket. He slid his credit card across the bar.

She pushed her empty glass to the edge of the bar and smiled. "If you don't want to drink down here, do you want to come up to my room? I really have missed you."

The bartender handed him his receipt.

He slipped it into his pocket and nodded his thanks. "Stopping by your room isn't a good idea."

Her smile transformed into a pout, and her shoulders slumped forward. "All right, I get it. Will you at least see me to my room? Walking alone in the hallways at night is creepy."

He stood on wobbly legs and braced himself on the back of the chair. He focused his gaze on Bridgette's face. Straightening his spine, he forced his feet forward. Getting to his own room would be enough of a feat—let alone helping Bridgette.

A husky laugh purred from her throat, and she wrapped her arm around the small of his back.

Her fingers found his hand on the chair, and she loosened his grip. She laced their fingers together. "Let's get you upstairs."

He shifted his weight and leaned on her. A warning blared in the back of his mind. He didn't want to be alone with her—give her the wrong idea of what he wanted—but the alcohol in his blood made it impossible for him not to go along. He stepped into the long hallway, and the hard, wooden floors morphed into thick carpet. His legs wobbled like jelly, and his feet stumbled beside Bridgette's. He shouldn't have had that last drink. His brain was mush—his body numb.

"Here's my room." Bridgette slid her room key from inside her bra and swiped it through the lock. The light changed to green, and she opened the door a crack. Her hand stayed on the silver handle, and she arched her back against the edge of the door. "Are you sure you don't want to come inside for a minute?"

His gaze lingered on her long neck. He swallowed hard. He was tired of feeling like garbage. For one damn minute he wanted to forget Emma. He grazed Bridgette's neck with the tip of his finger.

She moaned.

Leaning forward, he captured her mouth in his. His body pressed into hers, and the door banged open. He wrapped his arms around her, pulled her into the room, and kicked the door shut behind him. He spun her around, and he pressed his body against hers, flattening her against the door. He braced his arms on each side of her body.

Emma might still have his heart, but she didn't want it. He didn't need to be in love with Bridgette. He only needed to lose himself in her for tonight, even if the guilt of being with her stayed.

Chapter Seventeen

The orange and pink swirls of dusk glowed above the horizon. Emma leaned against the comfortable chair in front of the fire and settled Anderson on her shoulder and wrapped a blanket tightly around them.

Anderson nuzzled his head between her cheek and neck, and a thin string of drool pooled on her collarbone while he slept.

The fire crackled in the pit in the back yard, and the smell of burnt marshmallows made her mouth water. "Don't burn it too much, Sophie." She glanced over at Dylan who sat beside Sophie as she crouched low beside the fire. "You might need to help her."

"I got her. Don't worry." Dylan grabbed the marshmallow off the stick and placed it on a paper plate. He picked up Sophie and set her on a hay bale.

Sophie stuffed the marshmallow in her mouth, and white goo smeared across her face. "It's so good." She circled her mouth with her tongue and cleaned away the sticky residue.

Emma chuckled. Moments with Sophie giggling and enjoying being a child were rare, and she was overjoyed to spend this time with her daughter. "I hope you enjoyed your sugary treat, because it's your last one. We have to head to bed soon."

"Bed sounds good." Meg rested her head on the back of her chair. "I've never been so exhausted in my life."

"We've had a busy weekend." Dylan stretched his arms above his head. "I can't believe how many people showed up at the farm. Thanks so much for everything you did, Emma."

Her heavy limbs weighed her down, and she yawned. She'd spent the past three days on her feet, helping to make the grand opening of Gilbert Farms a smashing success. "I was happy to be there." She mentally cringed. "If you need me tomorrow, just call." She had a peaceful Sunday filled with baking cookies and playing in the yard planned with the kids. Hopefully Meg and Dylan wouldn't need her, and she could spend the time she so craved with her kids.

"We don't open until the afternoon since most people will be in church. We should be fine." Meg smiled wide.

Gravel crunched, and headlights peeked around the side of the house. A car door opened and then closed. Emma cuddled Anderson closer, and the scent of baby shampoo and sweat tickled her senses. The backdoor squeaked open, and she craned her neck to glance behind her.

Annie stuck her head out the door. "Emma, Antonio's here to see you."

The door banged shut, and she met Meg's amused smirk. "Will you hold Anderson? I'll get him ready for bed after I see what Antonio wants." She stood and placed Anderson in Meg's arms.

He gurgled, turning his head from side to side, and then settled into Meg's arms.

Stepping around the fire, she shielded her eyes from the billowing smoke. Her heart sputtered. She hadn't expected to see Antonio until later this week. She hurried around the side of the house then slowed her pace as she approached the front steps that led up to the white-washed porch.

Staring into the descending darkness, he buried his hands in the pockets of his jacket and hunched forward his shoulder.

Shadows washed out Antonio's face. A shiver ran through her. "Hey."

His body tensed, and he met her gaze before dropping it back to the floor. "Sorry to drop in, but you didn't answer my calls."

"My phone's inside." She took a step toward him, and adrenaline spiked in her gut. Something was wrong. "Is everything okay?"

"My parents are coming into town tomorrow, and they'd like to meet you." He lifted his chin but darted his gaze around her. "I told them about the baby."

"Okay." She rested her hip on the railing. "Are you sure nothing else is going on? You're acting weird."

Tightening his jaw, he snorted and rocked back on his heels. "I'm perfect. Let me know if you can stop by tomorrow. I've gotta go." He moved around her toward the stairs.

She grabbed the forearm of his jacket. "Wait. What's with attitude?"

"I don't have to explain myself, Emma." He pulled free his arm and faced her.

The light from the rising moon highlighted his strong cheekbones. She narrowed her eyes and leaned closer. A long scratch tore down the side of his face. She reached out to touch it.

He backed away.

"What's the scratch from?" She squinted, studying the mark.

He covered his cheek with his hand, and then traveled it down to rest on the side of his neck. "Nothing."

"Damnit, Antonio. What's going on?" She yanked away his hand from his neck and stood on her tiptoes. A quarter-sized red mark blemished his olive skin. Her stomach dropped. "Do you have a hickey?"

Antonio took a step backward. "I said it's nothing."

Her heart pounded. "You have a hickey." She threw her hands in the air. "What kind of grown man walks around with a hickey on his neck? Oh my God…is that how you got the scratch? From the woman who sucked on your neck?" Nausea rolled in her gut.

"Why do you care? You've made it clear you don't want to be with me. If I want to spend my time with another woman, it's none of your business." He glared and jammed his hands in his jacket pockets.

Pain pierced her chest. She cared more than he knew, but now wasn't the time to jump into a relationship. "We talked about this. I'm not ready to be in a relationship. I need time. You said you'd wait for me, and you didn't want to be with anyone else." She turned her back and closed her eyes. Tears stung her eyes, and she bit into the top of her lip to keep them at bay. "We're having a baby. Is a little time to sort through everything too much to ask?"

Antonio snorted. "Not when I thought the only man I was competing with was dead. Things changed when you decided to be with someone else."

His words slammed against her like a hurricane. She spun on her heels and fisted her hands. "Excuse me?"

He shook his head and rubbed a hand over his chin. "Don't play innocent. I'm not buying it any longer. I saw you with Travis at the farm, and it sounds like you've spent quite a bit of time together."

Confusion clouded her mind. She hadn't seen Antonio all weekend. When had he seen her with Travis? Confusion morphed into anger, and her blood pressure spiked in her ears. "Travis is a guest at the inn, who happens to know my mother. He's been here over a week and won't leave for a while. I don't know what you saw, but you obviously contorted it into a twisted version of what it was and made me the bad guy."

Antonio widened his eyes and craned forward his neck. "What?" He took a step toward her.

She took two steps back and held up her palm. His misunderstanding or confusion over her friendships with other men didn't give him an excuse to be with another woman. "No...don't. I can't believe you did this."

He pinched the bridge of his nose and sucked in a large breath. "But you were with him. He had his hands on you, and the kids and you were so comfortable with him. I swear, it looked like you were a family...like the two of you had been together for years."

"You sound ridiculous." She bit her cheeks to keep her voice from cracking. His jealousy was unfounded, even if it showed the extent which he cared.

He dropped his hand, and his gaze bore into hers. He drew his mouth down into a tight frown, and wrinkles creased his brow. "Do I? You've dragged my heart all over the place, and I've tried to be understanding. You pushed me out of your life after we slept together, you told me I got you pregnant and then stormed out of my house, and then you didn't even bother to tell me about your doctor's appointment. You've shut me out of everything." He sliced his hand through the air. "After getting nothing but one conversation I dragged out of you, I see you all sunshine and smiles with another man. How should I feel?"

"You're supposed to talk to me about it like an adult. Not fall into bed with the first woman you find." Nausea swirled around her stomach, and bile slid up her throat. Antonio couldn't have betrayed her like this.

"Because you've made speaking with you so easy in the past." His hand snaked around and rubbed the back of his neck. "I've tried so hard, and I'm tired. I know you've been through a lot, but do you ever think about what I've been through? How I feel?"

A sliver of guilt sliced through her, but she ground together her teeth and pushed it back. No. He was in the wrong. What he did wasn't her fault. She straightened her back and planted her feet into the white planks. "I'm sorry my past is an inconvenience, but you knew where I stood when this started. I will not apologize for grieving for my husband. The fact you couldn't keep it in your pants long enough for me to be ready shows me the kind of man you really are."

He flinched. "Don't say that. You know who I am, and you know I would never purposely hurt you."

She folded her arms across her chest and arched her brows. "You're right. I do know what kind of man you are. You're the kind of man who runs and does something stupid at the first sign of trouble—just like you did with Jillian. You left her to take care of your son because things got too hard to handle. I don't know why I assumed you'd be any different with me."

His chest expanded as he inhaled, and his nostrils flared. "You don't know what you're talking about."

"Don't I?" She huffed out an irritated breath.

He jabbed forward a finger. "You have no clue what it's like to be married to someone who doesn't love you—to wake up every day knowing you're her second choice. It eats you alive."

"True." Her voice grew quiet. "My husband loved me with every fiber of his being. I was his life, and he was mine. He was a good man, and he treated me with respect and kindness." She shook her head and swallowed the bile filling her mouth. "You're nothing like him. I will spend every day of the rest of my life wishing he was here with me instead of you."

Her hands shook, and she stormed to the front door. Nothing but crickets sounded behind her, but the heat of Antonio's gaze burned through the back of her head. She wouldn't turn around. She wouldn't feel anything but anger toward him. Her chest tightening, she opened the door. Tears gathered at the corners of her eyes. Her heart split in two, but it wouldn't hurt so bad if anger was all she felt. For the second time in less than a year, she'd lost the man she loved.

She stepped through the door and closed it behind her. Sighing, she rested against the hard wood, her knees buckling, and she sank to the floor. She didn't wipe away the tears that overflowed from her lids and slid down her cheeks.

"Emma?" Meg crouched in front of her. "What's going on?"

She hitched up one corner of her mouth and sniffed

back her tears. Bracing her hands on the floor, she pushed herself to her feet and peered through the living room curtains.

Antonio stood with his back to the house. He kicked a toe against the railing.

"Where are the kids?" She kept her gaze fixed on Antonio while she spoke to Meg.

"I put down Anderson, and Dylan's reading Sophie a bedtime story." Meg stood behind her. "Antonio seems pretty upset."

"I don't care if he's upset." The force of Antonio's feet pounding down the porch steps vibrated through the small living room.

He stormed to his car and yanked open his car door, slamming it shut once inside.

She winced from the force.

His car roared to life, and gravel flew as he peeled out of the driveway.

"What happened?" Meg rested a hand on her shoulder.

"He ruined everything." She leaned her forehead against the cool glass and stared into the night. "We're over." The clock ticked on the wall as the minutes passed.

Meg cleared her throat. "How can a relationship be over if it never started?"

"What's that supposed to mean?" She whipped around to face Meg. Heat invaded her cheeks, and her pulse pounded in her veins.

Meg's face relaxed. "Emma, you never gave him a fair chance. I understand why you kept him at arm's length, but the poor guy's followed you around like a lovesick puppy since you moved back. You spouted the same story to everyone…you two are friends and nothing more. How could he mess up your friendship?"

Her throat constricted. She rubbed the base of her neck, took large gulps of air, and tried to catch her breath. She stumbled to the sofa and sank into the cushions. "I can't handle this drama. I can't do it…it's too much. I've been through enough. I just want things to be easy."

"How do you know life can't be easy with Antonio?" Meg sat next to her, and the cushions dipped low.

Emma shook her head. "Not after tonight. I can't trust him." Tears clogged her throat. "I can't trust anyone to stick around."

Meg clasped their hands together on her lap. "What do you mean? You have me, and Mom, and Jonah. Hell, now you have Dylan."

Moisture clouded her vision and blurred the lines of Meg's face. "I've given my heart completely to two men in my life, and they both left me behind. First Dad, and then Luke. How do I know that won't happen again?" A small sob broke from her parted lips. "Antonio's already proven he'll leave when things get tough. He's not worth the risk."

"Oh, honey." Meg wrapped her arms around her. "This isn't the same thing. What happened to Dad and Luke—those were accidents. They didn't have a choice. But Antonio…he loves you and wants to be with you. Anyone can see how much you mean to him. If you keep pushing him away, you'll regret it."

Meg's words made sense, but she couldn't make her heart believe them. She pulled away, and her gaze met Meg's. "How do I know he won't hurt me?"

Meg cocked an eyebrow and smirked. "How do you know he will?"

"This whole situation sucks." She leaned her head against the back of the couch and pressed her hands against her stomach. "It'd be different if I only had myself to worry about. But I have the kids, and a baby on the way. I have to think about what's best for them, too."

"You're having a baby? Mommies only have babies with daddies, and Daddy's in heaven."

Knots twisted in her stomach, and her heart fell to the floor. She shot up her head from the couch and stared at the wide eyes of Sophie. This night could not possibly get any worse.

Chapter Eighteen

Antonio sped along the deserted country road and tightened his grip around the steering wheel. The blanket of black clouds hid the moon and stars. Empty fields flew by in a blur. He shouldn't have gone to the inn—not with the stupid marks Bridgette left still visible on his skin.

Not like it mattered now after what Emma said. His blood boiled, and rage clouded his vision. He clenched his teeth and held onto the rage. He'd rather have the anger pumping through him than the sharp stabbing in his chest—the guilt fisting his heart. He drew in a ragged breath and concentrated on the anger. The anger fueled him, instead of the pain in his heart that threatened to break him. She pushed him away and avoided him…then got mad when he ran to someone else—someone who actually wanted him.

A brown blur ran into the road.

He slammed the brake to the floor. A cold sweat gathered at his brow. His elbows locked, and he yanked the steering wheel. The car bounced over the centerline and veered toward a telephone pole. His brain screamed. His heart thundered, and he jerked the wheel farther to the side. Nothing happened. The tires locked, and the car skidded. The pole rushed toward him, and time stood still.

The gruesome sound of crunching metal filled the

air. He lurched forward, and then smashed back against his seat. The tinny smell of blood entered his nostrils. He gingerly placed his fingertips to his temple. Sticky blood covered his hand. He needed to get out of the car…needed to call for help. Emma, and then Sam, flashed in his mind. He reached for his phone. Pain shot through his arm, but he closed his fingers around the smooth plastic case. He screamed. Darkness outlined his vision. He couldn't close his eyes. He had to get help. He unlocked his screen with shaky fingers and brought up the last number he'd called. Emma. Her brilliant smile and sapphire eyes flashed before him, and then darkness pulled him under.

****

Beep-Beep-Beep

What the hell was that sound? Antonio's heart beat along with its rhythm, but so did the pounding in his head. His eyelids were heavy, and he concentrated all of his effort into lifting them. The pungent scent of antiseptic stung his nostrils. A small shaft of light beamed through the tiny slits and burst in his brain. He closed his lids again. Muffled voices caught his attention, but he couldn't focus on their words. Who was with him? Where was he? The dark fog closed in around him and fused his eyelids shut.

The tips of his fingers twitched, and panic seized him. He couldn't move his hands. He tried to lift his leg, and nothing happened.

Beep-Beep-Beep-Beep-Beep

A frantic flurry of light and dark clashed on the back of his eyelids. His muscles tensed. The muffled voices became clearer, and the sobs of his mother echoed in his ears. A sound he'd heard too often in his youth to forget. He focused on the light that burned his eyes, but the darkness grabbed him again. He was too tired to fight. He relaxed his body, and he faded into oblivion.

Time stopped while he retreated into himself, until the warmth of a hand on his stirred him. He darted out his tongue and moistened his cracked lips. The dryness in his mouth made swallowing hard. He worked hard to lift his eyelids, and this time the blinding light didn't penetrate his skull. He parted his lips and cleared his throat. "Water." His voice was full of grit, and he winced.

He wrapped his lips around a plastic straw and sucked. Searing pain stabbed his side, and the cold water in his mouth trickled down his chin. Moaning, he glanced up and locked his gaze with Jillian.

The lines around her mouth lifted, and she wiped the moisture from his chin. "Drink slowly."

He darted his gaze around the empty hospital room and then landed back on her. He searched his memories but came up blank. "What happened?"

Jillian placed the clear, plastic cup back on the table beside the bed. "You were in a car accident. You're hurt pretty badly. Do you remember anything?"

The last words Emma said lingered in his mind, and they hurt more than the cracked ribs. "I was with Emma at the inn. We had a fight, and I left."

Jillian cringed. "You must have been pretty upset because you wrapped your car around a telephone pole."

He groaned and closed his eyes. Memories of the accident slammed into him with the force of a tidal wave. "A stupid deer ran out in the road. I swerved to miss it."

She quirked her lips to the side. "You idiot. You always hit the deer. I've told you this."

He opened one eye, and then the other. "How bad is it?"

"You or the car?"

His chest tightened. The white cast on his leg and the pain in his shoulder told him much of the answer. "Both."

"The car's totaled, and you're lucky to be alive." She drew in a shaky breath. "You have a fractured tibia in your left leg, and you sprained the acromioclavicular in your right shoulder. You cracked a couple of ribs, and you have a pretty bad concussion. They want to keep you for a few days, but you shouldn't need surgery."

"Oh, man. I won't be able to fly."

Jillian pressed together her lips, and her chin dipped down. "You'll be lucky if you can wipe your own bottom."

A memory flitted in his mind, and he widened his eyes. "Did I hear my mom earlier?"

Jillian chuckled. "Things got a little crazy. Apparently, I'm still listed as your emergency contact, so I was the first one called. I rushed here, and when I found out what was going on, I called your parents. Your mom insisted they come straight here. I assured her everything was okay, but she wouldn't listen."

"Imagine that." He rolled his eyes. His mom loved drama, and if she could be in the middle, no one could keep her away. "Where is she now? Wait…what time is it?"

"It's late. I had Jonah and Sam drive your parents

to your place for the night."

Using his good arm to pull on an overhead bar, he tried to sit, and his bones burned from the effort. Gasping on each breath, he struggled to take in air. Each inhale shot bolts of pain to his side. "Did Sam see me like this?"

She shook her head. "He stayed in the waiting room. I didn't want him to see you while you were asleep."

"Well, look who's awake." A large, middle-aged nurse entered the room. "You should have hit the call button as soon as he woke up." She aimed her words at Jillian. "How's your pain level?"

He winced and shifted on the bed. "I feel like I was hit by a truck."

"Close enough, sugar." She pushed buttons and scanned the monitor. "I'll increase your pain meds to help you sleep tonight."

"I feel like I've been asleep for hours." He glanced around the room, and his gaze landed on a clock in the corner. "Holy cow. It's three in the morning. Jillian, go home."

The nurse chuckled. "This pretty little thing hasn't left your side since she got here. You're a lucky man to be married to her."

Jillian folded her right hand over her left and shielded her wedding ring.

He clenched his teeth. How many people would mistake his marital status this week? First, Emma's doctor and now, the nurse. It was getting old. "She's my ex-wife."

The nurse faced him with wide eyes. "I'm sorry. I assumed…"

Jillian smiled. "We're good friends, and there's nowhere else I want to be right now."

"How sweet, but he'll be out cold in another fifteen minutes. He needs sleep, and the best way for him to get rest is for you to head home."

His muscles melted, and he blinked to keep his eyes from closing. Whatever they gave him must be strong.

Jillian smoothed the creases from his blanket. "Do you need anything before I go?"

"I'm fine." A heaviness settled over his body, and all he wanted was to close his eyes and escape the pain.

She tucked her top lip between her teeth. "You scared the hell out of me. Don't do it again."

Closing his eyes, he lifted his lips. "You've always been so bossy."

She kissed his cheek. "Good night. I'll see you tomorrow."

"Umm hmm." He surrendered to the soothing calmness of sleep.

Soft footsteps scurried around his bed. He wanted to put a pillow over his head to block out the noise, but he couldn't lift his right arm, and the memory of the pain in his left side prevented him from attempting to move his other arm. A soft moan escaped his lips, and he opened his eyes.

Nancy, the nurse who had knocked him out with meds, smiled. He shifted in the bed and winced. "What time is it?"

Nancy checked her watch. "A little past 9:00 a.m. How did you sleep?"

"All right." He squeezed shut his eyes and then blinked rapidly to fight through the lingering fatigue.

"Will I go home today?"

"The doctor will be around soon, and he'll have some answers. One thing's for sure, you'll need someone to stay with you for a while. Your injuries are extensive, and you can't get around much. Do you have anyone to help you?" Nancy flashed him a sad smile.

"Of course he does. I'll move in for as long as I need to." His mother stepped through the door.

Jillian and Sam followed.

He groaned. He couldn't handle his mom taking care of him for weeks on end.

Nancy stepped to the end of the bed. "I'll be back in a little bit to check on you."

"Hi, Dad." Sam took a slow step toward him, and then stopped. He clasped his hands in front of him, and his gaze stayed glued to the floor. "Do you hurt?"

All the pain faded to the background, and a fist squeezed his heart. "I'm okay, buddy. Come here, and let me see you."

Sam glanced back at Jillian.

"Go on, Sam." She shooed him forward with her hands.

Tears filled Sam's eyes.

Antonio cleared his throat to push down his own tears. "Really, buddy. My injuries appear worse than they are."

Sam stepped up to the bed and rubbed a hand up and down the blanket. "I was really scared last night. I thought you might die."

Antonio inhaled deeply, and then winced. These ribs would be the death of him. "I'm sorry you were scared, but everything's all right. I'll be back to normal in no time."

"Yes, he will." His mom stood behind Sam. She placed her arms around his neck and pulled him close. "I'll make sure you have everything you need."

"I can't ask you to stay and help, Mom. Dad would hate being away from home, and he wouldn't know how to survive without you fussing over him. I'll hire someone to stay at the house."

"You don't want a stranger taking care of you." She raised her brows. "What about Jillian?"

"What was that, Gloria?" Jillian stepped around to the other side of the bed.

Gloria shrugged. "Well, it makes sense. Don't you think? You live practically around the corner anyway. What would the big deal be if you just stayed with him for a few weeks?"

Jillian's cheeks sunk in.

He bit down on his tongue to keep from laughing. His mom had always made Jillian's life miserable. Playing nice in front of Sam must be killing her.

Jillian smiled. "I don't think my husband would like that very much."

Gloria's brow creased, and she pursed her lips. "Oh, right, dear. You got yourself a new husband. I forgot."

"I can take care of you," Sam said.

"You have school." Jillian ran over his mop of hair. "I can come by during the day to check on you, but I can't commit to being there twenty-four hours a day."

"What about Emma?" Gloria bounced her gaze between Antonio and Jillian. "She sounds like a lovely girl…one who understands loyalty."

"Absolutely not." What kind of hell had he ended up in?

His mom narrowed her eyes.

He narrowed his back, refusing to budge. "She has two kids. She doesn't need someone else to take care of."

"She better get used to it. The baby will be here before you know it." Gloria crossed her arms over her chest.

Sam scrunched his face. "What baby?"

Antonio locked his gaze on Jillian.

She shrugged. "You might as well tell him."

"Tell me what?" Sam cocked his head to the side.

Antonio's heart slammed against his chest. "Emma and I are having a baby."

Sam's face lit up, and his gaze darted from Antonio, to Jillian, and back to Antonio. "I'll be a big brother?"

Relief flooded through him, and he hitched up his lips. "Are you okay with that?"

"Abso-freaking-lutely!"

Sam's enthusiasm was infectious, and Antonio's smile grew. "I guess I shouldn't have been so nervous to tell you."

"Are you and Emma getting married? Are Sophie and Anderson my sister and brother, too?" Sam bounced up and down on his toes. "Emma should definitely move in. She'll be there anyway with the baby. And Sophie can pick out a room. This is awesome!"

He shot his gaze to Jillian's and pleaded for her help. Sam had too many questions he didn't have the energy to answer.

Jillian drew in a small breath. "Sam, honey, calm down. Your dad and Emma have a lot to figure out over the next couple of months, and this might not be the best idea."

"I agree with Sam," Gloria said. "Emma moving in with Antonio now sounds like the most logical plan."

Sam's lips drooped into a frown. "Wouldn't she want to help you, Dad? If you're having a baby, doesn't she love you?"

His question was like a kick in the gut. What was he supposed to say? *No, actually Sam, I fell hopelessly in love with her and then found out she's callous and cold. Your dear old dad is an unlucky sonofagun who keeps falling for women who are in love with other people.* Slowly, he found Sam's hand. "This problem isn't for you to worry about." He travelled his gaze above Sam's head and rested on his mom. "I'll figure out what needs to be done, and everything will be good."

Everything wouldn't be good. Hiring a stranger to come into his house and take care of him would be awful. But he'd do what he had to. One thing was certain, no way was Emma taking care of him. Hell would freeze over first.

Chapter Nineteen

Emma sat at the kitchen table staring at table decorations for a shabby-chic barn wedding on the Internet. Meg told her she didn't care what the reception looked like, but she knew her sister. Meg wanted simple, yet classy. She picked up her pen and jotted down notes on the yellow legal pad. Setting down the pen, she shifted her attention back to the computer screen. She scrolled through hundreds of images, and her focus wavered.

Her mind shifted to the previous night. Sophie's big, watery eyes and quivering lips haunted her. She'd explained she was having a baby, but the baby would have a different daddy than her and Anderson.

Sophie buried her head in Meg's neck.

The conversation had been awful.

"Hey, Emma."

She glanced up. "Hi. What are you doing here?" Jillian's red-rimmed eyes and firm mouth set alarm bells blaring. Bracing herself, she closed her laptop and stiffened her spine. "What's going on?"

Jillian grabbed the back of the chair beside her and placed it in front of Emma. She sat, and her knees brushed against Emma's. Jillian drew in a deep breath. "Antonio was in a car accident last night."

The icy fingers of fear gripped her heart. Her throat closed around a ball of panic, and she gasped for breath.

Her lungs burned, and her hands shook. "Is he okay?" Her voice was soft and tentative. Her gaze searched Jillian's for answers.

"He's okay." Jillian grabbed her hands and squeezed. "He's pretty banged up, but he'll be all right."

She covered her mouth with a hand. "Oh my God…did this happen after he left here? Was this my fault? I shouldn't have let him leave when he was so upset. I didn't even think about how unsafe it was for him to drive after a fight. Why don't I ever think about anyone but myself?" As she stood, the legs of her chair scraped against the wooden floor, and she began to pace.

Jillian moved her head from side to side and followed her with her gaze. "Emma, the accident wasn't your fault. A deer ran out in the road, and Antonio swerved into a telephone pole. No one's to blame."

Her heart fell to the pit of her stomach. Tears stung her eyes. "A deer?" Her voice shook, and her whole body trembled. "Did the accident happen after he left here—after the horrible things I said? He could have died. He could have been ripped away just like Luke… except Luke knew how much I loved him." She squeezed shut her eyes and let the tears roll down her cheeks. "I was so cruel."

"I'm sure Antonio knows how you feel about him. And if he doesn't, you still have plenty of time to tell him. He's not going anywhere."

Emma shook her head, and wisps of hair stuck to her cheek. "You don't understand. He made me so mad last night. I went for the jugular." She leaned the small of her back against the island and rubbed her temples.

189

"I don't know what to do."

"Do you want to see him? I'll go with you." Jillian's lips tucked in, and the lines around her eyes softened. "I'll even suffer through another encounter with his mother if it will help you."

She winced. "I was supposed to meet her today. Now I can approach her and say 'hi, I'm Emma. I'm the woman who broke your son's heart and sent him flying down the road. He's in the hospital because I'm a horrible person. Oh, and I'm carrying your grandchild, even though I've only known your son since August. I'm pleased to meet you.' What a great impression." She choked out a sob.

Jillian chuckled and leaned beside her. "Trust me, his mom would find a reason not to like you no matter what. Don't let her keep you away."

She stared into space with her feet rooted to the spot. "He won't want to see me. I've pushed him away since we met. It doesn't matter I'm in love with him. He'll never forgive me for what I said."

"Did you tell him you love him?" Jillian bumped Emma's shoulder with her own.

Guilt pierced her heart, and a strangled laugh slipped from her mouth. "Never. I told him I wished Luke was here instead of him, and those feelings would never change. I said he was unreliable, and I could never trust him."

Jillian's shoulder tensed. "Ouch."

"Yeah." A few moments of silence passed as the horrible things she had said played on repeat in her mind. "Do you think he'd believe me if I told him now? I don't want to lose him."

"Telling him how you feel is worth a shot. And if

he doesn't believe you, you'll just have to prove your feelings."

She met Jillian's gaze. "How?"

Jillian's lips curved into a grin.

A flash of yellow flared in her green eyes—never a good sign.

"I have an idea. You might not like it, he sure as hell won't, but it could be the answer you're searching for."

She leaned forward and waited for Jillian to enlighten her. Her pulse raced, and her palms grew damp. She had to fix this. Meg was right. Her situation with Antonio was different. If Luke could have chosen to spend another fifty years with her, he would have. But he didn't have a choice, and she had to move on. She couldn't punish Antonio because of the cruel twist of fate that changed her life. She loved him, and she would do everything in her power to prove it.

Jillian glanced around the room. "Where are the kids?"

"Napping. They should be up any minute."

"Could your mom keep an eye on them while we go to the hospital? I'll explain the situation on the way."

Anxiety rippled in her gut. "Is it a good idea to see him now? Maybe I should wait until he gets home."

Jillian's brows dipped together. "Emma, if you really love him, you have to show him. You need to start now."

She blew a breath through parted lips and sunk lower on the side of the island. "You're right."

"She's right about what?" Annie stretched her arms around three brown paper bags filled with groceries.

"Help me with these, girls."

"Sure thing." Jillian pushed off the island, grabbed a bag, and set it on the counter.

"Thank you." Annie set the other two bags beside Emma. "What are you two gabbing about?"

Emma locked her gaze with Jillian. She opened her mouth, but no words came out.

"What's wrong, Emma?" Annie placed a hand on her shoulder.

Her mother's reassuring touch caused the floodgates to open. A sob broke loose, and she buried herself in her mom's embrace. Two strong arms wrapped around her.

Jillian rested a hand on her back. "Antonio was in an accident last night. I stopped by to let Emma know. He'll be okay, but he has a long recovery ahead."

"Oh my goodness. Oh, Emma…everything will be fine." Annie's voice cracked, and she squeezed her tighter.

She sniffed back her tears. "Jillian offered to take me to the hospital. Could you watch the kids?"

"Go. He needs you right now, and you need to see him with your own eyes." Annie tucked a strand of hair behind Emma's ear and cupped her cheek with a hand. "What happened to Antonio is not the same as Luke. Antonio's still here. You need to make the most of it."

She nodded and bit her lip. "Okay. Thanks, Mom. I won't be too long."

"Take all the time you need."

She pulled Annie in for one more hug, and then grabbed her purse from the hook by the door. "Let's go." She stepped into the autumn breeze and cringed at the blinding beams of sunlight. How could the day be so beautiful? The heavens should open, and rain should fall. Instead, picture-perfect clouds dotted the blue sky, and birds sang cheerfully overhead. She sighed and climbed into Jillian's car. The world always kept spinning when everything crashed down around her.

Jillian started the car and let it idle at the end of the driveway. "Do you want me to go a different way into town?"

She snapped together her brows and frowned. "Why would I want you to drive a different way?"

"Because we'll pass the site of the accident."

Her stomach rolled. "I'll be fine."

Jillian nodded and turned onto the road.

Emma kept her gaze glued to the front window as the empty fields passed by. Black tire tracks stained the pavement ahead of them, and she sucked in a breath. The path of the marks landed on a battered wooden pole. Bits of metal littered the ground. Saliva pooled in her mouth, and her body grew warm. She grabbed hold of Jillian's arm. "Stop. Please."

"You don't have to see this," Jillian said softly.

"I'm going to get sick." She swallowed hard and switched on the air conditioner. The cool air slammed against her face, cooling her skin. She took shallow breaths.

"Can I do something?" Jillian slid to the side of the road.

"I just need a minute. Maybe it will pass." She angled the vents to hit her squarely on the face, and then pressed her hands against her stomach. She squeezed shut her eyelids and concentrated on breathing in and out. "The cold air is helping."

"Do you want me to start driving again?"

"Yeah. I should be fine if I keep my eyes closed and the vents blasting. Are you cold?"

"Don't worry about me. Relax until we get to the hospital. If you need me to stop again, just let me know."

The sound of cars rushing by rang in her ears. She let her mind wander to who was driving past and where they were going. Anything to keep her mind off the dipping in her stomach…and where she was headed. She had no idea what she'd say to Antonio, or how he'd react to seeing her. Maybe almost losing his life would give him a different perspective. Hopefully it would make him focus on what was important and help him forgive her. Lord, she hoped so.

The car bounced as it passed over a speed bump. She opened her eyes, the county hospital coming into view, and dread burrowed in her stomach lining.

Jillian drove to the drop-off zone and put the car in park.

"What are you doing?"

"I'm dropping you off. I'll find a parking spot and give you two a little privacy. You don't need me in the room with you."

She widened her eyes. "Yes I do."

Jillian dropped her gaze. "Don't look up."

"What? Why not?" She glanced over the dashboard.

"Stop." Jillian slapped her side. "Antonio's mom is exiting. I don't want her to see us. Trust me, the last thing you need is her following you in there. The woman's a nightmare."

Emma dropped her gaze. "How are we supposed to know when she's gone?"

"You check. She doesn't know who you are yet." Jillian shielded her face with her hand and stared out the window. "She stepped out a second ago and was wearing a black trench coat. Her dark hair was secured in a bun at the nape of her neck, and she wears tortoise shell glasses."

Emma slowly lifted her neck and peeked around the parking lot. An older woman matching Jillian's description climbed into a tan Buick and backed out of her parking spot. "Coast is clear. And she left a close spot, too, if you want to snatch it really quick."

Jillian's lips turned down in a frown. "You'll be fine. You don't want an audience in there. If his mom is gone, he shouldn't have any other visitors right now. I told Jonah to keep Sam home for the afternoon so Antonio can rest."

She drew in a large breath, and then slowly released it through her nose. The rapid beat of her heart pounded in her head, adding to the dull ache already there. She could do this…she had to see him for herself. "What's his room number?"

"116. Good luck. I'll be in the waiting room when you're done."

Emma freed herself from the car. The automatic doors in front of the hospital swooshed open as she stepped in front of them and across the threshold. Bright, fluorescent lights shone down, and the sterile scent of disinfectant stung her nose. Small green plaques worked as guides, pointing in the direction of the private rooms.

She kept her head down, ignoring the stares of nurses and visitors as she followed the arrows. Her footsteps echoed off the walls until she stopped in front of Room 116. The door stood ajar, and the beeping of the machines drifted to her ears. The beeps meant life. Antonio's life. She took a deep breath, knocked softly on the door, and stepped into the room.

"Oh my God." She covered her mouth with her hand. Jillian told her he was pretty banged up, but nothing could have prepared her for the extent of his injuries. She rushed to the side of the bed, and her chest tightened. Antonio lay motionless on the bed—his eyes closed in sleep. A large goose egg took up half of his forehead, and dark purple bruises circled both of his eyes. Red gashes slashed up his cheek and into his hairline.

His eyelids fluttered, and then lifted.

He peered through long, thick lashes. Her heart stopped. Recognition dawned in his eyes.

"Emma?"

Moisture clung to her lashes, and she took a step forward. She gently rested a hand on his. She feared her touch would hurt him, but she needed to feel him.

His muscles tensed, and he tried to pull away. He grimaced.

"Don't move, please. I needed to come and see you. I have so much I have to say." Her voice was thick and quiet. "I'm so sorry, Antonio."

He closed his eyes and turned away. "I don't care what you have to say, Emma."

"But, Antonio, I love you."

He snorted out a sharp laugh. "Isn't that convenient? I get into an accident, and then suddenly you love me? You said everything you needed to say last night. Now get out of my room."

Emma reeled back as if he'd slapped her. His

words stung and cut through her soul. She opened her mouth, and then snapped it closed. He was right. Coming here was a mistake. Straightening away, she ducked her head and strode for the door. She needed to hear Jillian's plan because no way would Antonio believe her words. Another way to show him how much he meant had to exist.

Chapter Twenty

The car jostled back and forth, and he gritted his teeth. He secured a hand around the leather handle of the door and squeezed. "Geez, Mom. Are you aiming for every pothole?"

Gloria's chocolate brown eyes stared back from the rearview mirror. "Watch your mouth. It's not my fault these roads haven't been maintained properly. These potholes are so big my car will fall right into one."

Great, just what he wanted to hear. The way his luck was going, he'd get into another accident on the short ride home from the hospital. His mom had never been the best driver. "You should have had the nurse I hired drive me."

"She's meeting us at the house. I haven't even met her. Jillian took care of it. A friend of hers is a nurse, and she had some recommendations." Gloria huffed. "I don't understand why you don't want me to take care of you. I kept you alive for eighteen years under my roof."

Rolling his eyes to the ceiling, he pushed his tongue against the roof of his mouth. He'd had the same conversation twenty times in the past five days. "It'd be too much for you. Dad's already gone home, and I'm surprised he's managed without you there." Besides, he needed someone who'd only do what things he absolutely couldn't, not coddle him. As tempting as it was for his mom to bustle around the house and do everything, her presence wouldn't help him in the long run. Not to mention she'd send him right to the loony bin.

"I guess. But make sure to call if you change your mind. Maybe this nurse can do something about all of those unpacked boxes littering your living room. You've lived in that house long enough. There's no reason why things shouldn't be put in their proper place."

He kept his mouth closed before he snapped at his mother for treating him like a child. He had every intention of throwing everything in those boxes on the curb. Reminders of Emma filling his house were the last thing he needed. The furniture she ordered would be enough.

Jillian's blue Honda sat in front of the house. He peered through the window. Where was the nurse's car?

Gloria stepped out of the driver's side door and rounded the back of the car. The trunk popped open.

The screech of metal scraping against metal sent chills down his spine. He opened his door and waited for his mom to come around with the wheelchair. He hated being in it, but he didn't have much of a choice. His cast wouldn't be off for at least a month, and he couldn't hobble around on crutches with his arm in a damn sling.

Gloria appeared beside him with the chair. He braced his left hand on the seat and shifted his weight. Despite his pain medication his ribs ached, and the top of his shoulder burned from the movement. He ground together his teeth, pushed off his good arm, and plopped on to the chair. The sun shone brightly against his sunglasses, and he closed his eyes. Bile sloshed in his stomach. He needed to get inside and go to sleep.

The chair bounced along the uneven terrain of the brick sidewalk that led to the front of his house. A stick lodged under a wheel, and his body lurched forward as the wheelchair stopped suddenly. Widening his eyes, he bit into his bottom lip to keep from screaming.

The door opened, and Jillian stepped outside.

A wide grin spread across her face like the Cheshire cat.

"Welcome home."

He landed his gaze on his stoop, and his jaw dropped. "What the hell?"

His mom cleared her throat. "What did I say about your mouth?"

"Sorry, but look at my house." Irritation heated his face at his mother's condescending tone. He pointed a finger toward the front porch. A wooden ramp covered the top of the stairs. "Where did the ramp come from?"

Jillian descended the ramp toward him. "Jonah built it. We figured climbing up and down the stairs would be too hard if you wanted to leave the house. No reason you need to be cooped up inside."

Annoyance flared inside him like a freshly stricken match. "He didn't have to build anything."

Jillian shrugged. "I know, but it wasn't a big deal."

"Tell him I said thanks." The words tasted bitter in his mouth. "Can you get me inside, Mom? The light is killing me, and I just want to lie down."

"Sure, *mi amor*."

Jillian stepped back inside the house.

His mom rolled him up the ramp. The wheels slid effortlessly over the wood. Damnit all to hell. The ramp would come in handy, and the fact Jonah did something nice only soured his already bad mood. Having bigger issues to deal with, he pushed it from his mind.

He rolled over the threshold and rested his sunglasses on his head. Blinking, he adjusted to the shadows in the house. No light peered in through the large windows in the front living room, and he craned his neck to gaze into the room. "Why is it so dark? And why is a hospital bed set up in my living room?"

"Your bed sits up too high for you to maneuver in and out."

The hair on the back of his neck stood at attention, and the blood in his veins turned to ice water.

Emma stood beside the bed with wide eyes. "The living room will make a good temporary bedroom since you haven't done anything with it. I carried the boxes to the office and have been working at getting those unpacked." She crossed the room to the window and ran a hand down the dark material covering the glass. "I had Jonah and Dylan hang blackout curtains on all of the windows on the first floor. With your concussion, the light will bother you. This way, you can keep the curtains drawn and don't have to worry about the sun."

"Why are you here?" His voice was as tight as the ache in his chest.

"I'll take care of you until you can get by on your own." She clasped her hands in front of her waist, her gaze unwavering.

"Oh, how wonderful! Why didn't you mention Emma agreeing to take care of Antonio to me?" Gloria skirted around the wheelchair and strode toward Emma. She hugged her, swaying back and forth while she squeezed. Gloria turned toward him, one hand remaining on Emma's arm. "This girl has been amazing. She's been here day and night getting this place in order. I had no idea she planned to stay once you got home."

"I didn't ask her." He ground out each word through clenched teeth. He couldn't cause a scene in front of his mom. "I wanted to hire a professional."

Jillian rested a hand on his good shoulder. "The physical therapist will be here tomorrow to work on your shoulder. You don't need a nurse here, too. Emma has the time, and she wants to do this."

He glanced up and narrowed his eyes at Jillian. The muscles in her face twitched, giving away her guilt. *Traitor.* He tilted his head and glanced at Emma. "What about your kids?"

She shrugged. "They'll stay here, too. Sam and Sophie already picked out her room, and most of her stuff is moved. Anderson can sleep in your room with me. Tonight, they'll stay with my mom so you can get settled."

A fist squeezed his heart. He wanted nothing more than to have his house filled with children and a family he loved. But not in this way. Not because a woman who he accidentally got pregnant felt sorry for him. Not because the woman he loved was consumed with guilt due to the heartless things she'd said. He shook his head, and the bile in his stomach rolled up his throat. He pushed the back of his hand against his mouth until the sensation faded. "We'll talk about this later. Right now, I want to take my meds and go to sleep."

"Here, honey, I'll help you." Gloria retrieved a paper bag from her purse and read the labels from the bottles she fished out from inside. "Once you're situated, I'll take off."

He sighed. At least he'd have one unwanted woman out of his hair soon. "Thanks, Mom."

Emma took one step forward. "Do you need help getting into the bed?"

"Not from you." The words flew out of his mouth before he could stop them. Her mouth fell open, and the color of her eyes deepened with pain. He released a heavy sigh. "Sorry, Emma. I'm tired, and everything hurts. My mom can help me right now. I'll talk to you later."

She nodded then passed on her way out of the room.

He wouldn't feel sorry for her. She was the one who had caused this rift. How could she expect him to be all right with her waltzing into his house and inserting herself in his life? When he woke up, he'd deal with her.

"I'll head out, too. If you need anything all you have to do is call," Jillian said.

"I think you've done enough."

Her lip tilted up, and she chuckled. She wiggled her fingers in good-bye and retreated out the door.

He shook his head and bit his tongue.

Gloria stepped behind him and wheeled him to the side of the bed. He shifted his weight to his good arm, just as he'd done in the car, and swung himself over to the bed. Bright, intense pain burst inside him like fireworks. He grabbed the two little pills from his mom and threw them in his mouth. Without water, the pills burned his esophagus.

His pillow dipped down and nestled his head on its feathery softness.

Gloria pressed her lips against his forehead. "Go to

sleep. And be nice. Emma's here because she loves you. I can tell."

"How?" The word scratched against his throat, and his eyes misted.

She smoothed back his hair. "A mother knows these things. Now close your eyes and go to sleep. I love you so much. You hurry up and get better, and I'll be back soon to see you."

"I love you, too." His eyelids drooped closed, and an image of Emma, smiling and full of sweetness, invaded his mind. He was a fool to have fallen in love with her. He'd been a convenient person when she'd needed something and nothing more. She didn't love him. She'd said it in more ways than one. His heart ached, but he breathed through the pain. You can't make someone love you...he'd learned that lesson the hard way.

He jerked awake, and a cold sweat gathered on his brow. He flitted his gaze around the dark room. Only the faint glow of a nightlight in the hall filtered into the room. Anxiety pitched back and forth in his stomach like the giant swells in the ocean. A memory flashed in his mind. His car skidding across the road...the telephone pole speeding toward him...and total blackness sucking him under. The nightmares started the night after the accident, and they were getting worse. He blinked in rapid succession, and his mind snapped back to the present as pain zinged around his body. A gentle caress tickled his arm, and he whipped his head to the side.

"Shh, everything's okay." Emma placed a cool washcloth on his forehead.

His muscles relaxed, and he focused on the smooth

ceiling overhead. His breath came out in short gasps, and he clutched a pillow to hug to his body. The motion helped to ease the agony in his ribs as his chest expanded…even if only a little. He caught his breath, and his nerves settled. "Why are you here?"

She slid the washcloth over his brow and down his neck. "I want to help you."

"I told you to go home. I don't want you here." The washcloth stopped on his collarbone, and he closed his eyes as the coolness battled against the constant burning in his sprained joint. The moisture seeped into the tape that wound around his injury, but he didn't care. The physical therapist would have to change it tomorrow anyway.

"Please, let me do this for you. Me taking care of you is the best solution."

He choked out a strangled laugh. "How do you figure?"

"I'll stay out of your way as much as possible. Meg and Dylan's wedding reception is in two months, so I have a ton of work. I'll make sure you're fed, you're getting around okay, and nothing more."

He swallowed past the lump in his throat. "I don't know, Emma."

"The best part is Sam can still spend time here. If you hire a nurse, you can't expect her to take care of Sam, too. I love having him around, and so does Sophie." She lifted the washcloth.

He wanted to protest, but stubborn pride stood in his way. He didn't want to admit she was helping him.

A soft laugh poured from Emma's mouth. "Sam's so excited about the baby. He's been fun the last few days. He even has Sophie excited for another little brother or sister. I'm so grateful."

A reluctant smile touched his lips. "I don't know where he got such a great personality. Must be from Jillian, because it certainly didn't come from me."

"I wouldn't be so sure. He's like you in every way. The more I'm around him, the more I see it." Silence stretched between them, and she cradled her stomach. "I hope the baby is a boy. Another mini Antonio."

His heart slammed against his ribcage. He'd dreamed of a little girl, but he kept the dream to himself. He sighed. She was right. Having her here was better for Sam. He needed to stop protesting. "Fine. You can stay, but it won't change anything."

Emma nodded and dropped her gaze. "If that's what you want."

"You made sure that's the way it had to be." He returned his focus to the ceiling. He couldn't look at her. She was too damn beautiful, and seeing everything he'd lost hurt too much.

"I am sorry for what I said. I was angry and selfish. I wanted to hurt you as badly as you hurt me."

"Well, mission accomplished." He shifted in the bed, squeezing the pillow harder as the ache in his side screamed in protest. "I don't want to talk about it anymore. If you're staying, fine. But you're here to help get me back on my feet and nothing more. Now, can you please give me my pain pills and some water?"

"Okay." She hurried out of the room.

He tried to ignore the pain in her voice, but it rang in his head. He couldn't let her wear him down. The only reason she was here was because she pitied him. She didn't love him. No one could change their mind so quickly. Even if she had tender feelings for him, he'd always play second fiddle to another man. He refused to play that role again.

Chapter Twenty-One

The next morning, Emma rolled her neck back and forth, and the muscles screamed in protest. She cradled a cup of hot coffee in her hands and fixed her gaze out the window that looked out into the spacious backyard. The sun wasn't up yet, but the outlines of the wooden swing set stood out against the inky sky. Sophie would love climbing the rock wall and flying down the slide. A large yawn tore through her, and she blinked to keep her eyes open.

She should go back to sleep, but what was the point? She lay awake for hours in Antonio's large, king-sized bed. Images of Antonio flashed in her mind until her eyes were grainy and her nerve endings throbbed. The night she'd spent with him meant more than she'd admitted. She'd grabbed a pillow and blanket and spent the rest of the night in a chair beside his hospital bed. The idea was good at the time, but this morning her stiff muscles told a different story.

She sighed and sank into the leather armchair in the family room off the kitchen. A slight chill nipped the air, and she wrapped a blanket around her legs. She'd talk to Antonio about turning on the heat. October had arrived, and the cooler weather was here to stay. She lifted her cup. Sweet coffee hit her tongue, and she moaned. This would be her only cup of the day. Limiting her caffeine intake during pregnancy was never an easy feat. She'd sit and enjoy the hot coffee, along with the stillness only the start of a new day brought, before tackling what needed to be done.

A loud buzz vibrated off the marble countertops. So much for enjoying a quiet moment before starting her day. She stood, and the dark green, cashmere blanket slipped to the floor. Ignoring the blanket, she hurried and unlocked the phone screen. A text message from Jillian popped up.

—*How'd it go last night?*—

Emma carried the phone to the chair and sat again, tucking her feet underneath her. Her mouth twisted at the memory of Antonio's attitude, and she moved her thumbs over the screen.

—*Okay. He woke up once, got crabby, and then went back to sleep.*—

A few seconds passed and the phone vibrated in her hand.

—*Lol, I'm not surprised. Do you want me to bring over the kids when I drop off Sam?*—

—That would be great, thanks. His therapist is coming this morning, so I can't get them until later. I'll let my mom know.—

Good, she could cross one thing off her list. Jillian was a lifesaver.

Her phone buzzed again, and she glanced at the screen.

—*See you later. Call if you need anything.*—

Emma set her phone on the arm of the chair and took another sip of coffee. Nerves danced in the pit of her stomach. How would Sophie react to staying here? She was excited about having her own room, but her enthusiasm might change when Sam wasn't around.

"Darn it."

Antonio's shout of pain sliced through the silence of the house. Her nerves morphed from dancing to zipping around her stomach in a dead sprint. Good thing she hadn't tried to go back to sleep. She set her coffee on the end table and hurried to the living room. "Is everything all right?" She stopped beside Antonio's bed.

He curled onto his side with a hand clutching his fractured ribs. "No, everything's not all right." He clenched his teeth. "Get my pills."

She wrung her hands. "You need to wait about an hour."

Antonio hissed, and he shifted in his bed. "Well, do something. Isn't that why you're here?"

His gruff tone stiffened her spine and constricted her chest. "First of all, stop squirming." She fisted her hands on her hips. His irritation was understandable, but she wouldn't let him treat her like dirt. "Do you need to go to the bathroom?"

He glared.

Heat invaded her cheeks, but she didn't waver.

"Fine. Help me to the bathroom."

She narrowed her eyes and ground together her teeth. "You don't have to be a jerk."

"You're the one who wants to be here. If you don't like my attitude, you can leave."

She inhaled a deep breath, drew herself up tall, and approached the wheelchair. If he wanted to play hardball, bring it on. Dealing with bratty children was her specialty. Placing the chair on the side of the bed, she supported him while he sat. She helped him swing his legs over the edge and offered her shoulder as a brace to transfer into the chair. She wheeled him across the hall, through his bedroom, and into the master bathroom, then turned to walk out of the bathroom. Let him figure out the rest.

"I need help."

She glanced over her shoulder. "And?"

"What do you mean 'and'?" he snapped.

She faced him and crossed her arms over her chest. Frustration threatened to raise her temper, but she fought to keep her cool. "Even Anderson knows not to be so rude, and he's only sixteen months old. You don't have to be happy about my being here, but you won't be disrespectful. Do you understand?"

He dropped his gaze.

His cheeks burned red. Whether from shame or anger, she wasn't sure.

Cringing, he lifted his gaze. "You're right. I have no reason to get nasty."

"If you speak that way in front of Sophie, you'll have to explain why you think having an attitude is okay. You're the male role model in her life right now. I expect you to take that seriously."

"Okay, I understand." He nodded along with the words

She narrowed her gaze. "Good. Now say please."

He lifted his eyes to the ceiling. "Please help me."

"Of course." She flashed him a bright smile, got him situated, and then left to give him some privacy. Sitting on the edge of the bed, she hung her head in her hands. Light spilled in through open curtains. The day had officially begun, and all she wanted to do was curl into a ball and hide under the covers. Winning over Antonio would be harder than she'd expected. He was angry and in pain. The last thing he wanted was to open his heart right now. Maybe moving in wasn't such a good idea, but she couldn't do anything about her decision. She'd committed herself to showing Antonio she loved him, and she'd stick to her commitment, no matter how hard he resisted.

"Emma?"

His voice was quiet and tentative. Sympathy burrowed deep in her heart. Being dependent on someone who had been so cruel had to be difficult. She needed to let his anger bounce off her and do whatever she could to make things easier.

She pulled out clean clothes from the dresser and left them for the therapist to assist Antonio get dressed then hurried into the bathroom. When Antonio was back in his wheelchair, she stepped behind him and wheeled him down the hall. The smooth wheels glided over the floorboards, making them creak. "Are you hungry? Want some coffee?"

"Coffee would be good, and maybe an ice pack for my shoulder."

"You got it." She prepped his coffee, and the machine chugged to life. As it brewed, she stepped over to the freezer and grabbed an ice pack. The frozen bag sent chills up her arm. "Do you want to hold it on your shoulder, or do you want it wrapped up?"

He reached for the ice pack. "I'll take it."

"I was enjoying my coffee in the family room when you woke up. Would you like to join me?" She held her breath and busied herself with his drink.

"I'd rather drink it in the living room. I want to relax and ice my shoulder before the physical therapist gets here."

"Oh, okay." A stab of disappointment pierced her heart. Her eyes burned, and she turned her back so he wouldn't see her tears. Of course he didn't want to have coffee with her. He didn't want her here at all. He'd change his mind eventually. She just needed to be patient. She'd win him over in time.

****

The front door banged open. "Dad! I'm home! Where are you?"

Emma ran out from the office. "Shh, honey, your dad's asleep. He had a tough morning."

"Oh." Sam's face fell. "I really wanted to see him."

Jillian stepped inside with Anderson on her hip and Sophie by her side. "It's all right, buddy. I'm sure he'll be awake soon. Why don't you put away your backpack, and then we'll get a snack?"

"Hello, my babies," Emma cooed.

Sophie wrapped her arms around her mother's legs.

Anderson leaned forward with his arms open.

She grabbed him and squeezed him tight. "Did you have fun with Grandma?"

"Mama, Mama!" Anderson pressed slobbery kisses to her cheek.

"I helped Meg-Meg grow flowers and made cookies with Grandma," Sophie said.

"What a fun day. And now you get to have a sleepover with Sam." Emma circled an arm around Sophie's back. "Let's go into the kitchen so we don't wake Antonio."

"Too late." Antonio's voice drifted out of the living room. "You guys can come in."

Sophie's arms wrapped tighter. "The room is dark, Mommy."

Emma rubbed her hand over Sophie's hair. "The sun hurts Antonio's head, sweetheart."

Sam disappeared into the room.

Sophie glanced up.

Emma smiled and guided her toward the living room.

"How'd it go today?" Jillian asked.

Tucking in her lips, Emma shrugged. "Okay. Therapy was tough, and it was hard to watch. I had to step out. He hasn't left his room much today, so I've stayed busy by rearranging some of the things I'd unpacked while Antonio was in the hospital. I still can't believe he never opened any of the packages I'd sent him."

Jillian's chin dipped low, and she arched her brows. "I think he was waiting for you."

"Stop, Sam! He'll die!"

Sophie's shrill screams made Emma's pulse race, and she ran into the living room. Fear invaded Sophie's wide blue eyes, and tears stained her cheeks.

Sam stood by the bed, his chin quivering as he glanced from Sophie to Antonio. "Am I killing you, Dad?" Sam's voice cracked, and his shoulders hunched forward. He took a giant step backward.

"Sam, no," Antonio said. "Don't ever think you're hurting me by loving me."

Emma thrust Anderson into Jillian's arms and grabbed Sophie's shoulders. She crouched and faced Sophie. "Why would you say that to Sam? He was saying hi to his dad, baby girl."

"But he was hurting him. I could tell. He made a weird face when Sam jumped on the bed."

Her tiny voice shook from the force of her tears,

and Emma held her. She locked her gaze on Antonio and saw regret in his eyes.

"Oh, Sophie. Sam didn't mean to hurt me. I was just surprised."

Sam's head dropped down, and he shuffled his feet back and forth. "I'm sorry, Dad."

"Look at me, Sam." Antonio fixed his gaze on Sam. "Never apologize for giving me a hug. I love you, and I'm excited to see you, too. I'm okay. Now come here." He reached out a hand.

He took a step forward and then stopped. "Are you sure?"

Antonio smiled. "Abso-freaking-lutely."

Sam beamed.

Antonio grabbed his hand, and then glanced at Sophie. "Do you want to come say hello, Sophie?"

She shook her head.

Emma used the pad of her thumb to wipe away Sophie's tears. "Today's been a big day for everyone. Do you want to find a movie and relax a little bit?"

"Will you carry me?"

"Sure." She stood and lifted Sophie. "Sam, when you're done visiting, come let me know. I'll grab you a quick snack, and you can watch the movie with Sophie."

"If he doesn't have homework to do first," Jillian said.

Sam sighed. "I just have one sheet. I promise."

Antonio chuckled, and then winced and grabbed his side. "I've learned the hard way you always have to check his book bag."

"Good to know. Come on, Sophie. Jillian, will you bring Anderson out here?"

"Sure thing."

Emma left the room. Her pulse returned to normal, but the ache in her chest remained. Sophie lived through so much pain at such a young age. Her reaction to Antonio and Sam rattled them both. Her scars from her dad's death ran deep, and Emma's own experience made her all too aware they would never disappear. She wished she could absorb all of her daughter's pain, but it wasn't that easy. Sophie would need to learn to deal with the issues that would always pop up because of Luke's death. Emma hoped bringing another baby into the family, and hopefully Antonio as well, would help her to heal and not make matters worse. She set Sophie on the couch in the family room and kissed her forehead. "Are you all right?"

Sophie sniffled and used the back of her hand to wipe snot from her nose. "Yes. Can I watch Ariel?"

"An excellent idea. Do you want popcorn?"

Sophie nodded.

"Okay, love." Emma set up the movie, and then walked to the kitchen to make the popcorn.

Jillian sat on a stool with Anderson perched on the counter. She covered her face with her hands, and then quickly moved them out of the way. "Peek-a-boo!"

Anderson giggled.

The tension eased from her neck. Nothing in the world sounded sweeter. Emma put a pot on the stove, and then reached in the cabinet for olive oil and popcorn kernels. She leaned the small of her back against the counter and waited for the popcorn to pop.

"It'll get easier." Jillian gazed at Anderson.

"Did I make the right decision? You saw Sophie. Being around Antonio while he's injured is tough on her. Maybe I shouldn't have brought her here to see a busted-up man day in and day out." She rubbed her temples with her fingertips.

"What I saw was a little girl who showed concern for another's well-being. She might be a very smart little girl, but she's only three. She doesn't know how to express big emotions yet." Jillian picked up Anderson from the counter and put him in her lap. "In my opinion, her reaction was a good thing."

Emma reeled back her head and wrinkled her nose. "How do you figure?"

"Would she have gotten so upset if she didn't like Antonio?" Jillian planted a kiss on Anderson's cheek.

She tilted her head and twisted her lips. "I didn't think of it that way." She tended to the popcorn. Jillian had made a good point. Sophie must care for Antonio if seeing him hurt caused her to get upset. She straightened her back and steeled her resolve. Antonio had been hurt in the worst way…by her. She had to make it right. If he didn't want to be with her, she could live with his decision. But she had to show him she wasn't a heartless brat. She was wrong to treat him the way she had, and at the very least, she could show him kindness. Maybe, just maybe, they could share something more. Her happiness wasn't the only one at stake.

Chapter Twenty-Two

The itch on Antonio's calf intensified, and he curled his toes. Exhaustion and pain pills made his brain fuzzy, and the desire to give in to sleep was so strong he wanted to cry with frustration. If only he could scratch the maddening itch, he could fall asleep and put another God-awful day behind him. He darted his gaze around the room, searching for something to jam into his cast and relieve his agony.

A pen sat on his nightstand, but it was on the side of his injured shoulder. He twisted his torso, stretching his good arm across his body, and yelped as his ribs screamed.

"Do you hurt?" a voice asked from the doorway.

He leaned forward and strained his eyes against the darkness. "Sophie? Is that you?"

"You made a weird noise."

His heart twisted. "I'm sorry. I need to reach something. What are you doing down here?"

"I wanted to see Mommy." She took one slow step into the living room. "Do you want help?"

His chest tightened, and a smile touched his lips. "Sure. Can you grab the pen on my nightstand?"

"Are you going to draw?" Sophie took two steps closer.

He chuckled. "No, I need it to scratch my leg." The reminder of his leg caused his muscles to tighten.

She grabbed the pen from the nightstand. "Here you go." She took a step back but kept her gaze on him.

Antonio inserted the pen in the small crack between the cast and his skin. He plunged it down, scratching the itch that kept him awake for the past hour. A groan of satisfaction caught in his throat. "Thank you so much, Sophie."

"You're welcome. Do you feel better?" She clasped her hands in front of her waist.

"I do."

"So you aren't dying?"

Air wheezed from his lungs as if he'd been punched in the gut. "No, honey. I won't die. Why would you think that?"

She dropped her gaze to the floor. "You can't walk, and you have lots of purple spots on your face."

Sadness encircled his heart and pressed against his tender ribs. He wanted nothing more than to erase all the heartbreak she had suffered, but that wasn't possible. "The spots are bruises, and they'll be gone in no time. I'll walk again when the cast comes off my leg in a few weeks, and I'm already working on making my arm better. I should have this silly sling off in a week or so." His heart beat frantically. Maybe he should call for Emma. He wasn't equipped to handle this.

Sophie drew in a deep breath. "Well, my mommy's daddy and my daddy died. You're Sam's and the new baby's daddy. Doesn't that mean you'll have to go to heaven, too?"

He opened his mouth to speak, but nothing came out. His throat burned, and he wished like hell Emma was here. He glanced toward the doorway. She was just down the hall. Maybe he should call for her. His palms dampened, and he wiped them on his blanket. "Oh, Soph. I'm not going anywhere."

Her gaze met his, and one lone tear spilled from her lashes and rolled down her check. "How do you know?"

He swallowed hard, pushing back his own tears. "Come here, sweetheart."

Sophie stepped as close to the bed as she could.

He grabbed her small hand. "Life is scary sometimes, isn't it? People leave, and we miss them with our whole hearts. But our hearts are so big that if we're lucky, we'll find new people to love. People who will help us with our pain and our sadness. Because you'll always miss your daddy, won't you? And no one will ever take his place."

"But what if you leave me, too?" Her bottom lip trembled.

"Then you will have some awesome memories to make you smile. Do you want to sit?" He let go of her hand and patted the bed beside him.

Her eyes widened, and she roamed her gaze over his body. "Will it hurt you?"

"No, honey." He scooted over and let her climb up. All the moving around sent waves of pain through his body, but he hardened his jaw and refused to let it show. Sophie curled on her side and her long, golden hair fanned out on his arm. "What do you remember about your daddy?"

Sophie was quiet for a few minutes, and she wiggled her foot against his leg. "He was a silly dancer."

Her answer brought a sad smile to his lips. "He was? Did you like to dance with him?"

"Yes! We would play music and dance in the living room together. Me, Mommy, and Daddy. Mommy would hold Anderson, and Daddy would hold me."

Her voice rose with excitement. His heart cracked in two. "Did he have a favorite song?"

"He liked them all. Especially the fast ones where he could shake his booty." She giggled.

Her breath tickled his chin. Antonio laughed. "His booty, huh? He does sound like a silly dancer."

Tear drops fell on his shoulder, and he winced as he gathered her close to his side.

"I miss him so much."

"I know you do." He rubbed a hand along her small back. "Do you think when you get sad, I can be the person to help you through?"

"You're kind of big. Will you fit in my heart?"

He held back a laugh. He loved this little girl. "I think I can fit, if you'll let me."

"I'll let you. And I can help you, too." She cuddled closer.

"Oh, I'm counting on it. You're here to help me get better."

Sophie yawned. "Uh-huh. Can I stay here for another minute?"

Warmth radiated from his heart. "You stay as long as you want."

A few minutes of silence passed, and Sophie's breathing slowed until she fell asleep. He closed his eyes and focused on her even breathing until the sweet escape of sleep dragged him under.

A sharp kick to his side had him sucking in his breath. His eyes shot open, and he gnashed together his teeth to keep from making any noise.

Sophie wiggled, and then settled back into a quiet sleep. One arm stretched above her head, and soft snores drifted from her open mouth.

He pressed a hand to his side to ease the pain, and he drifted his gaze over Sophie to the chair in the corner. Soft light from the hallway filtered into the room.

Emma was curled into the chair fast asleep.

She was so damn beautiful. The lines of her face softened in sleep, and her wavy hair was a tangled mess. Shapely legs peeked out from the blanket she wrapped around herself, and his fingers itched to caresses the smooth skin on her calf. Her chest rose and fell in a steady rhythm, and he chuckled as her own snores rose in the air and matched Sophie's.

The two were alike in almost every way. If only he could trust Emma like he did her daughter. Sophie had the innocence of a child that was impossible not to love. Emma had shattered all of the illusions he had created in his mind about the future they could have. But right now, as she slept, the thought of forgetting the harsh words and losing himself in the dream of always having her and her children in his home was easy…in their home.

Emma's eyelids fluttered and slowly lifted. Her gaze narrowed.

His pulse spiked. He swallowed hard, and then lifted a hand in silent greeting.

A slow smile curved on her lips.

His toes curled.

She raised her arms above her head in a stretch, and the blanket fell to the floor. She stood and ran her hand through her wild hair. Her tank top exposed her bare shoulders.

He dropped his gaze, but her pretty toes with their bright pink polish were just as sexy.

"How did Sophie end up in here?" She approached the bed and swept stray wisps of hair from Sophie's forehead.

"She came downstairs and heard me make a noise. She checked to see if I was all right, and then we had a little chat. She asked if she could stay for a little bit and ended up falling asleep."

"I'm sorry. You should have called for me."

Her voice was thick with sleep. "Nah, we had a good talk. She's a sweet little girl." Emma's gaze found his. His nerve endings tingled. He hated the way his body reacted to one glance from her.

"She sure is."

He narrowed his eyes. "Why were you in here? The chair can't be comfortable to sleep in."

Emma's hand snaked around her neck, and she glanced away. "It's not too bad."

"The bed's better." A crimson blush tinted her cheeks.

"I know, but I like being close in case you need me in the middle of the night."

His blood warmed, and lust pooled in his belly. She would know. She'd been in his bed before. He cleared his throat. "I need to go to the bathroom. Can you help me?"

"Sure. Let me put Sophie in bed first." She leaned forward and scooped Sophie in her arms.

His gaze dropped to the subtle sway of her hips. He groaned. Having her here was pure torture.

Emma retuned moments later, and she replayed the

same morning routine as the day before. She didn't speak until he was dressed, in the kitchen, and both had a cup of coffee in their hands.

"Do you want to sit in the family room with me this morning? Or go back into the living room?"

Indecision tore through him. He'd been a jerk since his accident, and his bad behavior needed to stop. She was right about being a good role model for Sophie, not to mention Emma was having his baby. He still didn't believe she'd miraculously discovered she was in love with him, but they needed to get along. "Let's go into the family room. Spending so much time in my temporary bedroom is depressing."

"Okay." Emma hurried into the family room and set down her steaming mug then returned to the kitchen to push the wheelchair into the other room.

The curtains were drawn, but daylight hadn't broken yet anyway.

"Do you need anything else?"

"I'm good." He glanced around the room. Knickknacks littered the entertainment console, and the new coffee table held a galvanized tray that neatly contained all of the remote controls. Two green candles sat beside it. His heart stopped. The candles they picked out together. He closed his eyes and absorbed the pain crushing down.

"Are you ready for therapy this morning? Maybe you should take off a day and rest." Emma sat cross-legged in the brown leather armchair in front of him.

He took a sip of coffee, concentrating on the pain of the scalding liquid on his tongue instead of the pain in his chest. He balanced the cup on the arm of his wheelchair. "No rest. The doctor said I should only need this sling for another week. My shoulder hurts a lot, but it's getting better every day. Once I get off the sling, I can use crutches to get around."

Emma's brows arched high. "You'll drag that big cast around with a sore shoulder, cracked ribs, and crutches?"

He lifted his good shoulder. "Why not? My ribs are healing. By the time the sling is gone, the ribs won't be so bad. Then I'll get a walking boot instead of this stupid cast. I have a long road ahead, and I know everything will hurt for a while, but I'll manage. Then you can go home."

She winced. "Try not to push too hard. I'm here as long as you need me."

He didn't want to talk about his injuries or her leaving. He'd never admit it, but he liked having her here. Too much. That's why she needed to leave as soon as possible. "The room looks nice. You've been busy."

Emma lifted her chin and glanced around the room. "About time someone unpacked those boxes. They've been sitting untouched for over a month." Her chin dipped down. "Why didn't you go through the boxes?"

Not wanting to get into it, he sighed. "I wanted you to have an excuse to come over."

She lifted her mug and took a sip. Her gaze stared over the side as she lowered it slightly. "Did you ever plan to unpack?"

He shook his head. "I didn't want reminders of you all over my house."

Coffee sloshed over the side of her cup and landed on her bare thigh. She shot to her feet and set her mug on the end table. She wiped the brown liquid off her leg with the palm of her hand.

"I'm sorry. I didn't mean to upset you."

She took a deep breath and waved away his words. "No need to apologize. You've been very honest about how you feel. I can take it."

"Honesty is always the best policy, Emma." His words came out harsher than he'd intended, but he wouldn't take them back.

She stood straight and narrowed her gaze. "I agree, and the only time I wasn't honest was when I said those horrible things. They came from a place of anger not from the truth."

"I told you I don't want to discuss this," he snapped. Forgetting what she'd said and welcoming her into his life with open arms could happen so easily. But letting Emma into his life would be a mistake he couldn't make again. Doing so would kill him.

"Fine. I need to get ready before the kids wake up. Are you okay alone for a few minutes?"

"I'm not a child, Emma. I'll be fine."

She nodded, walked past, and out of the room.

Her angry footsteps pounded through the kitchen and down the hall to the bedroom. He should have kept his mouth shut. He leaned forward to place his cup on the edge of the coffee table. His body tensed, and his muscles screamed. He'd forgotten to ask for his pain pills, but he'd push through the discomfort. He wanted to stop taking the pills as soon as possible.

The handle of his mug slipped from his grasp, and the mug crashed to the floor. Hot coffee splashed everywhere, soaking into the new area rug under the coffee table. He choked out a strangled laugh so he wouldn't cry. So much for being all right on his own.

He leaned an elbow on the arm of his chair and cradled his head in a hand. If he couldn't make it five minutes without Emma by his side, he'd never make it for the rest of his life.

Chapter Twenty-Three

When the physical therapist arrived, Emma retreated into the office with Sophie. Antonio's agonizing groans penetrated through the French doors and into the office. Emma gritted her teeth and focused on the computer screen.

Sophie dropped her crayon and stared across the desk. "Antonio doesn't sound good. Should we help him?"

Emma forced a cheerful smile on her lips. "He's fine, honey. The therapist is helping him with his shoulder. He doesn't sound as bad this week. I think he's getting better. Don't you?"

Sophie shrugged, picked up her pink crayon, and filled in the unicorn on her coloring page.

She watched Sophie color for a second, impressed by how well she stayed in the lines, and then picked up her phone to call Meg. "Hey, how are you?" She clicked the mouse, and images of floral arrangements filled the screen.

"Tired, always tired. When does this feeling go away?" Meg asked.

Emma chuckled and squeezed the phone between her ear and her shoulder as she closed out of her browser. "I don't know. I've been tired for over three years."

"Great." Meg groaned. "How's everything over

there? Has Antonio lightened up about you being in his house?"

"A little bit." She eyed Sophie. Her head was bent low over her coloring book, but that didn't mean she wasn't listening. "He's been concentrating on his recovery."

"How are the kids doing?"

"Sophie loves seeing so much of Sam, and Anderson's been a pain in the butt. He's into everything. Nothing here is baby proofed, and he's constantly trying to climb the stairs. At least he's been sleeping well in the pack 'n play."

"But have *you* been sleeping?"

Her reflection bounced off the black computer screen. Heavy bags hung under her eyes, and she hadn't had the energy to do anything with her hair in days. Stringy bangs swept across her forehead, while the rest gathered into a stubby ponytail. She cringed. She was the poster child for an overwhelmed mother. Between having Anderson sleeping in the same room as her, and being up constantly to check on Antonio, she hadn't gotten more than five hours a night. "Not really, but I'm fine. I don't need a lot of sleep."

Meg snorted. "Yeah right. You're super-crabby when you don't get enough sleep."

"Gee, thanks." The baby monitor crackled beside her, and she waited a beat. Anderson shouldn't be awake for a while. She needed more time to get stuff done before he woke. "Before I get too crabby, let me tell you why I called. I'm looking at floral arrangements for the reception."

"Why?"

"Don't you want some ideas for the tables?"

"You're joking, right?" Meg laughed. "You know nothing about flowers, and I manage a nursery. I'll handle the flowers."

"You shouldn't have to work on your special day. Wouldn't it be easier to have someone else do it?"

"Dylan and I are already married. I love doing this type of thing, and if I need help, I'll ask Mom or Celeste. You can handle everything else."

"Are you sure?" Meg putting the flowers together for her own reception didn't sit right, but the decision didn't surprise her. Meg lived for her horses and helping Annie in the garden. And now for her little family.

"I'm sure. How's the rest of the planning going? Remember, I want this to be low-key."

Anderson's shrill cry pierced through the monitor. "Sorry, but I have to go. Anderson cut his nap short. I'll call you later. Love you." She stood and rounded the desk. She wrapped her arms around Sophie and leaned down to give her a hug. "I have to get Anderson. Do you want to come with me, or stay in here?"

Sophie's crayon kept moving. "I'll stay in here."

"Okay, love." She kissed the top of her head and pushed open the glass doors.

Anderson's wails grew more impatient.

Ding-Dong

She froze, one hand on the bedroom door handle. Who could be stopping by? The physical therapist was the only person to ring the bell since she'd been here. Everyone else walked in because they didn't want to disrupt Antonio if he was asleep. She hurried to the front door and came face-to-face with every man's fantasy come to life. Well, more like her face to dark-haired Barbie's collarbone. "Can I help you?"

The woman's eyes misted over, and her lips trembled. "I need to see Antonio. Is he here?"

The muscles in Emma's stomach twisted. She dropped her gaze to the woman's hands. Long, polished nails graced her elegant fingers—the kind of nails that leave scratches on a lover. She curled her hand around the doorknob and fought the urge to run a hand over her messy ponytail. It wouldn't help anyway. She could spend an hour primping, and she'd still fall far short beside this woman. She cleared her throat to break through her nerves. "He's in therapy right now. Please come in, and I'll see if he can take a break. I'm sorry. What's your name?"

"Bridgette. I… work with Antonio."

Yeah, she worked with him all right. Emma clenched her teeth and firmed her lips into a straight line. "How nice of you to visit." She opened the door wider and let Bridgette brush past her. She closed the door, and Anderson's screams caught her attention. "I'm sorry. I need to get the baby. Why don't you head into the kitchen, and I'll meet you in a second? Just walk straight down the hallway. You can't miss it."

Bridgette drew in a shaky breath and ran a hand over her heart. "Thank you so much. Are you his nurse?"

She pressed together her teeth harder, and a dull ache throbbed in her jaw. "Not quite. Excuse me." She headed into the bedroom.

Anderson stood in the pack 'n play with outstretched arms. Tears streamed down his face.

"I'm coming, baby boy."

As he caught his breath, Anderson whimpered

softly in her arms. He wrapped his arms around her neck.

She nuzzled her nose on the top of his head and hummed softly. "See, buddy. Mommy's here. You're okay. Now let's go out there and play nice to the mean old lady."

Okay, so Bridgette hadn't been mean. She'd been friendly and clearly concerned about Antonio. Emma glanced longingly toward the master bathroom. She could smooth down her hair, add a little blush, and maybe cover the dark circles under her eyes. But what was the point? The makeup wouldn't help, and that she primped would be obvious. She steeled her spine, gathered her courage, and prepared to greet Bridgette in the kitchen.

Her steps slowed to a dead stop. Antonio must have heard the doorbell.

Bridgette was crouched in front of him, teetering in her five-inch heels, as he sat in his wheelchair. She had Antonio's cheek cupped in her hand while her other hand rested on his thigh.

Red, hot jealousy scorched her veins, but she couldn't tear away her gaze.

"Who's the lady, Mommy?" Sophie snuck up beside her and leaned her head against Emma's leg.

Antonio's head snapped up, and his gaze met hers.

Her heart pounded, but she refused to glance away. His brown eyes rounded, and his irises darted to Bridgette, back to her, and then dropped to his lap. One look told her everything she needed to know. A rock lodged in her throat, and she bit the inside of her cheeks to keep from crying.

Clearing her throat, she grabbed Sophie's hand and

walked into the kitchen. "I won't intrude on your time. I just need to get a bottle for Anderson. He gets cranky if he doesn't get his milk after he wakes."

Bridgette stood and wiped her cheeks. "No intrusion. I needed to yell at Antonio for not calling to tell me about his accident. I had to find out from Nate last night and couldn't get here until today."

As she opened the refrigerator and grabbed a bottle, Emma lowered her brows and stole a glance at Antonio. He didn't appear pleased to see Bridgette, but he might be fighting off the pain from his therapy session. "Where's Pam? I thought you had more time left with her today?"

"I sent her home so I could talk to Bridgette."

His tone spiked Emma's blood pressure.

Bridgette flashed her white, straight teeth. "I'm sure she was happy to leave a little early. I have to say, your house looks amazing, Antonio. Last time I was here it was so bare."

So, she'd been to his house before. Emma slammed the microwave closed a little too hard and heated the bottle. "Sorry." Her hands shook, and her pulse raced. Sweat gathered between her breasts, and she fought to rein in her temper.

Bridgette waved a hand through the air. "Did you hire someone to decorate? I have to get their number."

"My mommy did it," Sophie said. "Do you want to color with me?" She slid next to Antonio's wheelchair and placed her tiny hand in his.

A small smile touched his lips.

Emma melted into a pile of mush. Sophie appointed herself Antonio's guardian in the last few days, and his easy acceptance made her love for him grow.

"And who is this lovely little lady?" Lines creased Bridgette's smooth forehead.

Her forced smile was comical, and Emma coughed out a laugh.

"I'm Sophie."

Emma stepped around the island and sat on a stool.

Anderson greedily accepted his bottle.

"She's my daughter, and this is my son."

Bridgette glanced down at Antonio and quirked her lips to the side. "Your nurse is your interior designer? And she brings her kids to work?"

Sophie rocked back on her heels. "She's also having a baby. I'll be the big sister, but we'll have different daddies. My daddy died, but now I have Antonio just like the baby."

Bridgette's jaw fell open, and her face turned white.

Emma jumped to her feet, and the bottom of the stool scraped across the floor. "Okay, I'll get out of your hair now. Come on, Sophie. You can color in the office." She avoided Bridgette's wounded gaze, grabbed Sophie's hand, and dragged her out of the kitchen.

Sophie scrambled up on the chair in front of the desk in the office and picked up a blue crayon

Emma widened her eyes and stared at her daughter as if she had just dropped an atomic bomb. She sank into the chair behind the desk with Anderson on her lap. A tiny stream of milk pooled down his chin, and she dabbed it with a cloth.

His mouth smiled around the rubber nipple.

Her heartrate slowed to normal. Staring into his sea

green eyes, she lost herself for a moment. She didn't take enough time to enjoy spending time with her kids. She glanced at Sophie, and her singular concentration to stay in the lines, and her muscles relaxed as she leaned back in the chair.

Click-Click-Click

Heels tapping on the wooden floors grew louder. She leaned forward to peek out the door.

Bridgette stared through the glass of the closed French doors. Her shoulders lifted.

Emma waited. She couldn't possibly be considering coming in to talk.

Bridgette faced her again. "Do you have a second?"

"Um, sure. Sophie, why don't you see if Antonio needs anything?"

"Okay." Sophie jumped off the seat and ran out of the room.

Emma gestured toward the vacant chair with her free hand. "Do you want to sit?"

Bridgette chewed on her bottom lip, and tears glistened on her lashes. "Sure." Sitting, she crossed her long, lean legs and played with a strand of hair. "I didn't know about you. Antonio and I…we hadn't seen each other in a while. I tried, but he always resisted. But something was different the night I was with Antonio. I couldn't put my finger on it, and honestly, I didn't really try."

Her stomach rolled. "I didn't know about you either." Emma's mind drifted back to the night she fought with Antonio. "Well, not really."

A strangled laugh escaped Bridgette, and her gaze found Emma's. "Nothing to tell. We kept each other company a few times, and I wanted more. He was clear he wasn't interested in anything else, and I was stupid enough to think I could change his mind."

The corner of her mouth hitched up in a half-hearted smile. Her jealousy faded, and sympathy ebbed through her. "I'm sorry he hurt you."

Bridgette shrugged. "He was honest with me."

"He would be." Antonio had always been blunt. He wouldn't manipulate someone to get what he wanted.

"He loves you, doesn't he?" The tears in Bridgette's lashes spilled over and ran down her cheeks.

Emma shrugged and smoothed the lines of her face, fighting the emotion Bridgette's observation evoked. She didn't want to hurt the other woman any more than she'd already been hurt. "I hope so."

Bridgette nodded and tucked in her top lip. "He does. I've known him for a long time. I don't know what's going on between you two, and I'm sure I helped to screw up things, but he's in love with you. Don't give up, Emma. He's a good guy."

"You know, Bridgette, I really thought I'd hate you." She ran a palm over Anderson's soft hair. A husky laugh rumbled from Bridgette's throat.

"I hear that reaction a lot." She stood and smoothed her linen pants. "Good luck. Make him happy." Walking out of the office and to the front door, she cast one glance over her shoulder. Then she stepped outside and closed the door behind her.

Anderson spat the nipple of the empty bottle out of his mouth.

Standing, she placed him on her hip and returned to the kitchen.

Sophie sat in front of Antonio's wheelchair, telling him a story from one of her books.

He nodded along with her words.

She threw the bottle in the sink and moved to stand behind Sophie.

He glanced up.

She winced. The lines in his face tightened with pain, and his eyes were heavy with fatigue.

He waited for Sophie to stop reading. "Can we talk later?"

"Sure." Her pulse beat loudly in her ears. She'd given him the space he'd asked for the first night he'd come home from the hospital. She had so much she wanted to say.

"Good. For now, can you wheel me to my bed? I'm exhausted and need to ice my shoulder."

"No problem." She set Anderson on the floor and chuckled as he toddled into the family room. "Sophie, keep an eye on your brother for a second. Yell if he gets into anything." She gripped the back of the wheelchair.

Antonio covered her hand with his.

Heat engulfed her body, and she pushed him down the hall.

"Thanks for everything, Emma. I know being here hasn't been easy for you." He kept his face forward while he spoke.

She swallowed past the lump in her throat. This was the first time he'd offered her any gratitude. Maybe Bridgette's visit opened his eyes to what he wanted in life. Hopefully what he wanted was her.

Chapter Twenty-Four

The long day finally ended, and all Antonio wanted was to lie in bed and rest his aching body. But rest had to wait. He couldn't put off talking with Emma any longer.

Emma pressed her cheek to Anderson's as she paced around the bedroom, cradling him in her arms like a tiny baby. A soft hum purred from her throat.

Antonio's blood warmed. She was such a great mom…and it was sexy as hell. He sat in the doorway and remained silent until Anderson was sound asleep in her arms.

She bent low over the pack 'n play.

To stop from groaning, he bit into his lip. The shorts she wore to bed rose high on her thighs.

She lifted a finger and tiptoed toward him. "Okay, both kids are down. Did you still want to talk?"

"If that's okay." He needed to explain his relationship with Bridgette. Their relationship had always been casual, and he needed Emma to understand.

Emma hesitated, and then glanced toward the bathroom door. "Do you want to talk in there?"

His brow furrowed. The bathroom wasn't exactly his ideal setting for a serious talk. "Why?"

Her big toe traced circles on the floor. "I thought you might want me to wash your hair. It hasn't been washed since you came home from the hospital, and you can't lift both your arms above your head to do it yourself."

He ran a hand through his hair and cringed. "It's pretty greasy. How can you wash it without getting my cast wet?"

She wiggled her eyebrows. "We'll think of something." She wheeled him into the bathroom.

His pulse raced through his body like a freight train. "You could grab my crutches, and I can stand. I'm better now with the sling gone."

Emma placed the tip of her finger on her chin and glanced around the bathroom. "You've had a long day. I don't want you to fall because you've done too much. Plus, you're too tall." She stepped into the tiled shower. "Is the showerhead detachable?"

He peered up, even though the showerhead was shielded by the frosted glass door. "I think so."

"Perfect. Pam sent over a shower chair. You can sit on that, and I'll stand in the shower with you and wash your hair. The floor might get a little wet, but I'll clean it when we're done."

"You'll stand in the shower with me?" His voice rose high, and he squirmed in his chair.

Pressing her lips together, she raised her brows. "Don't worry. We'll both have clothes on. I'll help you take off your shirt, though."

His pulse jumped in his neck. "Okay." His hair did need washed, and he'd face the wall. He'd concentrate on his conversation about Bridgette, and then get out of there.

Emma stripped off his shirt, helped him into the shower chair, and then rolled him backward into the standup shower. Water sprayed from the showerhead. "Ack, the water's cold." Emma screeched with a laugh.

He glanced over his shoulder, and his jaw dropped. Water dripped down her neck and soaked her T-shirt. The white material clung to her damp skin. He whipped back his head, and the muscles in his stomach clenched. "You'll get soaked, Emma."

"I needed to shower before bed anyway. I'll hop in after I'm done with you."

Warm water pounded lightly against his scalp. He cleared his throat and focused on his words. "I wanted to explain about Bridgette."

"You don't have to explain anything." She lowered the spraying showerhead to the ground and massaged shampoo into his scalp. "She seems nice."

He sucked in a deep breath and searched for the right words. He needed to lay all his cards on the table—needed Emma to know exactly where things stood. "She is, and she's a good friend. I haven't been fair over the past year. She wanted more than just a causal relationship, but I couldn't give her more. First because I was caught up on Jillian, and then…"

"And then me?" Emma's fingers stopped moving.

"After we became friends, I stopped spending time with her because in the back of my mind, I wanted more with you. But then she found me drinking alone the night I was so upset, and one thing led to another." He took a deep breath. "It shouldn't have happened. Not just because of you, but because I knew how she felt about me. I used her."

The tips of Emma's fingers dug into his scalp again, and suds dripped onto his neck. Her fingers traveled lower down the back of his head and rubbed the base of his neck, and he groaned.

"I'm sorry she was hurt. She didn't deserve it. But you were honest with her. Everything else...well, what happened between you two is in the past and none of my business."

"I wanted to tell you so we could move forward with a clean slate." His voice was thick, and lust sparked in his body like jolts of electricity.

Her fingers tensed. "Is that really what you want? A completely clean slate?"

"I don't know what I want anymore." The lie slipped from his tongue. He knew exactly what wanted. He wanted Emma. He wanted them to build a family together and live happily ever after. But he still didn't know if he could trust her. Damnit, he couldn't think with her warm, wet body so close to his and her fingers doing wicked things to his scalp.

The curve of her breast brushed against his skin and scalded him. He bit into his bottom lip and flexed his fingers on the tops of his thighs. She placed a slender hand on his shoulder and bent over to pick up the showerhead. Warm water washed over his hair and down his back. The water pooled on the bottom of the chair, and his shorts molded to his legs. "Emma, can you cover my cast with a towel or something? The water is getting everywhere."

"Oh, sure." She lowered the showerhead again and stepped in front of him to grab a towel. She reached into the cabinet then faced him with a pale blue towel in her hand. "Will this work?"

Sucking in a breath, his gaze met hers, and he nodded.

She stepped toward him.

All of his blood left his brain. Her T-shirt hugged her so tight he couldn't tell where it stopped and her soft, supple skin began. Her damp hair matted around her face, and beads of water skimmed over her skin. "Wrap my leg and then hang up the showerhead. Angle it so the water comes down on the right side."

She narrowed her eyes, bent down, and carefully wrapped his cast. She stepped into the shower to reattach the showerhead. "Now what?"

Water rushed down, hitting the tiles and echoing around him. "Now help me get to the bench in the shower. This chair is wobbly and not steady enough for what I have in mind right now."

She rushed to his side.

He braced himself on her shoulder as she twisted him to the side and set him on the smooth, tiled bench. His bad leg stuck out to the side, the towel soaking up any moisture that rained down. The water pulsed between them.

Emma widened her eyes, and her breath puffed out in short, quick pants. "Now?" Her voice shook, and she clenched her hands into fists.

All his resistance melted away, washing down the drain. He loved this woman, and he couldn't resist her anymore. "Come closer."

She walked through the downpour and stopped in front of him.

He tugged the hem of her shirt and pulled her close. Her chest pressed against his, and his heartbeat matched hers. He lifted his hand and brushed a damp strand of hair behind her ear. The pad of his thumb caressed her cheek.

She closed her eyes on a moan. "Antonio."

"Open your eyes, Emma. Look at me." He wiped his tongue across his lips. "I want you."

Her lips curved in, and she raised her brows. "Are you sure?"

He curled his hand around the base of her neck and lowered his lips. He parted her mouth with his tongue and deepened the kiss.

She wrapped her arms around his neck.

The minty taste of her kiss mixed with the pulsing water. He broke away and fought to catch his breath. He was tired of fighting his feelings for this woman. She'd moved into his home to take care of him and prove her love. His soul ached to believe her—to give them a chance to be a real family. "I want to be with you, Emma."

She brought her forehead to his and inhaled a deep breath. "I want to give us a chance. We owe it to this baby—to us."

He ran a finger along her jawline, relishing the feel of her soft skin. "We have a lot to talk about, but it doesn't have to be tonight. We have plenty of time to figure out things."

Her eyes filled with tears, and her bottom lip trembled. "Okay." She shut off the water.

Her damp skin glistened, and desire stirred in his gut. "You better wrap up yourself in a towel, or we won't get around to sleeping for a while."

She fisted her hands on her hips. "Sorry to tell you this, but a little man is asleep in your bedroom right now. If you plan on sleeping with me, you won't get a chance to do anything else."

He laughed and lifted his hands. "You're right. I'm sorry." Warmth spread through him. She was so happy now…so full of life. The Emma he fell in love with. God, he hoped she was sincere about being in love with him. He couldn't take another blow.

Emma helped dry him and hobble to his wheelchair. He glanced around at the mess. Puddles of water covered the tiled floor. "Should we clean up first?"

"I'll get it tomorrow. Another day, another mess to clean. The story of my life." Emma grinned.

He grabbed her hand and pulled her onto his lap. "Thank you for everything you've done around here. I don't know how I would have managed without you."

She pressed her lips to his then curled against his chest. "I did it because I love you. I hope you know that."

"I do." He ran his fingers through her hair and closed his eyes. She loved him. A burst of joy pulsed in his heart. For the first time since his accident, he had hope.

Chapter Twenty-Five

Emma sat in the waiting room for her sonogram, and a sense of peace settled over her. The last few days brought nothing but happiness and laughter. She hadn't brought up the future yet, but like Antonio said, they had plenty of time to figure out the details. Now, she just wanted to enjoy this moment in time.

"This waiting room needs more magazines for guys." Antonio tossed a copy of *Pregnancy Fit* onto the oak end table beside him. He leaned back in his chair and stretched his arm over her shoulder.

Emma nestled into him and glanced at the cover of the magazine. "You mean you don't want to read about fitness and the pregnant woman?"

He leaned down and nibbled on her ear. "I think I've learned plenty the last couple of days."

Her breath caught in her throat. She laced her fingers in his. "Are you excited to see the sonogram?"

He rubbed a hand over his chin. "Yeah, but will the picture even look like a baby yet? You're only twelve weeks."

She shrugged. "I'm not sure. I've never gotten a sonogram this early before. I was twenty weeks along with my other two pregnancies. This one might appear to be nothing more than a bubble." Warmth bubbled inside her at finally having a normal conversation with Antonio—finally looking forward to a future together.

"Aren't babies always weird on these things? Even when Jillian was farther along, I could never tell what was what in the pictures. Sam was like an alien."

Emma laughed and slapped his chest. "Our baby won't look like an alien."

"Not when it comes out, but it might when it's still in there." Antonio rested a hand on her stomach. "Do we see the doctor after this?"

"Yeah. This part shouldn't take too long."

"Hey, strangers. How've you two been?" Meg strode across the waiting room.

Her long blonde hair was braided down her back. She wore dark jeans and a loose T-shirt, hiding any evidence she might have of her pregnancy. Emma lifted the corners of her mouth. "Hi, Meg. I didn't know you had an appointment today. Is Dylan with you?"

Meg sat in the empty chair beside her. "He's talking to the receptionist about the farm. She wants to bring her kids over the weekend. Are you seeing Dr. Dressler today?"

Emma nodded. "After an ultrasound."

Meg clapped her hands under her chin. "You brat. You get pictures already. Dylan," she called when he stepped into the room.

He lifted his other hand in greeting.

"Can we stay while Emma gets her ultrasound? I want to see the first picture of my niece or nephew."

"Sure." He sat next to Meg and rested a large hand on her knee.

The door to the back room opened, and a technician stepped out. Her gaze roamed the waiting room. "Emma Harris?"

"Right here." Emma stood and glanced down at

Antonio. "Do you need help?"

"No thanks. I got this." He grabbed the crutches and set them in front of him. He braced one hand on the arm of the chair, the other grabbed the top of the crutches, and he pulled himself to his feet. "Go ahead. I'm right behind you."

She picked up her purse and turned toward the technician. "Let's get this started. I've had to pee for the last twenty minutes."

The technician laughed and opened the door wider for her and Antonio to step through. "Keeping your bladder full for an internal ultrasound is torture. Go ahead and step into the room on the right. Since you're so early and we need a good view of the cervix, this will be an internal ultrasound. Take off your pants and climb up on the table. There's a gown in there to cover with. I'll be in shortly."

"Thanks." Emma stepped into the room with Antonio on her heels. As soon as the door closed, she wiggled out of her jeans.

"I'm liking this appointment already." Antonio leaned forward, his crutches under his armpits, and grabbed her wrist. He gathered her close, and his mouth crushed down on hers.

She sagged against his chest. "All right. Enough." She leaned back and stared into his warm, chocolate eyes, trying to catch her breath. "She'll be back any minute."

The corners of his eyes crinkled, and dimples deepened the center of his cheeks. "You can't take off your pants and expect me not to react."

She raised her brows. "Trust me, I know exactly how you react when I take off my pants."

A deep laugh rumbled from his throat.

She hopped on the table and wrapped the gown around her waist as the door opened.

The technician stepped in. "Everyone ready?" She closed the door and sat on a stool in front of the ultrasound machine beside the bed.

Emma leaned back on the bed with Antonio standing by her head and watched the screen in front of her spring to life. She shifted slightly as the technician used an internal wand to examine her.

Antonio sucked in a breath. "Is that the baby?"

"The image is of Emma's cervix. I need to check and make sure it hasn't shortened at all."

Emma gritted her teeth and tightened her muscles as the wand moved around to get a better perspective. "Is everything okay?"

"Everything appears exactly like it's supposed to at this stage in the pregnancy. Now, do you want to see the baby?"

Emma held her breath, oblivious to the uncomfortable motion of the wand, as a small sack appeared on the screen. Two connecting circles lay within it. The image of her baby filled the screen, and joy burst through her heart. Tears gathered in the corners of her eyes, and her cheeks hurt from her smile.

"The heartrate is a steady one hundred sixty beats per minute."

She glanced over her shoulder at Antonio. "Anderson's heartrate was the same around fourteen weeks. Maybe we're having a boy."

Antonio's gaze met hers, and moisture clung to his lashes. "Whatever it is, it will be perfect."

Her chest tightened, and she swallowed past the

lump in her throat. She nodded, and then rested a hand on her stomach. Their baby was in there. This little miracle brought them together and opened her eyes to how full her future was. She turned back to the screen, watching the tiny flutter of the heartbeat.

Antonio's hand covered hers, and his fingertips grazed the tops of her fingers.

Goose bumps rose on her arm, and shivers of anticipation rippled in her gut.

His fingers stopped, and his body tensed.

Her heart dropped to the floor, and she searched the screen. Had he seen something? Was something wrong? Nothing stood out, and the technician wore a bright smile as she studied the monitor.

All the color had drained from his face, and his wide eyes burned a hole in her finger. She followed his gaze, and a weight dropped in her stomach. Panic bubbled in her chest. She yanked away her hand and covered the gold band on her left hand.

"You're still wearing your wedding ring." His gaze was glued to her hand.

"Wearing the ring is a habit. I don't even think about it. The ring never comes off my hand." She reached for him.

He jerked away.

His wild eyes darted around the room, landing everywhere but on her. "Antonio, don't read more into this than what it is."

He fisted his hand in his hair and turned toward the door. "I can't do this right now, Emma. I've got to get out of here." His balance faltered as he tried to get to the door quicker than his crutches could keep up.

"Are you kidding me?" she shrieked.

The technician set her mouth in a firm line and cast a quick glance to Emma. "Do you want me to step outside? I just need to hit Print, and I'm done. I can give you two some privacy."

"Don't bother." He touched the doorknob.

The bubble of panic burst. "Please, let her step out. We need to talk about this." Her muscles relaxed as the technician removed the wand. She grabbed the gown and covered herself as the technician brushed past Antonio and left the room. She sat as still as stone on the table, unable to move unless she wanted her bare skin to peek through the flimsy paper gown. Now was the worst possible time to have this conversation.

"We can't keep doing this." She'd put him above everything the last few weeks to prove herself. She couldn't do it anymore. At some point, he had to let go of his insecurities. "I'm tired of walking on eggshells around you, hoping I don't slip up and do something to upset you. I know I screwed up, but I've done everything I can to show you I didn't mean what I said. You've got to get over your insecurities to move forward."

"What if I can't?" His voice cracked, and he hung his head. "I want to, God I want to more than anything. But the emotions are always right beneath the surface. I'm not your first choice, Emma, and I don't know if I can live with that knowledge."

Fear clawed through her veins. "You are my choice…right now I choose you. I love you. Isn't that enough?"

His lip quirked down in one corner, and he shook his head. "I don't know if it is. I need to figure out what I want, and I need some space. Maybe you and the kids shouldn't be at the house for a while. I need some time."

She opened her mouth to speak, but he left the room before she could find the right words. Numbness encased her, and she stared down at the gold band on her finger. The ring was a symbol of her love and commitment to Luke. She would never forget her love for Luke, even if she took off the ring, and she didn't want to. Luke's memory would always be a part of her and her kids. If Antonio couldn't live with her past, they'd never be together.

Tap-Tap-Tap.

She straightened her spine and wiped the tears from her face. "Come in."

The technician stepped inside. "You might want these." She offered a stack of printed pictures. "Once you get dressed, you can head back to the waiting room. You'll be called back shortly so you can speak with the doctor."

She grabbed the pictures and forced a small smile. "Thank you." The door closed, and she stared down at the picture. The grainy white circles surrounded by black stared up. Her baby. Tears filled her eyes once more. Stupid hormones. She grabbed a tissue from a box on the counter and blew her nose.

Tap-Tap-Tap.

Her heart picked up its pace. Maybe Antonio had come to his senses and realized what an idiot he was. "Yes?" As the door swung open, she held her breath.

"Hey." Meg stepped through the doorway with wide eyes and closed the door behind her. "Are you okay? What happened?"

All the air left her lungs, deflating her. She held up

her fingers, showing her ring to Meg.

"I don't get it. What are you doing?" Meg grabbed her hand, turning it palm up, and studied it.

"My wedding ring, you idiot."

"Oh." Meg dropped her hand and raised her brow. "Haven't you always worn it?"

"I haven't taken it off since the day Luke and I got married. Well, except when my fingers turned into sausages while I was pregnant with the kids, and then I wore it around my neck."

"Antonio asked Dylan to take him home. He was pretty shaken up." Meg sat down on the stool the technician had been on moments before. "Has he never noticed it before?"

"I guess not." Exhaustion weighed her down, and she lay back on the table. "I can't keep fighting for him if he expects me to forget Luke. Asking me to forget the father of my children isn't fair."

Meg took the pictures from Emma's hands and was silent for a moment. "Did he ask you to forget about Luke?"

Conflicting emotions weighed her down. Antonio might not have asked her to forget Luke, but he was threatened by her deceased husband. "No. In fact, in the beginning, he was the only person I could talk to about Luke. But after we fought, Luke has been an issue."

"Have you two talked at all about how to handle Luke's memory?"

Emma sat, and her cheeks grew hot. "We agreed we had plenty of time to talk about everything. We've just been a little…busy."

Meg chuckled.

Emma glared.

"Sorry." Meg rolled her eyes and pressed her lips together to hide a smile. "Well, I think the time has come to discuss this. I can see his point a little bit. He loves you, but you're wearing another man's wedding ring. That would be a tough pill to swallow."

Emma twirled the band around her finger. Guilt washed over her. She didn't want to upset Antonio, but she also couldn't just slam the door on her past. "I can't just erase Luke from my life."

Meg placed a hand on Emma's arm. "Honey, he never asked you to. But if he did, he's a jerk and not worth your time anyway."

"It might not matter anymore. We've gone around and around this problem and keep ending back in the same place. He can't get past this whole him being the second choice thing, and I can't keep pushing him along. He needs to get there on his own."

"Give him some time."

She sucked in a large, shaky breath. "Maybe it'd be better to cut our losses and figure out where to go from here. I can't keep dragging Sophie and Anderson from house to house. If Antonio wants us to leave his house, then we won't be back." Her heart cracked in two. She'd woken this morning with a future of possibilities laid out before her. Now, she had been abandoned at the doctor's office and forced to face the impossibility of a future without the man she loved.

Meg held up one of the sonogram pictures. "Just remember, no matter what happens between you two from here on out, you made this happen. And this little baby will be loved by so many people, and you will never regret the time you spent with Antonio that led to this new life. Even if it does look kind of like an alien right now."

A strangled sob caught in Emma's throat. If only Antonio would have been there, he would have loved hearing Meg's words. A pang of despair stroked her heart. How many times would she wish Antonio was still by her side in the years to come?

Chapter Twenty-Six

Antonio sat in his driveway in Dylan's idling truck. He shoved open the passenger side door, and shrill shrieks reached his ears from the backyard of his house.

"Thanks for the ride." He nodded at Dylan, and then froze. Annie was probably outside with the kids. He'd forgotten she was here with them. He could sneak in, but he doubted he'd be stealthy enough. He didn't want to deal with Annie or the kids right now. "I hate to ask you this, but can you take me to the bar?"

Dylan furrowed his brow. "Are you sure? You just left Emma at the doctor's office during her appointment, and now you want to go drink at the bar in the middle of the day?"

Hesitation made his words come out slow. Spilling his guts to Dylan was the last thing he wanted to do, but he needed Dylan to take him away from his home. "Emma's mom and kids are at my house. So I either pretend like everything's okay, which Annie will never buy, or I act like a jerk and ignore them. I don't like either option, so yeah, I want to go drink in the middle of the day."

Dylan gripped the steering wheel with both hands. "Dude. Your life's complicated."

He pinched the bridge of his nose. "You don't know the half of it."

"Why don't you fill me in?" Dylan backed out of

the driveway and drove toward the town square.

"You don't want to hear my problems." He leaned his head against the seat and steadied the bouncing crutches with his hand.

"Someone's got to hear them, and I'm the only one around. You're in a world of trouble right now."

He groaned. Leaving Emma probably wasn't the smartest decision, but the air had been squeezed from his lungs when he'd seen the wedding band. One glance at the physical reminder of her dead husband had brought all of his stupid insecurities crashing down. "My troubles are complicated." He stared out the window. Houses, large and small, passed by as they drove along the tree-lined streets of his neighborhood.

"Then uncomplicate it, man. What made you leave today?"

He glanced over at Dylan, whose gaze stayed fixed on the road. "Emma's still wearing her wedding ring."

Dylan spared him a quick glance and narrowed his eyes. "And?"

His blood pressure spiked. "Are you serious? How would you feel if Meg was still stuck on her fiancé?"

Dylan chuckled. "Dude, this is totally different. Before you even bring up your first marriage, this situation is different from what happened with Jillian, too."

He slumped his shoulders. "Really? Because it feels exactly the same."

Dylan parked across the street from the bar. He let the engine idle and faced Antonio. "Jonah and Jillian never should have split up. They were two stupid kids who didn't know how to deal with life. Unfortunately, you were caught in the middle. Emma's husband died.

He won't swoop in and take her back."

"I know," he snapped. "But just like with Jillian, she'll always love someone else more. I don't want to deal with playing second fiddle again."

Shaking his head, Dylan snorted. "Don't you think we've all got stuff to deal with?"

He picked a piece of lint off his pants. "This is bigger than most issues. I've been down this road, and I know where it leads. Maybe calling it quits before anyone gets too hurt is best." His heart was already cracked in two. If Emma left it in too many pieces, he'd never put it back together.

"That's the dumbest thing I've ever heard." Dylan snorted.

Antonio glared. "Thanks for the support, man."

"Hey, you seem like an all right guy, but Emma's family. She's been like a sister to me my whole life. Trust me, I like her a lot more than I do my own sister. She's already been put through the wringer this year, and if you split now because of some stupid grudge you're holding about Luke, then you're an idiot."

Irritation at the insult had him clenching his jaw. "I'm not holding a grudge."

Dylan arched an eyebrow. "Are you sure?"

He squeezed his eyes and rubbed his temples. "It sucks always being second place. For once, I'd like to be someone's first pick."

"You end up with a gorgeous woman who loves you, a new baby, and two beautiful little ones who will adore you forever…that seems like a good place. No matter how you got there."

Antonio dropped his hands and tilted his head to the side. "I've never looked at the situation that way."

"You might not want to hear this, but Luke's the one who got screwed. He'll miss seeing his kids grow up, and he'll miss being a part of all the milestones in their lives. You're the lucky one."

"I know." He blew a long breath through parted lips. Guilt ate away at his stomach lining.

Dylan slapped a hand on his shoulder. "Listen, Emma and Luke were together for a long time. They met in college and got married a month after graduation. You can't expect her to throw everything out the window. Hell, you shouldn't want her to. She's loyal, and she loves with her whole heart. She'll love you the same way."

Loyalty. That was one characteristic that didn't exist in his last marriage. He wanted a loyal partner more than anything. "I don't want her to forget about him. I'm not a monster. Those kids are amazing, and they need to know their father somehow. Emma's the only one who can share memories of Luke."

Smirking, Dylan shrugged. "Then what's your problem?"

"I need to know she's not with me because she has no other option. Seeing her wedding ring on her finger today…it messed with my head." He snaked his hand around his neck and kneaded his fingers into his flesh. "Does she wear it out of habit? Or is it something more?"

"What more could it be?"

"She doesn't want to break her vows." He hung his head, and nerves danced in his stomach.

Dylan nodded toward the windshield. "You see that jerk?"

Antonio glanced out the window. Blake strolled

down the sidewalk, hands in his jacket pocket, hunched against the brutal wind. His head was down, and he nearly knocked a middle-aged woman with arms full of groceries to the ground. He rose his head slightly, scowled at the woman, and then disappeared into the bar. "I see him."

"If you want my opinion, you have two choices. One, you can get over your stupid hang-ups with Emma and Luke. Trust what she's telling you, let go of the stupid stuff, and build a beautiful family together. Or end up like him." Dylan narrowed his gaze as he stared at the door to the Village Idiot. "A sad, sorry sonofagun who didn't appreciate what was right in front of him. He doesn't have a damn thing going for him, and he wastes all his time getting drunk and acting stupid."

"I want to trust her. More than anything."

"So do it." Dylan faced him with raised brows. "Did you give her a chance to explain the ring?"

He winced. "Not really."

Dylan chuckled and ran a hand through his beard. "Man, you really are an idiot."

"I really screwed up." He drew in a deep breath, and then regretted it as his nearly healed ribs throbbed beneath his skin.

"At least you realize it, but what will you do?"

Hope bloomed in his chest. He could fix this. He could make Emma see how much he loved her and wanted a future together. "I need to do the same thing Emma's done since I got in my accident. I need to show her how much I love her. Can you do me another favor?"

The corner of Dylan's mouth hitched up in a smirk. "Sure. I've got to see how you dig yourself out of this."

Antonio chuckled. "If you take me somewhere first, I'll let you watch me grovel."

"If I get to watch you grovel, I might have to let Jonah get in on this adventure. He'd hate to miss it."

Antonio rolled his eyes. He'd forgotten for a minute Dylan was Jonah's best friend. He'd poured out his heart to one of the least likely people in the whole town. But he didn't care, the guy gave great advice. "Call Jonah for all I care. As long as you get me where I need to go."

A grin split Dylan's face as drove out of town.

Antonio's nerves knotted in his stomach. His plan had to work. He didn't want to think about what would happen if it didn't.

Two hours later, Antonio balanced on his crutches and leaned forward to grab the door handle. He closed his eyes and steadied his breath as the cool air whipped around his face. His heart pounded like a racehorse out of the gate. He opened the door and stepped into the quiet house. The hairs on his arm stood on end. The house was too quiet. Had Emma already left?

He glanced around and spied a sparkly pink shoe beside the door. His heartrate slowed. Sophie wouldn't have left without her favorite shoes. He stepped farther into the house, and a motion in the corner of his eye caught his attention. He spun toward the office, and relief seeped through him.

Sophie sat at the desk, her feet dangling from the chair, her hand moving quickly as she colored.

"Hey, Soph." He stepped inside the office.

Her eyes stayed on the page in front of her. "Hi."

"What are you coloring?" He peered over her shoulder. A princess coloring book sprawled open on the desk. A smile tugged at his lips. He should have guessed.

"Ariel." She bit her bottom lip and concentrated on her work.

He leaned down farther, and his gaze zeroed in on a dainty chain around her neck. "Did you get a new necklace?"

She glanced up and beamed. "Mommy gave it to me." Her hand dipped into the front of her shirt, and she held up a simple gold band.

He sucked in a breath. Emma's wedding ring.

"She wants a piece of my daddy's love to always be close to my heart."

Antonio rested his crutches against the wall and crouched as best he could in front of Sophie. Unshed tears lodged in his throat, and his heart pounded. "That's a pretty special gift."

"I know." Sophie widened her eyes and nodded. "I promised Mommy I wouldn't lose it. She was sad when she gave it to me."

His mouth went dry. "She was?"

Sophie dropped her gaze to the ring she held between her thumb and index finger. "She was crying. She said she always wanted me to feel my daddy's love close to me, and she should have given it to me sooner. Now she's packing. We have to go to Grandma's for a sleepover for a few nights. Mommy said she wants me to help her find a new home to live in."

A fist squeezed his heart, and he pushed a lump of fear down his throat. "Where is she?"

"In your room." Her gaze met his, and she widened her eyes. "Why do we have to leave? I like it here. I want this to be my home."

"I want this to be your home, too, sweetheart." He lifted her with one arm onto his knee and wrapped his arms around her.

Her arms squeezed around his neck.

He coughed to catch his breath. "I love you, Sophie."

"I love you, too."

Bursts of happiness exploded in his chest, and he hugged her tighter. "I need to talk to your mom. I'll fix this. You aren't going anywhere, okay?"

"Yay!" She buried her face in his neck.

He inhaled the scent of baby shampoo and vanilla lotion. She wiggled in his arms, knocking him off balance, and he crashed to the floor. Her giggles filled the room. "Silly girl, you knocked me over." He found her tickle spot and dove in.

She laughed and shrieked until she rolled over on the floor. She stood, her hands out in front of her, and panted for breath. "Please stop."

He chuckled. "Okay, I'm done." He sat on the floor. "I'll talk to your mom. Wish me luck." He pulled himself to his feet.

Sophie wrapped her arms around his waist. "Good luck."

Emma would listen. She had to. He couldn't lose her or the kids. Determination set its stubborn grip on his backbone as he grabbed his crutches, rushed out of the office, and toward what he hoped was his future.

Chapter Twenty-Seven

The top of the suitcase closed with a soft thud. Emma zipped the bag, lifted it off the bed, and placed it on the floor. Sophie's giggles carried in through the open door, and she stopped and strained her ears toward the doorway. She sank onto the edge of the bed and rested her forehead in the palm of a hand. Pressure tightened her chest. Sophie loved being here, and she was about to rip her away. But if she'd learned one thing in the past year, it was Sophie was resilient. Sophie would bounce back from the pain of losing Antonio a lot quicker than she did.

Emma pushed herself off the bed and glanced at the alarm clock on the nightstand. Two hours passed since Antonio left her at the doctor's office. She had no idea where he went or when he'd be back, but she wanted to be gone before he returned. She didn't have the strength to rehash the same problems.

She'd packed the kids' things, and all she had left was clearing out her toiletries. She turned toward bathroom, and all the air left her lungs. Her heart dropped like an anchor, and her feet planted to the floor.

"Hi." Antonio stood in the doorway. "Can I come inside?"

She took a deep breath and bit down on her cheeks as she let the air out through her nose. She couldn't let him see how upset she was. "It's your house. You can go wherever you want."

His gaze scanned the room and then landed on the suitcase by the bed. "Sophie says you want her to help you find a new house?" He hobbled into the room and leaned against the armoire in front of the bed.

"We'll stay at my mom's until we buy a place, but finding a house shouldn't take too long. We need a home of our own. Bouncing around isn't good for the kids." She grabbed her black travel bag from the bed. "I've got money set aside, and Meg wants to hire me as the event coordinator at the farm, so I think now's a good time."

Antonio's lips curved into a small smile. "Really? I didn't know you were interested in working at the farm."

"We haven't done a lot of talking lately." She shrugged. The zipper on her bag dangled between her fingers, and she dropped her gaze to the floor. "I've enjoyed planning Meg's reception. I think it'd be the perfect job."

"That's great, Emma. Take the job, but please… don't leave."

His smooth voice caressed her skin. She lifted her gaze until it met his, and her heart lodged in her throat. Tears burned her eyes, and she forced them to stay. "We've tried this relationship, a couple of times, and I can't do it anymore." She hurried into the bathroom.

The bright lights beat down, and she threw the bag on top of the marble vanity. She rested her hands on the countertop and stared in the mirror. Dark circles hung under her eyes, and her messy waves curled in every direction. She didn't need to waste time worrying about her appearance. She picked through the products and hair tools to find what was hers and shoved them in the bag. Irony made her laugh as the bag bulged at the seams. Had she even used any of them while she was here?

Taking a deep breath, she steeled her nerve before she returned to the bedroom. Everything was packed and ready. She needed to say a quick good-bye, and then get out. Once she was back at her mom's, she could hide away and fall apart. She shuffled her feet toward the bedroom.

"Are these from today?" Antonio held up the sonogram pictures.

Wonder filled his brown eyes, and the goofy grin on his face tugged her heartstrings.

"I knew the baby would look like an alien."

A half-hearted smile touched her lips. "Meg said the same thing."

Antonio placed the pictures back on top of the armoire. "I'm sorry I left. I never should have abandoned you at the doctor's office."

Emma sighed and threw the bag next the suitcase. "We don't have to have this conversation again. We're like two dogs constantly chasing their tails. I won't apologize again for what I said, and I sure as hell won't feel bad about still loving Luke. I will always love him, and you obviously can't handle those emotions."

"I was an idiot for reacting the way I did. The ring…it doesn't matter. I have no excuse for what I did."

"You're right. You should have let me explain instead of acting like an injured child."

Wanting to believe he was truly sorry, she inhaled

a sharp breath.

He leaned his crutches against the wall and took an awkward step forward. "Again, you're right. You've been here day in and day out taking care of me and two children. You've tended to my injuries, cooked for me, and on top of everything else…you've finally made this house I've lived in for over a year a home."

She lifted her eyes to the ceiling. Her pulse thundered through her veins. To steady her nerves, she breathed in and out. "All I did was add some stupid knickknacks around the house and pick out new furniture."

Antonio shook his head. "You and the kids made it a home. The way you sing off key when you're folding laundry, Sophie and Sam running around making more noise than I ever imagined two kids could make, and Anderson's giggles anytime he plays peek-a-boo. All those things made this a home. I don't want to lose all those little things I've come to love. I don't want to lose you."

Her eyes misted, blurring her vision. "Your pretty words don't mean anything."

The corners of his mouth tucked in. "They shouldn't. But maybe this will." His hand dipped into his front pocket, and he pulled out a blue, velvet ring box.

Emma pressed a hand to her chest. "What are you doing?"

"Something I should have done a long time ago." He opened the lid and handed her the box.

She lifted her brows, and a stab of disappointment pierced her heart. A proposal wouldn't fix their problems, but he could have tried to be a little more romantic. She held the soft box in her hand and stared at the ring nestled in the white pillow inside. She dropped her jaw and questions filled her mind. The ring was beautiful, but not what she expected. She jutted forward her chin and tilted her head to the side. "What's this?"

Antonio reached for the box and took out the simple gold band with a square cut sapphire shining from the center. "This is a promise I want to make you."

Her pulse pounded in her ears. "A promise?"

"Did you know the sapphire is the stone associated with the month of September?"

Her breath caught in her throat. September was the month she married Luke so many years ago. "I didn't."

He winked.

Her knees turned to gelatin.

"I just found out myself. I also was told today you and Luke were married in September."

"Yes," she whispered.

"When you and I first became friends, I told you I wanted to be someone you could always talk to about anything. I wanted to hear about your life with Luke, about the struggles you had with his death… everything."

She nodded, her gaze fixed on the ring.

Antonio took a deep breath. "I'm sorry I forgot about my promise. I let my own hang-ups get in the way of our relationship. I don't want you to forget about Luke, Emma. He was your husband and the father of your children. You will always love him, and you should. I understand your loving him doesn't mean you'll love me less."

He grasped her right hand and slid the ring on her finger. "I'd love for you to wear this as a reminder to always keep alive his memory. I don't want you to walk on eggshells around me. I want you to feel comfortable telling stories to Sophie and Anderson about their dad, and for them to know how much he loved them. They deserve to know their dad, Emma."

The ring slid into place, and her hand trembled. She stared down at it, and the tears she'd kept at bay rolled down her cheeks. She opened her mouth, but no words came. The ring was beautiful, but it dimmed in comparison to the meaning behind it. The warmth of his hand slid from hers, and she glanced up as he shifted his weight. "Thank you."

He raised his eyebrows.

His eyes sparked with mischief.

Planting a hand on the side of the bed, he braced himself as he lowered to one knee. He pulled a black velvet ring box from his other pocket.

Her palms grew damp.

He opened the lid.

She lifted her hands to her mouth and gasped. Tears clogged her vision, and she wiped them away.

Antonio locked his gaze on hers and licked his lips. "Emma, I started to fall in love with you the night I took you home from the fair. You exude this warmth and confidence that makes people around you happy. You're caring and loving, and damnit…you're the most beautiful woman I've ever laid eyes on. I don't know how I was lucky enough to get your attention, but I want to spend the rest of my life making you feel as lucky and loved as I do. I love you with my whole heart. I've already vowed to keep alive your past, but now I vow to be your future. Emma, will you marry me?"

Her knees buckled, and she sank to the floor. Her heart fluttered like the wings of a hummingbird. She traced the soft skin of his cheek, and then travelled down to rest on his rapidly beating heart. "Is this real? You really love me?" He hadn't said those sweet words in so long. The warmth of his hand covered hers, and the heat consumed her body.

"I love you more than anything. You, and this crazy family we're building together. Please…will you be my wife?"

Her lips curved into a slow smile. "Abso-freaking-lutely." She threw her arms around his neck, knocking him sideways to the ground. His hard chest broke her fall, and his arms circled the small of her back. "I love you." She pressed her lips to his, and her heart filled with so much joy it threatened to burst.

"Can I come in now?" Sophie yelled from the hallway.

Emma chuckled and rested her head on the side of his neck. "What's she doing out there?"

"She's my good luck charm. I told her she couldn't come in until I gave her the cue." Antonio's lips touched her forehead. "Come on in, Sophie."

Little footsteps padded into the room. "Is he tickling you, too, Mommy?"

"Not yet," Antonio said. "Should I?"

Emma grabbed Sophie and yanked her down with them, tickling her sides. "Don't even think about it. I'm the only tickle monster in this house."

Sophie's eyes widened. "Does that mean we're staying? Antonio said he'd fix everything. I want this to be our home, Mommy."

"Yes, honey. Antonio fixed everything." She met Antonio's gaze over Sophie's blonde head. "This is our home now."

Frantic cries crackled through the baby monitor, and Emma sat upright. "It sounds like Anderson wants to join the celebration." She stood, and then helped Antonio to his feet.

He grabbed the ring box from the floor. "We forgot something." He lifted the thin pave band with a brilliant, cushion-cut diamond and slid it on her left hand.

The weight of the ring shifted on her finger. "The ring is perfect."

He leaned forward and kissed her. "You're perfect."

"What about me?" Sophie asked with a pout.

Emma laughed and gathered her into a hug. "You're perfect, too, sweetheart."

Anderson's cries grew louder.

"All right, ladies," Antonio said. "Let's go tell Anderson the good news."

"That we're finally home?" Emma's heart exploded with joy.

Antonio grinned. "That he's finally getting his own room."

Emma threw back her head and laughed so hard her stomach ached.

Antonio linked their fingers.

She hurried out to quiet the screaming Anderson. She glanced down at the ring on her right hand. The past year had been unbelievably difficult, but they'd pulled through. She lifted her gaze, and it landed on

Antonio. He had been her rock in the darkest time of her life, and now, he offered her a future with limitless possibilities. A future filled with love and family. A future filled with a happy home.

Epilogue

The car bounced along as Antonio drove at a snail's pace through the quiet streets of Smithview. Emma didn't mind. Sitting in the back seat, she rested her fingers on the smooth, soft skin of the beautiful baby asleep in his car seat. The back tire dipped into a pothole, and a dull ache quickly turned into a sharp pain. She hissed.

Antonio's gaze met hers in the rearview mirror. "I'm sorry. Are you okay?"

"I'm fine. Just a little sore." She settled her gaze back on the baby. "What are the chances he'll keep sleeping as well as he did in the hospital?"

Antonio chuckled. "Slim to none. Meg said the minute they brought Lucy home, she decided sleep must be overrated. We'll probably be in for the same nightmare."

"Did you already call our son a nightmare?" Their gaze locked again. She firmed her lips into a straight line, but she couldn't keep the amusement out of her voice.

The car slid into the driveway, and warmth radiated from her heart at what waited. A welcome home banner flapped in the gentle breeze in front of the house, and blue balloons bobbed above the mailbox. Her whole family, baby Lucy included, stood on the front porch waiting for their arrival.

"Did you know about this?" she asked.

"I might have told them what time we were leaving the hospital. I also told them they have ten minutes to visit and then have to leave so you can rest."

Appreciation ebbed through her. All she wanted was to snuggle with her babies and fall asleep for three days. If she was lucky, she might get twenty minutes. "Well, if they want to cook or clean, they can stay a little longer."

Antonio parked the car, shut off the engine, and walked over to open her door. His hand touched hers.

As his wedding ring grazed her skin, she smiled. "Thanks, but I'm good. Why don't you grab Matthew?"

Lines etched the corner of his eyes. "Are you sure? I can help you to the house first."

"I'm sure." She closed the passenger door.

Antonio jogged to the other side of the car to lift out the car seat.

She closed her eyes and lifted her face to the sun. The temperature was hot for April, and the warmth spread from her face all the way down to her toes.

"Mommy! You're home." Sophie ran down from the porch stairs and wrapped her arms around her waist. "I've missed you so much."

Emma laughed. "I've only been gone two days, baby girl. Are you excited for the baby to be home?"

Sophie's head bobbed. "I'll help take care of him, and Anderson will help, too. But he's not as big as me."

At the sound of his name, Anderson hopped out of Annie's arms and ran over. Gone was the toddler who stumbled as he walked from place to place. He was a little boy now, with hair as blond as his sister's and eyes the color of his father's. Eyes that always gave away his orneriness. "Mama, you here. I wuv you."

She bent down and gathered him close, kissing his chubby cheek. "I love you, too, buddy." She stood, watching Antonio as he bent his face close to the baby, whispering something in his ear.

Matthew never stirred.

Antonio straightened and locked gazes. He walked forward.

Sophie and Anderson ran with as much exuberance as they had when they'd greeted her.

Turning, she faced the rest of her family and waved. As if a dam had burst, they all poured off the steps and surrounded her, Antonio, and the kids on the lawn. "Oohs" and "ahhs" rang in her ears as the sleeping baby was passed around in his carrier. Emma reached for Antonio, and he stepped beside her, an arm snaked around her waist. Happiness seeped into every corner of her being, and a peacefulness settled in her core. She glanced at every member of her family. This was what life was all about—surrounding yourself with loved ones. She nestled against Antonio's side and stared at his adorable dimples. He'd given her everything. He'd completed her family. He'd given her a love to always come home to.

A word about the author…

Danielle M. Haas resides in Ohio with her husband and two children. She earned a BA in Political Science many moons ago from Bowling Green State University, but thought staying home with her two children and writing romance novels would be more fun than pursuing a career in politics. She is a member of Romance Writers of America, as well as her local North East Ohio chapter. She spends her days chasing her kids around, loving up her dog, and trying to find a spare minute to write about her favorite thing: love.

Danielle can be found blogging about her adventures in writing at www.daniellemhaas.com, via her Facebook page under Author Danielle Haas, or you can follow her twitter handle, @authordhaas.

http://www.daniellemhaas.com

Other Titles by this Author
A Place in This World
Second Time Around

Thank you for purchasing
this publication of The Wild Rose Press, Inc.

For questions or more information
contact us at
info@thewildrosepress.com.

The Wild Rose Press, Inc.
www.thewildrosepress.com

www.ingramcontent.com/pod-product-compliance
Lightning Source LLC
Chambersburg PA
CBHW051534260626

47170CB00003B/926

9 7 8 1 5 0 9 2 3 8 0 7 1